Nick Corble first started watching football when the only writing on a player's shirt was the name of his club, the First Division was just that, teams were only allowed one substitute and it was still possible to move around the ground at half time. Although his first ever match was watching Luton he soon saw the light and caught the magic at Watford just as Graham Taylor and Elton John were starting the revolution that led from the fourth division to the boys in yellow playing in Europe, and culminated in that day of days, an FA Cup Final appearance.

Since then he's suffered the ups and downs of fandom and come to realise that following your team isn't all about glory, although on those rare occasions when glory is achieved there's nothing quite like being part of it, even if it is as a spectator. In the meantime he's forged an eclectic career as a writer, publishing fourteen books ranging from a travelogue, through walking and travel guides (he's a bit of a specialist on the canals), biography and a history of the Wall of Death. He's also written dozens of articles for titles as diverse as The Times and Practical Motorhome. Golden Daze is his first novel but probably not his last.

Nick can be contacted via his website www.nickcorble.co.uk and would like to make it plain that Golden Daze is a work of fiction and that any similarity to any characters, living or dead, is unintended and entirely coincidental.

NICK CORBLE

GOLDEN DAZE

Matador
9 De Montfort Mews
Leicester LE1 7FW, UK
Tel: (+44) 116 255 9311 / 9312
Email: books@troubador.co.uk
Web: www.troubador.co.uk/matador

ISBN 978-1848760-240

A Cataloguing-in-Publication (CIP) catalogue record for this book
is available from the British Library.

Typeset in 11pt Palatino by Troubador Publishing Ltd, Leicester, UK
Printed in the UK by TJ International Ltd, Padstow, Cornwall

Matador is an imprint of Troubador Publishing Ltd

To Golden Boys everywhere

Contents

Programme Notes

Some days are just different from all the rest. Like the right spice in a perfect curry, they contain the essential ingredient needed to make them memorable. Very rarely that ingredient can be so exceptional that it moves beyond the simply memorable and morphs into something life changing. I'm talking about pivotal moments, those times when fate applies electrodes to your life and BANG, everything changes. Most of us have moments like these. The trick is in knowing how to spot them.

Let me explain the Westlake Theory of Pivotal Moments. As I see it there are two extremes. At one end of the spectrum there's the Big Set Piece - births, marriages and deaths, that sort of thing. These are your standard off the shelf pivotal moments where we have a conditioned reflex on how we should feel and react; so that while they can qualify as bona fide pivotals they skulk in nonchalantly through a crack in the door, like a cat entering a crowded room. Unlike cats however, they are largely predictable.

More shocking are the pivotal moments at the other extreme that creep up behind you and apply a sharp jab in your kidneys. What makes these more interesting is that they can happen anyplace, anytime. They may happen to take place at a big event, it's just that you thought you were going along to enjoy yourself not to have your life changed forever; or they may just as easily happen in situations so ordinary they barely seem credible as a suitable setting for a pivotal moment.

These are the real shockers, the ones that make you think afterwards 'if I'd only got out of bed ten minutes earlier' or 'what if I'd worn a different pair of socks'. In fact, these moments can appear either at the time so ordinary or equally so bizarre that the fact that they were pivotal gets lost. Completely impervious to the fact that fate is hovering ghost-like on your shoulder, you go about your business, blind to the possibility of your life being transformed forever. Sometimes it can take years to realise that a particular moment was pivotal at all - take it from one who knows.

So, pivotal moments: tricky little blighters. Sometimes they're radioed ahead, other times they appear totally out of the blue. Sometimes obvious, at other times disguised. Sometimes in your face, other times sitting in the middle of a Russian Doll it can take years to peel the layers away from. Then there's something about the frequency with which they happen. In the same way that some folks can go all through life without ever falling in love, some people may lie on their death bed never having experienced a pivotal moment, whilst others, like serial romantics, get them all the time.

Me, I can remember two quite clearly, with almost exactly a year between them, book-ending a strange period when, on reflection, an awful lot was going on, although it didn't always feel that way at the time. The first falls into the ordinary camp, although ordinary isn't how I'd have described it at the time. Phrases like bloody irritating, stomach wrenching and totally desperate would have been more likely to have come to mind.

As for the other, well you're going to have to wait a bit for that.

TRAIN

1

ANYONE WHO WAS THERE will remember that the late 70s and early 80s weren't exactly what you might call jolly. In fact if we're being totally honest they were pretty bloody miserable. The country was like a punch drunk boxer standing up and waiting for the next blow to land. We were down and almost out, everyone seemed to sense it and quite a few were even happy to talk about it.

Being British though, most of us simply mumbled about our 'lot' and looked round for someone else to kick: Europeans, Argentineans, we weren't fussy, anything to avoid actually doing anything about it. Eventually, things got so desperate that we put our faith in a no-nonsense matron to sort things out for us, and even if most of us had severe doubts that the medicine she was administering would actually work, there was at least a sense of relief that at last someone was doing something.

Being pissed off seemed to be the national condition, and on the day my story begins, sometime early in June 1983, this was a pretty good description of the way I was feeling. It wasn't anything to do with the wider economic outlook, the state of the nation or the value of the pound; it was much more personal than that. My head was a mess, as if someone had just performed open brain surgery on me and had forgotten to put the bits back in the right order. Not unreasonably, therefore, I was feeling pretty hacked off, although like everyone else I didn't really know who or what to direct my anger at.

I also knew, deep down, that feeling this way wasn't exactly what might be called reasonable. After all, all things considered, I was in a pretty privileged position. White, middle class, just coming down from university with what I hoped was going to be a decent degree in Economics, I had a full stomach and a reasonable tan. To top it all my football team, Watford FC, the mighty Hornets, had just had their best season ever - second in the entire league having beaten top of the league Liverpool on the last day of the season, which to us fans at least made us the moral champions.

What made this achievement all the more remarkable was the fact that, like a snake easing a path through the branches of a tree, we'd spent the previous five years tenaciously working our way up from the lowest depths of the football league - with our arrival at the top having been about as welcome as the average boa constrictor to most outsiders. As if to rub our detractors' noses in it, coming second meant that European games beckoned. Little old Watford, playing the elite of Europe, a fantasy made flesh.

So really, all things considered, things weren't too bad. Dammit, the rest of my life beckoned, and looking back at it now through the misty windscreen of hindsight, you could argue that things were about as good as they could get, and you'd probably be right. Still, who ever said that life is reasonable, or that twenty year old white, middle class, soon-to-be-graduates are reasonable, especially if they'd just had a miserable job interview and were still virgins?

So it was that I found myself in deepest Surrey, my head staring down at the pavement and my hands deep into my trouser pockets, ambling disconsolately down an endless platform trying to find the train that could whisk me back into central London and then onwards to home as quickly as possible, my own personal dark cloud trailing like a vapour trail above me. I found my train and stepped in, the familiar smell of damp fabric enveloping my mood. Once inside the carriage I remember feeling a sense of satisfaction that I was alone before throwing my rucksack onto the seat beside me and sticking my feet up on the one opposite. I wasn't in a mood to be sociable; I was looking forward to turning up the heat on my misery stew too much.

Of course I knew the train wasn't running simply for my benefit and this was confirmed soon after when I began to detect from deep within it a vaguely familiar rumbling, like someone's stomach after a bad pint. The sounds grew more familiar and my first thought was that there must have been a match on somewhere, even though I knew the season was over.

It sounded like a group of travelling fans engaging in the familiar rhythm of a chant, the combination of repetition and discordant harmony sending out signals of comradeship. Kindred spirits perhaps? Curiosity got the better of me and I made my way up the carriage to the connecting door hoping to find the source of the noise. A thick film of grime covered the glass, which was further obscured by a faded No Smoking sticker, the edges of which had browned and curled. A quick rush of adrenaline pulsed through me as I peered through, but as the sound got closer and I began to make out the words, lubricated as they were with what I guessed was somewhere between six and eight pints of lager, my mood sagged.

'One Maggie Thatcher, there's only one Maggie Thatcher, one Maggie Thaaaaaaaaaaaatcher,' the note on the final word being held in a way that wouldn't have shamed a barber shop quartet, before ending with a final and confirmatory: 'there's only one Maggie Thatcherrrrr,' the note dropping at the end.

I had exercised my democratic right for the first time in a General Election a few days before, by post. The way I saw it, Watford was my true home and that was where I wanted my vote to count. Clearing out my room, packing, signing off at university and the prospect of the job interview I'd just come away from had, in the context of my life at the time, constituted a heavy agenda; and as such I'd completely forgotten that for most of the rest of the population it wasn't just another Thursday, but polling day.

The train was of the old slam-door type with vivid blue plush seats decorated with red and yellow diamonds. Triple seats sat either side of a narrow corridor, a typical commuter train with nets dangling over the seats to snare briefcases and umbrellas. It was mid-afternoon and I was alone, so naturally my greatest fear was that I was about to come up against a group of unemployed skinheads confident of victory for their chosen one.

I was wrong. Yes, they were celebrating, but this was no bunch of skinheads, but suits - fellow-supporters of the immaculately coiffured one, but at the opposite end of the evolutionary chain. I gradually made them out through the glass in the door. They were young, well tanked up on champagne (they were each holding a bottle which acted as a bit of a giveaway) and, as was their way, they had herded. At least a dozen I guessed, but more important than their number was the fact that they were heading my way.

As there were only two carriages I had no option other than to hope that they'd struggle with the door, it was that or negotiate a path through them in the hope that there'd be passengers on the other side and I didn't fancy that, not with my best jacket on. So it was that I ended up scampering to the back of the carriage and crouching down in my seat hoping they wouldn't be able to see me; like a grown ups' version of Hide and Seek.

I'd recently come across the word 'yuppie', so at least I could put a name to my enemy, although personally I preferred the more traditional term 'upper class twats'. Young certainly, upwardly mobile, I supposed so, but professional? Not really, just a bunch of wannabies pretending to be something they weren't. Whatever they were, my guess was they'd gone out to lunch and stayed there, at least in spirit. Half the day remained for people to cast their votes but they knew, as we all knew in our heart of hearts, what the result was going to be.

Maggie, slayer of the unions, defeater of the Argies, Churchill in a dress, was on her way to a second term despite mass unemployment and deep seated social unrest, and there was nothing the likes of me could do but grin and bear her for five more years.

At that precise moment though, I was more worried about the next five minutes. The unmistakeable sound of a door handle being rattled began to seal my fate, the future was inevitable and I was about to get an early taste of it. For a couple of minutes however there was hope. Different blokes tried to open the door, following a routine that went: rattle the handle, kick the door and swear (it being a matter of pride for each of them to find a different swear word) until one smart arse finally got the knack of it.

The singing - which until then had been muffled - suddenly assumed a greater clarity, as if someone had lifted a blanket off the loudspeakers. I could see them all reflected in a plastic cover over an advertising poster at my end of the train: it was as if the people at the office where I'd just had my interview had risen up as one, zombie like, and followed me.

Resisting the temptation to let them know that there was no such word as 'Yah,' I held my ground and my breath as the voices got louder and louder, competing with the rhythmic thumping of tracks outside and as they began their inevitable progression down the carriage. Gibberish poured from their mouths like crap out of a broken sewer pipe as the noise grew to unbearable levels, punctuated by neighing laughter which nearly always ended with a snort. I cowered behind the tall seatback, moving closer to the window to gain a cornered animal's spurious sense of safety.

'Maggie, Maggie, Maggie' came the cry from a solitary voice, followed immediately by everyone else chipping in with the refrain 'In. In. In.' Judging by the rhythmic braying this produced it seemed that this was the height of wit, turning on its head the chant those who were against her had been using over the previous three weeks. In fact, it was so good that they decided to repeat it - again, and again, and again, and again.

Then there was a pause, apparently while alcohol levels were topped up, followed by much theatrical belching. The whole situation had assumed some kind of sense of unworldliness, as if I'd been caught up in one of the weird new Channel Four productions so popular at that time, although the thumping in my chest had told me this wasn't a play, this was for real.

It was during this break that I made out the unmistakeable sound of a bottle hitting the floor followed by a series of clanks as it glanced off metal seat legs, no doubt spinning as it went, working its way inexorably towards me. Although I couldn't see it I could hear it, and I just knew it was heading my way, glug-glugging its contents over the floor as it went. After one of the longest minutes of my life it suddenly slammed against the end of the carriage as we picked up speed down a straight stretch, and the sound seemed to act as the starting gun for a stampede in my direction.

The moment the leader of the pack slid on the soles of his black brogues to reach the bottle first was the moment I discovered what a fox must feel like when confronted by a pack of salivating dogs. There was a moment's silence and then the guy I took to be the Master of the Hounds broke it.

'Well looky here chaps, see what I've found.'

He couldn't have been much older than me, but his sharply tailored suit and slightly padded shoulders seemed to give him an air of assumed authority. The emergence of his breed was something that had passed me by during my exile on campus and I wasn't sure how to react.

A sea of identical faces appeared one after another from behind every inch of the edge of my seat, not a chin amongst them, each supported by a bulbous-knotted tie ever so slightly yanked to one side, as if for effect, with most of them also sporting red braces.

As it happened, the initiative was taken away from me as one of the faces over the top of the seat simply yelled an elongated 'Hiyah' straight into my ear at full volume, while another, slightly out of time with the rest, offered a more subdued 'Wotcha' with a distinctly rougher accent, the dissident of the class.

'Hello,' I replied, with all the dignity I could muster, half raising a hand in greeting as if I'd suddenly decided to make a discrete bid at an auction. It seemed a matter of time before one of them suggested they de-bag me, but I dismissed the thought as quickly as it arrived. Everyone's eyes seemed to drift towards the Master of the Hounds as, with a dramatic collapse worthy of Norman Wisdom, he flopped down beside me in the seat. What might have happened next is anyone's guess, but after a few leaden seconds events began to take control and my new neighbour started to jerk his head and chest forward in regular spasms.

For a moment I thought he was going to have a heart attack and then the dreadful truth hit me - he was going to throw up. The previous three years had given me a lot of experience of this situation, and as the only sober person in the carriage I assumed an uncharacteristic air of leadership which could only have been driven by events, leapt to my feet and tried desperately to open the window.

Quite why British Rail windows at the time were designed so that you had to lean on them at the top before you could open them had always been a mystery to me, and luck being the fickle mistress she is, my particular window had decided to give me trouble.

'Come on you bastard,' I mumbled under my breath - cursing wasn't helping, but it gave me something to take my mind off what might be about to head my way. The chinless wonder in my seat had begun to dribble - we were on a countdown to disaster.

I turned to yell to the others to try other windows, but all I got was a chorus of giggles, as if I was the lead in a pantomime laid on especially for their benefit and they were watching to see what I might do next. The Master of the Hounds meanwhile was continuing his mock coronary thrombosis routine, with the intervals between contractions getting shorter and the spasms themselves getting longer, all the signs coming together to suggest that he was about to reach the puffed-out-cheeks stage. I guessed we had mere seconds before he presented us with a delivery - and I didn't mean the sort which would merit cigars all round. I gave the window one last shove - it wasn't having any of it - and spun round to issue what my instinct told me was going to be a final appeal for help.

At that precise moment a spume of porridge coloured vomit arched out into the air from below, describing an almost perfect arc as it homed in on, and deposited itself all over, the front of my beautiful black, brand new and never worn before, corduroy jacket. If it hadn't have been for the contents involved the whole manoeuvre could even have been regarded by an onlooker as something almost graceful.

The laughter now reached a crescendo as the Master's acolytes, all perfectly protected by the back of the seat, had got away scot-free. An encore was clearly demanded and as I saw the cheeks below me billow out once more I dropped my shoulder and performed a feint that wouldn't have shamed Watford's superstar John Barnes, only to find my view suddenly altering wildly as I slipped in the mess below me and, with a dreadful sense of inevitability, I began to topple.

Flinging both arms out I managed to grab the base of the seat opposite with one hand whilst the other, recoiling from touching my nemesis sitting there, secured a grip on the handrail at the top of what had been my seat. My balance was now a delicate trick to maintain, my legs spread apart, feet slowly sliding further apart, and arms stretched forward, I was caught in a nightmare game of Twister, my back presenting a table in front of the puke-dispenser.

It proved to be too much of a temptation. There was a short silence and then he convulsed once more and with an athlete's heave from his stomach sent a second, and I suspected not yet final, jet of vomit into the air, landing like a cow pat on my back, its warmth slowly permeating through the layers of my clothes until I could feel its dampness against my skin. It just wasn't my jacket's day. The general silence, so briefly broken, resumed, underscored by the sound of spitting up of after-birth from the chunder-king.

After a few moments a quiet and surprisingly sober voice, which I recognised as the same guy who'd offered me the 'Wotcha' earlier, whispered 'It was only wafer-thin' in a mock French accent. The fact that I recognised the quote as coming from Mr. Creosote in the new Monty Python film didn't really offer that much consolation.

'Fresh air everyone,' came a sudden braying shout from the crowd, and miraculously this time the order was obeyed, with windows opening all over the carriage in rapid succession, as if the assembled ranks were all back in their school's army cadet units and were responding to an order from their sergeant major.

'Nice one Bongo!'

'Brilliant shot old man!'

The entertainment, it seemed, wasn't yet over. I didn't know what to do next, whether to stand up first, or try to get my jacket off before the puke rolled down my back. Precariously balanced, a pool of regurgitated champagne across my shoulders and the front of my jacket trailing hopelessly in yet more of the foul smelling stuff, the decision was taken away from me as the train took a sharp corner and

I fell unceremoniously to the floor, glancing my face away just in time so that only one cheek landed in the rancid pool below.

From this vantage point I could make out the blue nylon of my rucksack on the edge of the widening stream of sick. Although all it held was a pile of dirty washing it rapidly became clear that even this had decided to engage in its own little disaster. From deep within it was giving off a stink of its own. Neither puke nor five day old underwear, it was the sweet and slightly tangy scent of Old Spice coming from the nearly full bottle I'd packed in one of the inner pockets and had, it seemed, smashed when the bag had hit the floor. As I wallowed around like a hippo in a mudbath, another sudden lurch caused the whole of my body to slide, and I whacked a temple and the whole of one side of my face on the metal leg of the seat.

It was the final insult. Things could get no worse. I rose onto my knees and lifted my jacket off of my back using only fingertips, by now retching myself as my nostrils were assaulted by the acrid and overpowering stink of alcohol combined with vinegar. At that point it was touch and go as to whether I might add the tuna and sweetcorn sandwich I'd managed to grab from the station kiosk to the mess below. By then the Master, who I now knew by his chosen name of 'Bongo', had been led off and had his head stuck outside one of the open windows - too little too late.

I remained poised in my bewildered position for a minute or two, just enough time for the numbness and general shock to subside sufficiently for me to feel a throbbing down the side of my face where I'd hit it against the seat leg. It wasn't only the side of my face, but also one edge of my nose, making the two thousand volts worth of pain that was now racing along the side of my skull feel even worse. The only thing in the pain's favour was it briefly took my mind off my predicament.

Without warning, the raucousness further down the carriage started up again, chants of 'five more years' echoing around the rattling tin box as if nothing had happened, and I was left to fend for myself.

Or not quite.

'Here mate, take this.' A pristine white handkerchief flew through the air towards me, a sticking plaster for a road accident but I took it anyway and wiped the worst of the sick off my face, away from my lips and out of my eyes and nose, wincing as I brushed the side of my nostrils. Glancing down at the linen I saw the interesting combination of textures and colours I'd managed to pick up with it, with crimson a dominant theme. Somewhere on the side of my head had started to bleed, a diagnosis confirmed by a huge blob of congealed blood, or it could have been something else, I didn't feel like speculating, landing on the front of my shirt.

For the first time I was able to put a face to my benefactor - who I identified as the guy who'd offered the 'Wotcha' earlier. He stood out from the others with deep brown, unfashionably long, sideburns and a moustache, whereas all the others were clean shaven to a man, almost certainly because they couldn't have grown much more than fuzz even if they'd wanted to. I noticed that his get up was the same as all the others though, a thin pin striped suit and, in his case, a light pink shirt with a white collar. No braces on this one though.

'Old Bongo never could hold his booze,' he informed me, as if this explained everything. 'You okay?' I gave him a glare that said in words of one syllable 'what do you think?' The truth was I felt like the biggest dickhead ever - only cubed.

'Sorry, dumb-ass question,' he acknowledged.

I nodded agreement and he wandered back to his kind, the maverick hound who'd stayed and had his curiosity satisfied before rejoining the pack. I didn't feel like thanking him and didn't have a chance anyway as by then the train was pulling into the station and the only thought in my head was to get off and get cleaned up.

2

THE JOB INTERVIEW was something my Dad had arranged. According to Mum, he'd 'pulled some strings' with an old school friend. Both of these crucial bits of information had put my defensive hackles up, but not enough to protect me against the experience itself. Obedience, like yawning through early morning lectures, is a hard habit to shake off though and I'd interrupted a perfectly satisfactory routine of getting up late, practicing my pool game and sunbathing to pack up my stuff and head back early to make the appointment.

On the other hand I'd recognised that the interview had provided the jolt I needed to actually do something, to start down the road that led to the rest of my life. My exams had finished early and most of my mates still had their heads down in the library so I was actually bored witless, wandering around campus like the solitary turkey who'd been given a reprieve for Christmas. There wasn't even any football to watch. More pressing was the fact that my grant had run out and I'd had to take advantage of my situation by getting in early on the final year student ritual of selling off most of my worldly chattels on the lawn outside the Union - the amp, the tape deck, the Wharfedales, the books and even the posters off my walls.

The whole process had actually proved to be surprisingly cathartic; a sort of personal Bonfire of the Vanities, but it had left a gap - and not just where my music system and posters used to be. I was ready to move on. The smell of stale beer and the sticky floor of the Union held little attraction in daylight and I didn't have enough spare cash for Space Invaders. I was playing a different kind of game, a waiting game, stuck in one purgatory between finals and results, and another between being a student and becoming a responsible tax-paying citizen.

The world of work was one I'd already tasted, and it hadn't been too bitter on the palate. The previous summer I'd worked at the local golf club, helping to keep the grass under control, and I'd got to know the satisfying feel of a pay slip made thick with notes in my back pocket on a Friday. I was ready for the next move, from what my old mate Marx would have called a wage slave to becoming a salaried professional.

The dark grey cloud of finals had obscured my vision for months as I'd consoled myself with the belief that I'd actually start applying for things once I knew what sort of degree I'd got. Far better, the rational half of my brain had told me, to focus on getting a good degree than to waste effort on applications. In amongst Maggie's three million unemployed someone waving an upper second might stand a better chance of being noticed, at least that was what I'd kept on telling myself. The exams themselves had come in a rush and were all over following a mad ten day sprint in May. Afterwards I seemed to suffer from some kind of battle fatigue, my mind and body going into shutdown as the rest of the world just carried on. I was like someone in a balloon looking down, drifting in an aimless but not unpleasant way, but not really going anywhere and probably heading for a hard landing.

With hindsight it might have been a good idea to have used at least some of my spare time boning up a bit on insurance before the interview with my Dad's mate. Up until then my only experience of it had been my annual Endsleigh student policy and to be honest I hadn't really understood that. Turning up with a rucksack full of dirty washing probably hadn't been the brightest move either, and if I'd known then what I know now I'd probably have gone home first and borrowed one of Dad's suits - but hey, that's hindsight, and given what ended up happening afterwards perhaps it was no bad thing I hadn't.

The office was tucked away down a side street in deepest Sutton and located in a modern office block probably built in the 70s. From the outside the building oozed potential, mystery and ambiguity in almost equal proportions, there could have been anything going on in there from a den of spies to an abattoir. I mounted the stairs to the third floor as directed where I was greeted by a small reception area with a central table covered with a selection of the day's newspapers. A lanky blonde with a bright red jacket and an unfeasibly flat chest sat behind a desk keeping herself busy rearranging bits of paper in a wire rack. She took my name, made a call and got back to the important job of ignoring me. I laid my rucksack down on the floor and waited.

Behind a glass partition I could see a huge open plan area with rows and rows of desks laid out in a grid, a modern day equivalent of a Third World sweat shop or something out of Dickens, the only thing missing being a raised dais at the end and someone poised with a quill in hand. Each desk had a small grey cloth-backed partition along its top edge. These partitions were no more than eighteen inches high and further inspection revealed them to be pinboards.

Pictures on the boards provided the only colour in what could only have been described as a depressingly drab room, the only other exceptions being four large overgrown Swiss Cheese plants sitting in red pots in each corner supported with bamboo canes, and an odd choice of posters of bland nature scenes and motivational messages blu-tacked on the coffee coloured walls. On closer inspection, I wasn't even sure the Swiss Cheese plants were real.

The other wall of the reception area was taken up with a mirror and I inspected my reflection while waiting for whatever came next. I certainly needed a haircut, with dark locks covering the top half of my ears and only just staying out of my eyes; but I was planning a visit to Luigi in the High Street sometime the following week. I had, however, taken the trouble to shampoo it the night before. The face gazing back at me looked relaxed and impossibly bronzed for so early in the year. Continuing with the inspection I noted that I'd arrived at university with bum fluff but was leaving it with bristles and noticed a patch under my chin I'd missed with the razor in my rush to get going that morning.

A round face I suppose you'd call it, an empty canvas waiting to have experience etched onto it. I didn't like my nose, I still don't, a real Pete Townshend of a conk, but you know what they say about people with big noses, big conk, big cock - well that was my standard riposte if anyone ever remarked on it, well blokes anyway. Hazel eyes and bushy brows, which maybe I could get Luigi onto as well, with high cheekbones and a slightly gaunt look - I could imagine Mum doing her nut later that evening, going into her whole 'not eating enough' routine.

The nose was a problem in another way too. I don't know why but for some reason the base camp from which it began its gradual ascent from my cheek bones had, for the last ten years or so, acted as some kind of unofficial gathering point for any grease and assorted bacteria in the vicinity, a sort of magnet for invisible filth. No amount of washing or Clearasil seemed to hold it back and the latter always seemed to do as much harm as good, leaving giveaway Red Indian smudge marks and a revolting chemical smell which together seemed to shout out 'Watch out, Spotty Herbert coming!'. Having either a vividly red, drunk's nose or feeling a nagging soreness on the front of my face had, it seemed, become my permanent condition.

15

I'd found myself gearing up for an inspection when a booming voice entered the room, just before the person it belonged to. I guessed this was Dad's mate. He thrust out his hand towards me as if it was a lethal weapon. I parried it, tucked my hankie into my pocket and swerved my wrist before taking his proffered hand in a smooth manoeuvre worthy of an Olympic fencer.

'Tim Grady,' he announced boldly, shaking my hand up and down as if he expected to pump some water from my mouth.

'Colin Westlake,' I replied, in what I thought was an equally determined manner, shaking not just my hand but the whole upper part of my trunk.

'Col. Good to meet you.' It seemed we were on first name terms, something that didn't bother me, other than I hated being called 'Col'.

'So, Col,' he continued, the time for preliminaries clearly over, 'What would you say is the greatest invention of the twentieth century?'

Leaving aside the fact that the twentieth century still had a little way to go, a point I felt would be nit-picky under the circumstances, I got ready to respond, confident in my answer.

'Insurance, Tim,' I announced, with an exclamation rather than a question mark, although I was immediately struck by doubt as to whether insurance *was* an invention.

'The telephone,' came the correct answer, as Tim ignored my clearly stupid reply as if he hadn't heard it, something that was entirely possible, and looking around I could see that to a man everyone in the vast warehouse of an office seemed to agree with him as they were all using one: black numbers with keypads.

'And tell me, Col,' he asked conspiratorially, 'what do you notice as you look round the room?'

This time I paused a little before answering, but there seemed no other obvious response than the realisation I'd come to moments before, except this time I indulged myself in a query. 'Everyone's on the phone?'

'Yes, obviously,' he responded, hiding a little soupcon of irritation. 'Anything else?'

'Everyone looks the same?' Tim looked at me quizzically, looking around to check, as if this was something he'd never actually noticed before. I was beginning to feel like someone who'd sat down in the wrong seminar and become the focus of the Tutor's questioning. Tim put me out of my misery.

'They all have a picture on their pinboards,' Tim announced, spreading his arms in a gesture of amazement that I hadn't spotted it. I glanced around. He was right, they did, although they weren't pictures of wives and girlfriends as you might expect, but of things. I didn't know a lot about cars but I did know that the cars in the pictures, and a good half of them did feature cars, were sporty numbers, Porsches at a guess, and the occasional MG. Other pictures featured large houses, villas in exotic locations, watches and other jewellery and bits of indeterminable fancy electrical kit.

Tim planted a hand in the small of my back and directed me into the room, where we were hit immediately by a babble of urgent voices half talking, half yelling; then half cajoling, half pleading into the phones. We started to walk amongst the desks like a Victorian mill owner and his sidekick patrolling his machinery. Occasionally one of the suits would look up and smile at Tim, the smile usually dissolving into a barely suppressed laugh as they looked me up and down, not seeing me, but my brown trousers and black corduroy jacket. The jacket had been a Christmas present from my Mum and although it wasn't the height of fashion, in fact I distinctly recalled Michael Caine wearing something similar in one of his early spy films, it was the smartest I had at the time. In this sea of suits I stood out like a rabbit at Crufts. Tim strode confidently amongst his men, dispensing slaps on the back and up-turned thumbs like largesse to his peasants.

17

'Smile down the phone,' he exhorted, and rows of teeth suddenly appeared, 'sell the benefits, not the product.'

'Know why they have these pictures?' he asked me, returning to his game of twenty questions, but by then I'd given up guessing and just shook my head.

'It's like that song last summer - you got to have a dream, if you don't have a dream, how you gonna make your dream come true?' Thankfully he didn't actually sing.

'Captain Sensible,' I offered; resisting the temptation to add that he was talking about the man who was formerly part of one of the greatest bands of modern times: The Damned. Before he sold out.

'Whatever.' He waved a hand, as if swatting a fly away. 'Do you get what I'm saying?' he asked, pausing in his perambulations and staring me in the eye. By then I was totally confused.

'Not really,' I confessed.

'These pictures represent their next target. This is what they're working towards, their reward. If they make enough calls, connect with enough punters, generate enough sales then they make enough money to buy their dream. Get it now?'

I got it alright.

It wasn't quite what I understood by a career though. Naively perhaps, my cursory reading had led me to the idea that a career revolved around a series of challenges, the fulfilment of one's potential, making a contribution to society and finding some kind of satisfaction and pride in your role. Sure, money was important but it was something that would follow, not lead. Somehow I didn't think this was the right moment to chew this thread over with Tim.

'Let me tell you how it works,' he offered, as if he was dealing with a six year old child, and he was into his spiel before I could tell him not to bother. I only half listened as he talked about the need for people to insure their health, to insure their cars, to insure their houses, holidays and even their life, it seemed a matter of time before he suggested the need to insure their insurance, it seemed that every aspect of modern life could, and in his eyes should, be insured.

There was no doubting his passion for his subject. I'd hate to have to be the one who pointed out to him that insurance was inherently dull, just as I'd hate to be the poor sod sat next to him on a long journey. Insurance was, he announced, the lifeblood of the economy, the oil that greased the wheels of commerce, but I wasn't convinced. He went on to explain how the agents, by which I took him to mean the suited drones in front of me, simply phoned people up and talked them into buying the protection his firm offered, although from his perspective the agents weren't so much selling but doing the people on the other end of the line a favour. It was a sort of modern day mafia arrangement, only performed with phones rather than violin cases. The agents got a straight percentage cut on each closed deal and this is how they bought their dream. It wasn't exactly rocket science.

I eavesdropped in on the conversations as we walked around. The range of emotions being expressed would have done justice to a Sixth Form drama production, with about the same level of success. Sympathy, humour, pathos: anything to build empathy and pave the way to a possible sale. Whilst the recipients of all this effort would only have words to go on, I could see the body language too, and this was enough to betray what most of them were really thinking: 'Give me your money suckers.'

Suddenly a yelp went up, followed quickly by a sort of klaxon that in any other circumstances might have been mistaken as the four minute warning and then I sussed that someone had reached their target. Everyone not on a call stood up to see who it was and join in the yelping (they were big on yelping, it seemed to be a secret code) whilst those still on a call seemed to become more urgent.

Tim turned to me and spread his arms and hands outward

as if to say 'there you have it'. From his point of view the klaxon couldn't have come at a better time, a perfect demonstration of the effectiveness of his operation. Someone had just made their dream and his whole body language seemed to be saying that I could do that too - who wouldn't want to?

Me.

'Look, you're kind of busy here. I'm not really sure this is what I'm looking for.'

Tim pulled a face like someone had just kneed him in the crown jewels. He probably wasn't the sort of person who took rejection well; after all, selling was his game and he'd been selling me the job. He was a pro though, I'll give him that, and he was quick to recover.

'First time?' he asked.

'I'm sorry?'

'First interview?'

'Yes,' I replied.

'Thought so. Look, I'm going to say a couple of things now and you might want to listen.' I sensed from his tone that he'd realised he wasn't going to convince me about the job but wanted to get the last shot in. From my side I felt as if we were two chess players who'd just fought out an honourable draw.

'Sure,' I offered, extending the metaphorical hand of acceptance.

'Think it over - there's some real money to be made here.' I nodded with what I thought was the right combination of deference and grace and turned to go. 'Oh, and another thing,' he added.

'Yes?'

'That jacket.'

'What about it?'

'If you were to come back, make sure you're properly dressed next time, I don't want people saying 'who was that scruffy bugger you were with in the office' - know what I mean?'

Perhaps it was that comment that put a hex on the damned thing?

And now I was standing at the sinks in the Gents toilet at Victoria Station scraping puke off that self-same jacket, and take it from me, this isn't a recommended activity. Not only were the sinks disgusting and inadequate but the hand dryer merely wafted a mere hot lover's breath over anything put under it to dry. Beige coloured tiles lined the walls, if it wasn't for the thin layer of condensation covering them it would have been easy to think I was in an old fashioned butcher's shop.

I'd got most of the solid stuff off using the side of my NUS card (I'd reasoned I wasn't going to need it anymore) and stemmed the bleeding with a succession of hand towels. The wire basket under the sinks looked like it belonged to a M*A*S*H unit by the time I'd got into my stride, and there was still some way to go. The remarkable thing was that at first no one seemed to pay me any attention, as if what I was doing represented a daily occurrence. That or they were all being terribly British.

'You look like you could do with a hand.'

It was a statement, not a question, offered by a Good Samaritan wearing an extraordinary light tangerine jumper and a benevolent smile just as I was reaching the end of my tether. I took it as a good sign that unlike most other people I'd come across that day he wasn't wearing a tie. My legs were gripping my rucksack as the last thing I needed was for that to be nicked and I was hoping the Old Spice might do something to negate the smell. I was running out of ideas on what to do next to the clothes I was wearing and those inside the rucksack didn't offer much of an alternative, especially when I thought of all the broken glass within. It was with some relief therefore that I handed him my jacket, gripping it between two fingers as if it was contagious, although by that stage it was probably beyond caring for. He took this as a 'yes' and offered a sympathetic grunt as confirmation.

He immediately pulled half a dozen hand towels out of the dispenser, wetted them under the tap and proceeded to scrub the back of the jacket efficiently like a washerwoman by the banks of the Limpopo. I froze for a moment in admiration, just relieved that something positive was happening and that some of the responsibility for moving things on had been transferred to someone else. Up until that point I'd been stuck on damage limitation. It was also a relief to be rid of the damned jacket - the thing seemed to represent everything that had gone wrong with my day.

Despite the situation, he was smiling as he worked and his smile seemed to give me permission to begin to see the funny side to my predicament.

'Been in the wars have you? Celebrating early maybe?' he fished.

'Christ no. I've got nothing to celebrate, I'm the victim here,' I replied; perhaps slightly too self-righteously.

He looked relieved to see and hear that I was coherent and that seemed to break the ice between us. I suspected he was similarly relieved to realise that I wasn't one of Maggie's men.

'Andrew Woodford,' he volunteered, 'I would shake hands but ...'

'Colin Westlake,' I replied. 'Look, thanks a lot I really don't know how to ...,' he waved away my clumsy attempts to show gratitude with a flick of the wrist which he combined with the despatch of a mass of sodden towels into the wire basket in a further display of efficiency. Maybe he was a full time guardian angel and got a lot of experience at this sort of thing?

'More required,' he demanded, and I obeyed.

'So, what's the story?' he asked, resuming his scrubbing while I began work on my trousers, which I'd left on for obvious reasons, this being a public toilet in one of London's main railway stations. I regaled my tale, which he soaked up with a mixture of sympathy and resignation.

'Bastards,' he concluded succinctly, and I didn't disagree as we both laughed a manly laugh and got on with our respective tasks, comfortable now that we were on the same side of the political fence.

'Looks like it's going to be a disaster, you know,' he threw in after a period of silence, holding my jacket up to what counted for a light in order to inspect his handiwork.

It took me a second to realise he was talking about the election not my jacket, but once I clocked what he was talking about I was off. It was late night at the Student's Union all over again, a full scale, hurricane force, half-formed but heart-felt student rant: the sheer fecklessness of the Labour Party and the barely-standing joke that was Michael Foot, the sheer unfairness of the electoral system and how it allowed people like Thatcher to foist her monetarism and unflexing arrogance on us. All the frustration I'd bottled up after the double whammy of the interview and Bongo, the barfing buffoon, and on reflection probably a lot longer than that, spilled out in a stream of consciousness that wouldn't have disgraced a Guardian editorial.

'But what's the answer?' my new friend asked, egging me on rather than trying to slow me down, although I didn't recognise this at the time. I needed no further encouragement. More rage with a generous side-portion of half-digested (if that wasn't an inappropriate analogy) theory followed. I stopped my scrubbing and vented my spleen on the need for more radical approaches, a plea for fresh ideas, something, anything, to change the way things were.

Poor sod, he was helping me out and all I could do was treat him to one of my lectures. By the time I'd run out of things to say I was actually spitting blood, but this was mainly because I'd reactivated the cut on my temple in my anger and a small vein-thin red stream was tracking a path down one cheek.

Andrew paused to wipe it away, licking a clean hand towel and brushing it away as if he was my Mum kissing away a childhood tear, before returning to his cleaning duties, nodding politely to each new point in my continuing rant as I sponged bits of regurgitated lunch off the front of my legs. By the time I got down to cleaning my shoes I began to feel the first tremors of embarrassment, but I was in too deep and lacked experience on how to stop so I carried on regardless, keeping my eyes pinned firmly on the floor and the straps of my rucksack.

It was his last act of kindness to provide me with an exit route out of the conversational dead end I'd carved for myself. Handing me back the jacket he took the top of my arm, looked me in the eyes and urged me to 'Keep the passion son, keep the faith,' as if we were two parting spies in a foreign land urging each other on in the face of insurmountable odds. As I gingerly put the jacket back on - he'd done a good job, but the unmistakeable smell still lingered - he handed me a card.

'Look, if you ever want to get together give me a call.'

I glanced down at the card awkwardly before slipping it into my top pocket.

GROOVY

3

HERE'S A TIP FOR YOU: if you ever want to make sure of getting a seat on the tube wander into the carriage smelling of stale puke, ideally with plenty of evidence still splattered about your clothes to confirm that it's more than just a suspicion. Well, there's only so much you can achieve in a public toilet.

If you really want to make sure I can recommend a liberal dosing of dried blood on your face too, and throw in some Old Spice just for confusion. You'll be surprised how quickly the hordes clear. What's more, for a bonus, you can spread yourself out a bit because no one will sit either side of you. It's as if you have your own personal ten mile exclusion zone. The occasional innocent soul may take the place opposite, but don't worry, they won't last more than one station.

There are twelve stops between Baker Street and Watford on the Metropolitan Line - but on Election Day 1983 it felt like an hour a stop. I'd had enough by the time we got to Pinner, the blood had dried to a cake by then and was beginning to crack. I'd tried scratching it off but hard black bits got under my fingernails. By the time we reached Moor Park my jacket was so dry and stiff I could have folded it in the shape of a flower, like a large cardboard origami model, put it on the floor of the carriage and it would have stayed there, a monument to my misfortune. Croxley meant we were nearly there and the need to put together a plan of action. Home was out of the question, so Groovy Greg's it was then.

"king 'ell Colin-mate!' Groovy yelled as he opened the door, loud enough for anyone within a radius of fifty yards to hear. 'What happened to you? Been on another of your Anti-Nazi League marches or somethin'?' I stood on the doorstep watching as his brain whirred for another suitable witticism. When he eventually decided he couldn't think of one he reverted back to normal conversation, as if the compassionate part of him had regained control of his mouth - a very Groovy-like sequence. 'What you doing back so early for anyway?' adding 'you'd better come in,' before moving aside in a silent gesture that meant that he didn't really need me to provide answers.

Let me get one thing clear before we go any further. Groovy is without doubt the best mate a bloke could ever want, although I'm glad I've never been asked to produce any evidence for this assertion in a court of law, as frankly it's pretty thin on the ground. On the other hand if asked to put forward instances of times when he'd let me down, got me down and even put me down in public I'd probably be able to rattle on until the judge ordered an adjournment and sent the jury off for a night in a local hotel, but somehow, despite of all this, he'd always been there. This was of course because he had always been there, and I mean there, right next to me.

Next to me in the park while our mothers chatted. Next to me at the kindergarten we both attended for half a term, until our parents got wind of the rumour that the old dear running it lived with another woman and that neither of them had ever been married (apparently the fact that both had had unnaturally short cropped hair and always wore trousers hadn't been enough of a clue), and next to me on our first day at school. Groovy and I shared a desk during our first year at primary school, although, in a radical departure from usual practice, he sat behind me during the second year, a position which gave him ample opportunity to flick my ears whenever Mrs Appleton turned her back to write on the board. And so the pattern was set.

Of course he wasn't called Groovy then, just plain old Greg, or Gregory if his Mum was within earshot, the nickname came later and stuck. It arrived probably the same time we learnt about irony. Think of all the reasons why someone might earn the appellation Groovy and then think the opposite and you have my best mate. No John Lennon glasses, no flowery shirts, peace symbols and 'cool man', just a straight down the middle 1970s middle class boy. From a distance his long horse-like face was pockmarked with a confusion of dots which, on closer inspection, revealed a collection of freckles, spots and spot scabs that rumour had it the Natural History Museum was thinking of putting a bid in for.

His hair, then as now, was butter blonde and invariably a day past its wash-by date, but never shoulder-length or in any style that could remotely be referred to as hippy. For brief moments it came dangerously close to his collar and peeked over the tops of his ears, and then would come the haircut. Groovy's Dad was of the school of thought that believed a damned good shearing had the effect of cutting back not only his boy's hairline but also the number of trips to the barbers he'd need, thereby saving money, regardless of the emotional cost paid in the hard currency of playground teasing. If it was his plan to help evade the genetic inevitability of hair loss I can tell them now that he failed. A definite ring of flesh arrived just as Groovy's teenage years departed.

As is the way of things, Groovy earned his nickname because it represented the very antithesis of what he was, but like a good caricature it was so appropriate it just stuck and it remained the name all his mates used. Groovy and I hung out together in the playground, played in the same teams, went to cubs and then scouts together, and shared tents together on camps. We'd even shared our first glimpse of a naked girl together. We hadn't understood at the time why we'd found that last shared moment so thrilling until later when we learned the facts of life from Chubby Johnson one rainy lunchtime - together, naturally. Chubby was that rare exception that proved the rule, his nickname fitted him perfectly. He'd ballooned out when he was nine, the hormones that had kickstarted the process apparently forgetting to switch themselves off. Chubby unlocked the mystery of human reproduction for us, one which offered a cocktail of emotions ranging from disgust, through to a disbelief that this act was something our own parents could ever have managed (let alone the Queen and Prince Philip), yet at the same time it had come as something of a relief, as it explained a lot of things.

Groovy and I passed the 11 plus together (I did much better than he did, but a pass was a pass) and we ended up at the same school. Groovy's own hormones seemed to regard puberty as some kind of competition and by the time he was thirteen he stood a good foot taller than most of us, but he didn't stop there. His escalating height came at a cost though and by the time we hit the third form he walked with a slight stoop, as if his body was somehow unbalanced and was looking for some kind of way to hide from what it was doing.

Almost inevitably he became ungainly, and although his long legs gave him speed this was more than counter-balanced on the games field by a worrying lack of hand-eye coordination. Although the Games Master's often-used description of him as a 'great blonde streak of piss' may have been a little harsh it did carry more than a grain of truth.

By this time our respective parents seemed to be echoing our closeness and when my folks first broached the idea of moving (we lived within a few doors of each other), Groovy's Mum and Dad picked up on the idea and within four months we found ourselves living next door but one to each other on a brand new housing estate out towards Leavesden, near the film studios, to the north side of town.

By then the die was cast and we set about growing up together, although there was nothing pre-ordained or planned about it, it just happened. We also found out about Watford Football Club together and alone, by which I mean it was something we discovered for ourselves, our Dads both being rugger men who would openly dismiss football as a game for 'oiks', even though they were barely one generation away from being working class themselves. Behind their backs Groovy and I called the rugger bugger crowd 'egg chasers', thereby beginning the process that all teenagers are obliged to go through of distancing ourselves from their parents' generation. The rest you can guess, birthday parties, discos, girlfriends, first puff on a cigarette - my last, his first of many until he gave up last year, this being the one and only thing I can think of we ever disagreed on.

Shoulder to shoulder we stood together on the terraces as an ever changing sea of faces represented our barely glowing hopes out on the pitch and assumed the mantle of heroes. We would have been too shy to speak to them if we'd seen them on the High Street, but out there on the terraces we shouted to them and cajoled them into ever greater effort on our behalf as if we knew them intimately, bound together by the firm belief that we were family, in this together. With their black shorts and dark yellow, almost orange, shirts, emblazoned with nothing more than the club's crest over their left breast, they were our buzzing hornets, our golden boys.

Saturday afternoons and midweek cup games we stood exposed to the elements with nothing other than a rather shabbily produced programme to protect us from the rain that always seemed to begin to fall when we were 2-0 down with quarter of an hour to play. It became our life, a triumph of hope over experience, but at least it was our own, unique, existence, shared with only a few thousand anonymous others. This was something we could do together that our parents hadn't told us to do. It wasn't school, it wasn't cubs, it wasn't swimming lessons. It was Watford Football Club, and it was ours.

We served our apprenticeship and then just as we were finishing the fourth form, and with the prospect of 'O' levels looming the following summer, everything suddenly changed: the club changed hands. The new owner was stubby, balding and probably gay but he had also been one of the biggest rock stars on the planet. He was Elton John.

We didn't know what to make of it at first but we were prepared to grant him the benefit of the doubt after his first and probably greatest masterstroke. He persuaded the man who'd taken Lincoln City to the fourth division title the previous season - scoring an inconceivable hundred plus goals along the way - to become our manager. Here was a simple man with an uncomplicated name - the sort of name you'd expect a boy in your class to have - and he had a manner to match. He was Graham Taylor, and he was about to become our Prince.

With form like that there was a chance he could get us out of the basement of the league, but together Elton and Taylor had a grander scheme. They offered to take our hands and lead us towards the sunny uplands of the First Division. 'Yeah right!' was the universal reaction, but we didn't really care, when you're young and someone as improbable as Elton John is in charge you're happy enough to go along for the ride.

'Elton John's Taylor-made army,' that's what they started singing down in the Rookery, the end where the hard core fans stood, their voices amplified by the fact that they were lucky enough to have a roof over their heads. The chant summed up the partnership. The pop star looking for some meaning in his life and the manager with something to prove: they made a hell of a double act. European football in five years was something else they promised, a prediction as outrageous as some of the outfits Elton had worn on stage. We were too young to know different though, we believed them and signed on the psychological dotted line.

As our testosterone kicked in and our respective Mums complained that we seemed to be going through a fresh shoe size every four or five months, so Watford began to reach for the stars. As we emerged from the innocence of the lower school so our football club began its climb from the primordial slime of the Fourth Division. We grew up together, the three of us, the success of the club only magnifying and accentuating the experience.

We started 1977 dreading the prospect of 'O' Levels the following summer, but we didn't let it get to us as the magic dust began to work its wonders and we found ourselves on the end of a winning streak that ended with us as champions - the Third Division beckoned. We felt ready for it, we had matured. Entering the Sixth Form seemed like a similarly natural progression. Suits instead of school uniforms, the freedom of the Sixth Form Centre with its snooker table, darts board and turntable, and some of us learning to drive, nothing fazed us. Likewise, the golden boys eased their way through the Third Division as if it had been created for their convenience, not champions this time but runners-up to Shrewsbury, but promotion was promotion and we waved goodbye to the likes of Blackpool and Plymouth Argyle - perhaps we'd meet again some time in the cup we sneered as we waved them goodbye? That season saw Watford overtaking Taylor's old club Lincoln, us on the way up, them on the way back down to the basement.

By then other mates had began to join us on the terraces, although at heart the whole enterprise remained a Groovy and Colin thing, a party we had to invite them to. Paully and Trev were particular stalwarts, although I'm not sure that Trev ever really got to grip with the finer nuances of the game, he came more because he enjoyed the whole vibe of being part of something successful. We were our own group, standing on the same spot by the same yellow painted crowd barrier at the Vicarage Road end under the new electronic scoreboard, every other Saturday at 3pm.

We were particularly pleased to have Paully along as he was the first of us to get through his driving test and proved to be a willing chauffeur to away games if we were prepared to share the petrol. So it was that we gained another level of independence and waved goodbye to Supporters Club coaches and football specials out of Watford Junction. Travelling the country with Paully introduced us to a new and sometimes intimate relationship with the country's motorways as the single defining characteristic of his car was the almost total absence of metal holding it together.

Rust was there in abundance and in places a mixture of clay and mud had been used to cover over a gap. This tended to dry in the hot sun when it would start to crumble or, if there'd been recent rain, to sprout grass; making Paully's the only car I knew which carried a pair of scissors in the glove compartment for cutting the lawn.

The one indispensable thing required to travel with Paully, if you excluded nerves drop-forged in Sheffield, was a sleeping bag, as these gaps in the bodywork looked out onto the fast moving tarmac below and in winter would send a draft through the car cold enough to allow frost to form on the insides of the windows. Like pensioners at the seaside, we'd sit across the back seat (none of us was brave enough to share the front with Paully), looking like caterpillars still in their pupae, clutching a hot water bottle on the inside and, if we'd remembered to bring one, a Thermos flask on the outside to keep our hands warm.

Paully was always easy to spot in a crowd because of the pork-pie hat that never left his head, although to be honest it was more of a Cornish pasty, because there's nothing we liked better than nicking it and then sitting on it, much to his annoyance. That's what friends are for, to sit on your hat. Trev had a more chiselled look, a certain perfect Aryan quality, all blond hair and sharp cheek bones as if he had just stepped out of a group photo from the local Hitler Youth, something that may not have been too far from the truth, given some of his opinions. The bastard also seemed to have perfect skin, even the girls seemed to admire it, so he was saved from the indignity of the ever wandering moonscape of blotches and scabs that seemed to plague the rest of us.

As Watford's notoriety grew so did the status of our manager, as in our eyes he morphed first from an ordinary bloke to a demi-God and then into a fully paid up Deity. And yet throughout he never really changed. Defeat or victory he told it like it was, with his flat worn-down East of England, verging on a Yorkshire, accent and his down to earth honesty. He was confident and it was infectious, although at the same time he was always telling us not to get too carried away, like your Mum telling you not to get too excited at your birthday party. We all knew though that our story still had some way to go and were conserving our energies for when it got really exciting.

The Second Division, like the Upper Sixth, came as a bit of a shock. We were expected to behave like grown ups, to prove that we were capable of holding a place in the society we were soon going to become members of. We had to earn respect. Parents frowned when we disappeared for midweek games, suggesting that surely we had better things to do - like homework for instance. Everything became so serious, the stardust began to settle as Watford flirted briefly with relegation and struggled to make a mark.

'Keep the faith', that's what we told each other, but while we told ourselves that the Promised Land was still within reach, things were changing between Groovy and me. Whilst we were equals on the terraces and in everything else we did there was no disguising the fact that Groovy wasn't exactly gifted academically. Watching him in exam season was like watching a cat trying to swim and he was about as successful.

Everything changed the summer after we left school. Supporting Watford through what was a challenging season while also swotting for exams proved too much for Groovy. On balance, the team probably did better, finishing a respectable ninth, the only consolation being that our nearest neighbours and therefore bitterest rivals, Luton also missed out on promotion, despite gathering five more points. He got three 'E's in his 'A' levels and I got a 'B' and two 'C's. My results matched my offer from Reading University, so my future was sealed. Groovy's was less certain and the fate we'd both probably always suspected awaited him, although neither of us had ever voiced it, duly came to pass. He got a job. At the time there was only one growth industry and he joined it. He became a clerk at the local DHSS, helping people complete their applications for unemployment benefit.

He fell on his feet in another way when his Dad offered to help him with the deposit for an ex-council flat, which was probably his way of sweetening the pill, as well as re-claiming the bathroom. Groovy wasn't the only one to stay in Watford. Paully started working with his Dad in his estate agency business while Trev did what we'd always known he would do when he finally donned the blue uniform of a policeman. His Dad was a copper and his Dad's Dad had been one as well. For all I knew his Dad's Dad's Dad's Dad may even have been a Bow Street Runner or something.

Trev was built, as our aphorism-ready gym master often said, 'like a brick shit house', loads of muscle where you could see it, less upstairs where you couldn't. Paintbrush-like eyebrows emphasised his wrinkled forehead and gave due warning of a general state of hirsuteness which, when seen in the changing room showers, suggested he'd be able to give Grizzly Adams a fair run for his money. Trev got through school by being brilliant at any sport that required brute strength and a complete disregard for your own personal safety. He was, needless to say, captain of the School rugger XV and it would have been a shame to have wasted all that knowledge he'd gained on taking people out without leaving any obvious scars so it was just as well he took up the family trade.

So it was that our respective ways parted, with me being the only one of our crowd to go on to further education. In truth it was only a partial divorce however, as we stuck together for the sake of the football. I discovered the power of my thumb and hitched my way to as many games as I could make, including a fair few away ones, which usually meant going on my own, the others now finding other things or even work to do on a Saturday.

We still managed most home games, with me often hitching up the night before and staying at Groovy's, the pair of us enjoying a few bevvies in the local down the bottom of his street on Friday night. These were our times again, my 'smash and grabs' - I never told Mum and Dad I'd been back and usually tried to get back to campus after the game in time to catch a band or a party. I always wore my scarf when hitching, it was amazing the power it had. The common man seemed to have adopted 'plucky little Watford' and our story, it was almost as if we were the people's team - us against the so-called pundits and sports journalists who had something against the way we played. 'Kick and run' they called it. We called it winning and having fun - sod 'em all.

At the end of my second year at Reading we finally managed it - promotion to the top division. UNBELIEVABLE. Once again we'd managed it without being champions, but that wouldn't have mattered if it hadn't have been bloody Luton above us. Still, the way we saw it, it was six easy points the following year, well that's what we told ourselves anyway.

The following year it was the Upper Sixth all over again. Pressure to revise and work hard but hey, this was the First

Division, the big boys, the Manchester Uniteds, Arsenals and Liverpools of this world - how could I not go? So it was that I stepped up efforts to get to as many games as I could and was rewarded by an extraordinary run of results leading to us ending up, where else, as runners-up. It had been gravity defying, electrifying, a crystalisation of all the effort that had brought the club, and me, to that point. The club had reached its pinnacle and I had reached the end of the first phase of my life. It was time to take a deep breath and get ready for the next stage of the adventure. Arriving back at Groovy's was a statement of intent.

As it turned out he wasn't alone in the flat. My chances of whipping in for a quick clean up before going home to meet the parents were scuppered by the sight of Paully lounging around on the sofa. This wasn't unusual; Groovy's flat was a sort of unofficial gathering point for our crowd, as if there'd been some kind of silent agreement that if the bugger had been lucky enough to be given the money to buy it then the least he could do was share it.

And share it he did. The flat was probably best described as a work in progress, furnished through a combination of bin-end sales from Habitat and a couple of secondhand auctions I'd gone to with him, in order to help lug stuff back. As a result, inside the flat was a curious mixture of Swedish chic and dead granny.

Large spherical lampshades made with white paper and held together with what looked like old coat hangers dangled from the ceiling, while bamboo blinds covered the windows. Revealing the floorboards had been intended as another money saving exercise, but wood splinters were a common complaint from anyone foolish enough to go around the flat in their bare feet. A massive dark wood sideboard dominated the front room, an item Groovy had fancied because it solved all his downstairs storage problems in one, but it had been a bastard to get back and we only got it through the front door by unscrewing the legs. Thankfully, the flat was on the ground floor and we hadn't had to carry it up any stairs.

Just as I closed the front door a toilet flushed and Trev emerged doing up his flies with a satisfied look of a man who'd just enjoyed a complete bowel evacuation.

'Fuck me, the professor's back in town then,' he announced, before remembering to give the more traditional greeting between fellow Hornets of 'You 'Orns!' bellowed rather than spoken, before landing on top of Paully on the sofa as if he hadn't seen him. Sarah, Groovy's sister, was there too, hovering in the background tidying something. She smiled a greeting, manoeuvring a strand of her shoulder length honey-coloured hair behind an ear as she did so. I waved a hand in the air by way of acknowledgement to everyone and stood there like a lemon, not knowing what to do.

'Bath?' Groovy suggested after a few moments silence.

'Christ yes, do us all a favour,' added Paully, his voice slightly muffled by the lump of meat on top of him as he grappled for air. Knowing Trev there was a very real chance he was about to be farted on big time.

'Bath.' I agreed.

'I'll see if I can find you some of Greg's clothes for you to change into as well,' added Sarah as she set off to raid her brother's wardrobe and I marched to the back of the flat to run the taps. Some kind of explanation was now unavoidable and a long hot wallow would allow me a chance to reflect on what exactly had happened, before sharing it with my friends.

VISITORS

4

DID I MENTION that Groovy and Sarah were, still are, twins? They're not identical, obviously, but when we were growing up there were a lot of similarities, at least from behind. The same lamppost lankiness and build, even the same way of holding themselves, and at times the same hair length and colour, which did lead to more than one embarrassing moment involving physical contact during adolescence - a time when you were allowed to notice that your mate's sister was, well, a girl, but not really meant to mention it in any way that might be construed as fancying her. There are boundaries after all.

Sarah had always been there in the background. We'd all gone to the same primary school and although our ways parted when we were eleven and she was despatched to the Girls' Grammar, it wasn't long afterwards that our families became neighbours and on top of that we all shared the same bus home. As time went on she acquired curves Groovy couldn't boast; their similarity in height gave her an aura of elegance rather than gawkiness and her once cute smile became more than that, something blokes might long for in the hope that it was directed at them. It was no surprise that as teenage dawned we found ourselves going to the same discos and hanging out at the same youth clubs before we were old enough to get away with going into pubs.

Once you knew they were twins it was obvious. They seemed to operate on the same wavelength and spent so much time in each other's company that people not in the know sometimes thought they were a couple. They had that kind of intimacy with each other, the non-physical kind, where they were comfortable in each other's personal space and knew instinctively when the other needed them and what kind of support they needed, as if they occupied their own private world.

Although Sarah would very occasionally join us at the football I'd often wondered whether, sub-consciously, this was an area of his life that Groovy deliberately steered her away from, as if it was something he had carved out that was distinctively his own, rather than theirs. Sarah was the only person I knew other than his parents who called him Greg.

All this is a long-winded way of saying that when you imagined Groovy you usually also saw Sarah somewhere nearby as his shadow. When the pair of them knocked on the door of my Halls of Residence room in the middle of my first term at Reading early one Friday night, the surprise wasn't that she was there too but that the pair of them were there at all. Groovy was dressed in a jacket and pencil-thin tie, as if he'd come straight from work, whilst Sarah had what seemed to be a party dress on, purple velvet I remember, with a pair of floral sashes that looked like mock braces down the front and back. Perhaps the most striking thing about her that evening was her eyes; turquoise smudges of eye shadow made her look a bit like an Egyptian mummy. No, not an Egyptian mummy, more of a Victorian doll, as she'd also done something to the top of her cheeks, reddening them up as if she was in a permanent state of embarrassment. As it happened the embarrassment was more mine, I wasn't sure why, I think it was because it didn't seem natural for them to be there, as if they were visitors from another world. I wondered if they were on their way to somewhere, Sarah clearly wasn't dressed for a night at the Union. I ushered them into my room almost like they were uninvited relatives on the doorstep at Christmas.

I'm normally a tidy person, it's been said that I'm so anal on the subject that I even comb my own arse hairs, but my room was an uncharacteristic mess; although thankfully I'd made the bed a few moments before. The industrial grade carpet was liberally scattered with open books, their backs spread like a whore's legs with covers gazing up at the ceiling to keep a certain place. The red sixty watt bulb I'd put in myself cast an eerie film-developer's glow over the scene, hiding its worst defects, including the rather tatty curtains, which I hurriedly drew, and the accumulated ink stains over the rather battered wooden desk that came with the room. At least the picture I presented them with was one of studious endeavour, although the truth was it had been like that for the last two days, a barely started essay held in a state of suspended animation below the desk lamp, out of which came the room's only pool of white light.

We hadn't seen each other for six weeks, probably the longest we'd ever been apart. What am I talking about? It was definitely the longest we'd ever been apart, and it was immediately apparent. There was an unaccustomed awkwardness between us, as if someone had died and none of us knew quite what to say. We stood rooted to the spot like a miniature Stonehenge, although without the caps to hold us together.

Things had changed, or more accurately I had changed, while they had remained where and who they were. The flow of communication between us, once so natural that it required no thought at all, had seemingly evaporated. They had trespassed into my new world and were suddenly strangers, these people I'd known all my cognisant life, and the emotion felt really uncomfortable.

What words might have rescued the situation after the initial formalities? A cry of 'Surprise!' from them perhaps, or a jokey 'What the hell are you doing here?' from me perhaps? Instead there was an awkward vacuum before Groovy finally remarked, with a voice that seemed to combine both shock and incredulity in equal measures, 'So this is where it all happens then is it?'

I felt a wave of guilt wash over me. It seemed so unfair. After all, I'd been practically living at his new flat the summer before and now I felt unable to offer the same level of hospitality when he was standing on what was my own sovereign territory. I wasn't proud of the thoughts buzzing around in my head, the mix of wanting the pair of them to leave, of wishing frankly that this wasn't even happening, but they were there all the same. I was just running through my options when Groovy dropped the bombshell: they thought they'd hang around for the weekend and sample the student life, see if it was all it was cracked up to be.

Like Groovy, Sarah had eschewed further education in favour of a salary and she'd joined one of the big building societies as a management trainee. In her case though the choice not to go to university was a deliberate one. There's no doubt she could have gone if she'd wanted to, it was just that she knew what she wanted to do and didn't see how a degree was going to help her. I admired her for that. The dress and make up were, I guessed, a sign of her changed circumstances and seeing her made me realise that I would have to get used to looking at her in a different light, defined less by her position as Groovy's sister and more in terms of who she was in her own right. She was a young woman now, making her way in the world; whereas me, I'd postponed any further growing up in favour of a three year extension to my schoolboy contract.

Groovy had his own car by then and had driven. They both had rucksacks and sleeping bags in the boot - my hospitality had been taken as a given. It says something about how I regarded Sarah as just one of the lads that it took me a while to clock that she wouldn't be able to stay overnight in the Halls, as girls staying overnight was something frowned upon by the Hall Manager, and, if I'm being honest, frowned on almost as much by the other blokes I shared the block with. Having girls stay over broke an unwritten rule around segregation which seemed to protect us from the pressures of 'having' to bring girls back and allowing us to behave as blokes tend to behave when left to their own devices. Girls did spend the night of course, but not as much as you might expect, being smuggled in and out rather than displayed as trophies over cereals and toast in the kitchen come the morning.

At least solving this dilemma gave me something to do and I was able to offload Sarah onto my long-standing girlfriend Andrea. It wasn't a perfect solution, I could imagine some pretty long silences between them, but it was at least some kind of solution. The two knew each other of course. Andrea and I had been going round together for years, although our relationship had typically oscillated between periods of intense and less intense phases. The demands on our time during the Sixth Form, what with studying and following the 'orns, had often made it difficult to meet regularly. Still, we'd been happy enough and we both quite liked having someone to hang out with and so we'd stayed together.

It had been a complete coincidence, and frankly a bit of a shock, that we'd both ended up at the same university; it wasn't something that we'd planned at all. In fact, whereas Reading was about right for me, Andrea had been aiming for higher things and her grades had been a bit of a disappointment. It was the unseen hand of the clearing system that had decided we should spend more time together. Neither of us was sure that this was something we welcomed, but we both lacked the confidence to challenge what had seemed like fate.

Neither of us had expected our relationship to develop the way it had. We'd met at a disco, got off with each other and then just carried on going out. She was from a girls' private school slightly out of town and as such a bit unusual amongst my friends, not being part of the bus stop crowd. It's true she could give off a slightly aloof air, but it didn't worry me; I actually quite liked the fact that she didn't try to be anyone else - she wasn't embarrassed by the fact that her family was obviously better off than most of ours, she just accepted it and carried on. I once joked that I was her 'bit of rough', but it wasn't a phrase she ever heard before so as a joke it was about as successful as a bacon sandwich at a Bar mitzvah, an allusion that she probably would have appreciated given the high number of Jewish families in her neighbourhood.

I wouldn't have gone so far as to say that Andrea and Sarah were friends, in fact I'd often sensed the girly-type tension that sometimes seems to happen. Let's just say I don't think they were on Tampax-borrowing terms. Andrea's upbringing as an only child of well-to-do parents and an education in a private school had given her a self-confidence that Sarah seemed somehow to be in awe of, and she never quite seemed to be herself when Andrea was around. At that particular moment, though, none of this mattered, I was just pleased to have some kind of answer to the problem I'd just been presented with.

The two of them looked totally different too. Sarah tanned well and usually carried a golden glow about her right into the New Year. Not exactly the farmer's daughter, but not far off it. She had a robust, rustic look, if you like, natural, as if she had no time for make up, or indeed any need for it; which was why her change in appearance had come as such a surprise. Her good looks were God-given, an almost Nordic beauty, with blonde hair held in check often with plaits, and strong cheekbones; almost as if nature had got the balance wrong and she'd been given Groovy's share of the looks in the womb. Other times she wore her hair long and she had an unconscious habit of forming an 'O' with her thumb and forefinger and running her locks through this ring before releasing them with a flick of the neck.

Andrea on the other hand looked almost delicate in contrast, which was odd as this was the exact opposite of their respective personalities. Her deep auburn hair was accentuated by her pale, almost paper white, skin, which provided a vivid canvas for the occasional blackcurrant purple skin blemish she was prone to. Not spots as such, they never actually came to a head, but they would linger for weeks before finally fading. Andrea had what is usually called a button nose, and ears that were prone to stick out from her hair if she let it get too long or too greasy. This was something she was particularly conscious of and as such her hair was rarely allowed to get much beyond a bob, which was a shame because long hair suited her, despite her ears' anarchic streak.

I got little more out of Groovy once I had him on his own, he was his usual laconic self, simply suggesting that it had seemed like a good idea to pop down - hadn't I said they must visit? Well yes, but a little warning would have been good, although it seemed churlish to tell him this. He was well into his job at the DHSS by then and wanted to share his experiences of the world of work with me, although it seemed as alien to me as my new world must have seemed to him. In fact I couldn't imagine it at all, I'd never worked in an office in my life.

A night in the Union, with them sticking out like away fans in the home end, having to explain them away to my new circle of friends, seemed like a step too far, so seeing as Groovy had wheels we went into town and had a few drinks down at a pub near the river. On neutral territory, things went reasonably well and some of the old camaraderie seeped a low level of warmth back into what had seemed like the cooling bones of our relationship.

I'd chosen the pub because I'd seen a board outside

saying they had some singers on. What the board didn't say was that they were using the word 'singer' in its loosest possible interpretation. The first act was some kind of folk warbler who perched on the end of a bar stool and stuck his finger in his ear when he sang as if there was an 'On' button there, although given the irritating whining he insisted on inflicting on us I was tempted to suggest somewhere else he could insert his digit. The other act was a duo, each with an acoustic guitar, who insisted we all joined in the choruses of their songs which had refrains like 'Far Canals' or 'Cunning Stunts', a ploy made all the worse when only a smattering of the crowd decided to play along. Sarah in particular didn't look impressed and I could see Groovy thinking that if this was what passed for student entertainment he was glad he'd taken the option of a life of sophistication with the DHSS.

Although the 'entertainment' gave us an excuse not to talk, this came at a price, with the whole evening slowly imploding into an act of sphincter-shrivelling embarrassment and no one objected when I suggested we leave early and head back to my block for coffees. It was when we eventually got there, that the evening, already half way down the hill, decided to make a dash for the bottom.

In the hours that followed I was boorish, unpleasant, probably more than a little drunk and a complete jerk-off; determined, it seemed, to show off in front of my freshly minted friends, mindless of the damage it may cause to deeply rooted relationships. Of course I know all this now, but I was blissfully unaware of it then. When we reached the kitchen a few of my new mates had formed a caucus and were, as was usually the case on a Friday night, discussing politics, specifically the forthcoming battle to succeed Jim Callaghan as leader of the Labour party following his resignation earlier that week.

I shudder to remember it now, and I don't really

remember the specifics of the arguments, just the way in which I conducted them. I do remember Sarah refusing to take part in the conversation though. Although she wasn't a shrinking violet by any stretch of the imagination she never liked discussing politics, preferring the practical to the abstract, she was definitely a doer rather than a thinker, which may have helped to explain why she'd decided not to go to university. I also remember insisting that Sarah express some kind of - any - opinion and refusing to accept her protestations that she really wasn't interested. This seemed to goad me on though and my demands that she get involved seemed to have the effect of setting her up as some kind of a whipping girl and the others, having scented blood, and having sensed from my attitude that she was fair game, duly laid into her.

To them - and to me come to that - not believing in politics was like not believing in life. To ignore it was an abdication of responsibility, a bottling out. I had always been politicised, but my short time at university had made it a legitimate activity and I was loving it, it was like I was normal, not some freak. Back home I had had to wait patiently for an occasion and the right circumstances in which it was okay to express my views. In contrast university seemed like heaven, a place where it was positively expected of you - *all the time.*

Groovy kept quiet while all this went on, and probably spent much of the hour shooting sympathetic glances over towards Sarah, as was his way - he had always hated confrontation. I do remember Andrea trying to get me to shut up, but by then I was in my element and she was in the dragon's den, a mens' block, so didn't feel able to push it. I didn't even have the nous to sense the damaging effect I was having when Andrea led Sarah away, although I was to learn pretty quickly. I found out, because Andrea told me afterwards, that I had shouted out 'You turn if you want to', after them as they left, in a parody of the Thatch's already famous phrase to her party conference the week before, in what I had regarded as a very clever piece of repartee, a view endorsed by the chorus of laughter it provoked from most of those left in the room.

Groovy and Sarah left the next morning. I immediately wrote a letter of apology, in fact I wrote several - their effect deadened by the fact that I never actually posted any of them. I felt dreadful for the next forty eight hours but as soon as my timetable kicked in again I found my memory of that evening became just that little bit more conveniently blurred with the passing of each hour until by the end of the week I'd filed it away under 'Best Forgotten' and got on with my life.

Suffice it to say Groovy never visited me at university again, with or without Sarah. A tacit agreement seemed to form that my university self and my home self were two different existences, Jekyll and Hyde, and the subject was strictly off limits. Things were a little frosty that Christmas, and although I did finally manage a mumbled apology of sorts on our traditional Christmas Eve pub crawl, being the coward I was I never took Groovy up on his hint that perhaps it wasn't him I should be apologising to. The whole incident was like waking up after a particularly raucous night and not quite believing the things you'd said and done. There was little doubt that something had been broken between Sarah and me in particular, an unseen bond, and I was the vandal who'd broken it.

Not even the football was enough to bring us together, although at that time the team was having a better season in the Second Division than they had the year before it was clear they weren't going to get promoted and I used this as an excuse to cut down on the 'smash and grabs.'

I decided it was probably best to serve a self-imposed exile and let things blow over. Of course having a bit more time at weekends provided the space for things with Andrea to move onto another level, and looking back, it was probably from about this time that the seeds began to be sown for everything that was to follow later between us.

HOME

5

'Trev?'

'Poof, no question.'

'Paully?'

'Bent as a three pound note.'

'Sarah?' a shout this time to reach Sarah who was in the kitchen, rinsing through some of my clothes. Groovy hadn't seen a washing machine as a priority when he'd kitted out his flat, and it hadn't got any closer to the top of his list at any point in the three years since he'd moved in.

'Well,' she hesitated, 'it doesn't look good.'

'That's it then, with my vote counted in that's unanimous. Young Colin here has just come away unscathed from an assignation in a public toilet with a turd-burgler, or shirt-lifter if you prefer. A close shave I think we'll all agree.' Groovy locked his fingers together and put on a serious face as if he was about to pass sentence, wincing visibly as he did so at the implications of the verdict that had just been delivered. Not having had the benefit of three years re-education in the school of political correctness, Groovy's flat remained a haven of what I had learned to call homophobia.

I was sitting on one of the dining chairs, still in a kind of quarantine, wearing an eclectic selection of Groovy's clothes, which had the effect of making me look like I'd just shrunk by two foot. My unfortunate jacket had been bundled into a plastic bag and was sitting on the draining board, my rucksack had been taken outside, safe in the knowledge that no one in their right mind would want to nick it. At that moment Sarah entered the room brandishing a bag of Findus peas wrapped loosely in a tea towel. Without asking, she dabbed it gently around my damaged eye before holding it still for a minute or so and then resumed the delicate swabs. Bereft now of conversation, everyone watched as if she was some kind of magician and I was the stooge from the audience.

All that stuff about time being a great healer is true. Although I hadn't deserved it, and entirely at her own behest, at some point in the previous two and a half years Sarah had decided to forgive me that dreadful Friday evening at Reading and in doing so had earned my undying gratitude.

A lot had changed in the time I'd been away. She seemed more in control of herself somehow, more confident, no longer the mousey one in the background; she had somehow acquired the knack to make heads turn when she walked into a room. Not just because of the way she looked - she had always looked good - but more because she was likely to make a positive contribution to the room's dynamic.

It was difficult to reconcile this woman with the Sarah I'd grown up with and I suspected that the image I had of her of someone perpetually in the shadows would always remain. Still, it was difficult not to acknowledge how different she'd become. She'd been through two promotions at the building society and was now in charge of a small team of her own. She was, it seemed, someone's boss, a position it was totally alien for me to imagine ever being in myself, at least not for a while yet anyway. People talked about how she'd matured, about how 'good for her' the job was, and I could see what they meant. For me the net result of all this was that she'd found herself able to forgive me and I was glad that we'd been able to regain our previous equilibrium. I felt like another brother to her. A proper brother if you like, not like Groovy, who was more like another version of herself, but one I liked to think she could share those thoughts and feelings with she would probably have found it awkward, if not impossible, to share with her twin.

It had of course occurred to me that the guy from the toilets at Victoria could have been gay, but unless he was some particularly strange kind of pervert who was sexually attracted to puke it hadn't seemed that likely. It was enough to banish him from my consciousness though. The whole gay thing and AIDS in particular was another world - thankfully not mine - and one I very naturally wanted to keep a million miles away from.

I took the ribbing in good heart however and it felt good to get stuck into banter with the boys again. The insults, the joshing, the whole feeling that it didn't really matter what you said because you all knew each other well enough for it not to matter. It felt comfortable and without pretension. I was reminded of something one of the tutors had once said to me when I'd first gone up to university which I'd found to be true - your real friends are the people you grew up with, the friends you make at university are more like temporary acquaintances.

Before too long the conversation turned to football, in particular how much we were going to miss our hero Luther Blissett next season. The First Division's leading scorer. The man we created and then sold for two million pounds to AC Milan. A legend. Paully and Trev had made a few of the games the previous year, Groovy and I a few more, but a sense of unfulfilled experience hung over us all, we had yet to really engage with football in what pundits insisted on calling 'the top flight'. The next season was going to be ours, we agreed, we'd shown we had nothing to fear, it would be just like old times.

Before we could get carried away, though, a glance at my watch revealed the inevitable. It couldn't be postponed any longer, I really did have to make tracks for home. Trev caught my eye and offered me a lift. He'd only popped in on his way back from a long shift and needed to get some shut-eye. A round of goodbyes followed with general agreement that we'd probably see each other the next day. It was as if the previous three years hadn't happened, the whole experience had been like finding a lost and once-loved pair of jeans and finding that they still fitted perfectly.

Outside, the light had begun to fade and I felt a slight chill through Groovy's old Grandad shirt. Retrieving the plastic carrier bag containing my jacket with one hand and lifting my rucksack from the doorstep with the other, I looked around for Trev's old Morris Minor van, which he'd bought as Post Office surplus when we'd left school. We passed Paully's Capri, which had developed a particularly fine crop of moss along one wing, and stopped beside a five year old MG in British racing green, its black canvas top folded down and showing signs of a number of inexpert repairs with insulating tape. It appeared that Trev had moved up in the world.

'Excuse me sir, is this your ve-hic-cle?' I enquired, in my best PC Plod intonation.

'Technically one third of her still belongs to Barclays Bank, but come December she's all mine,' he replied, rubbing his hands together both against the incipient cold and in anticipation of the day when it would become his. I was impressed.

Once we were inside the car no words were exchanged between us for fully three or four minutes: the comfortable silence of two friends left with their thoughts and each other. The months that had passed without us having seen each other were irrelevant, the roots of our relationship didn't need watering with small talk. Eventually Trev broke the silence as we sat at a T-junction waiting for the chance to join the traffic.

'Glad to be back?' he asked, his voice suggesting a genuine interest in my answer. I looked around at the familiar streets before answering, letting all feelings of nostalgia settle like the head on a pint of Guinness before giving him my considered opinion.

'Yes, yes I am,' I answered, honestly. 'Three years away was enough, truth be told.' Trev remained silent, his forward gaze towards the road removing the need for eye contact and opening the field to further reflection. He didn't need it, or indeed encourage it, but we both knew I had more to say. Counting off the familiar landmarks along the ring road, I tried to find the right words to express what it was I was feeling.

'I'm glad I'm back but I'm not really sure what happens next. It was easy at school you know, every year a fresh form, a ladder that led somewhere, but now I've been to that somewhere and I don't know where they keep the next ladder or indeed where it might lead to.'

Trev maintained his silence, proving that the best listeners aren't necessarily talkers too. Perhaps this was something they had taught him in basic police training? 'Coming home is kind of like stepping back down onto the top of the last ladder again and starting over, only without any idea of what I'm supposed to do now.' I had a feeling I was losing the whole ladder metaphor and decided to bring it to a close. 'Does that make sense?' I asked.

Out of all my friends Trev was probably the one least likely to have any clue at all what I was on about. His future had always been mapped out, the idea of not knowing what he was supposed to be doing was about as familiar as hunger to him - namely, not very familiar at all. He shrugged his shoulders.

'I guess,' he offered, eventually. 'But you've got a degree now, haven't you?'

'Sure.' I agreed. 'The question is, though, what with everything that's going on, does that make me more or less marketable?'

Another shrug, which seemed to confirm that he thought I was talking pretentious hogwash, but he'd had the patience to listen and I was grateful to him for that. By then we had arrived at my home and, with some difficulty, I extricated my belongings from the back of his car, thanked him for the lift and, taking a full lungful of fresh air, approached the still familiar door of number 49. On the way up the path I allowed myself a sneaky glance two doors down to Groovy's folks' house where I'd spent so much of my childhood and was probably as much a home to me as the place where I'd actually grown up.

My parents. Thomas and Gracie Westlake. Bastions of the community, the seed and womb from which I emerged. They're alright I suppose just, well, dull, really. Even the righteous halo they think shines a little reflected light into their ordinary dull lives is dull, as if someone put the wrong wattage bulb in a number of years ago and they'd just got used to it.

They called themselves non-conformists, but you'd struggle to find anyone more conformist in how they live. They'd have liked to have been thought of as pillars of the local Methodist church, although this seemed to represent more of an historical position than anything vaguely in touch with reality. Unfortunately, the period when that history was formed coincided with my childhood and subsequent adolescence and it was only after I left that, somewhat unfairly to my way of thinking, they'd decided to loosen up a little.

I've bored people to death with this countless times over the years so I won't go on about it here, but boiled down to its absolute basics my theory is that for them, while the confusion of the sixties and seventies whizzed around them, the church represented a refuge in which they could hide. I would have been just about walking and talking by the time the Beatles came onto the scene and getting ready to enter primary school during the Summer of Love. By hiding away in the church and immersing us all in their strictures and scriptures we could pretend as a family that it would all go away and that life would one day return to how it used to be, and in my parents eyes should be.

My Mum and Dad were big fans of Mary Whitehouse, the Royal Family and Ted Heath, and I don't mean the band leader. I tended more towards Pink Floyd, The Who and David Bowie. These weren't loves I could share, not at home anyway. For a start I had no brothers or sisters and Mum and Dad would have seen these people, icons to me, as devils incarnate. Cassettes and headphones, they were the solution.

My record collection lived at Groovy's, the deal being he could play what he liked so long as I always got the first, pristine, version on one side of a C90. I would then listen to it on the headphones back at home, the spiral wire linking me to the tape deck acting as an umbilical cord to the mother ship. I could play it as loud as I liked and block the world out as often as I liked, the inside of my skull acting as the perfect amplifier. It was a neat solution and seemed to suit all involved, especially during my 'difficult' adolescent years which, as a consequence, weren't really that difficult at all. Thanks are due then to David Jones, Pete Townshend and Roger Waters, for providing the escape tunnel that got me through the gaps between matchdays.

I say that things changed after I left, but this was based more on gut feeling than hard evidence. When I was around they seemed to revert to type. I felt they were keeping things hidden from me like I was the vicar in some Ben Travers farce. I often sensed an almost perceptible scurrying when I approached the house as things were taken down, put up and rearranged to what they had been before, both objects and opinions.

It was as if my leaving, or the prospect of it, had meant that it was okay for them to become different people. It wasn't that they set out upon a life of wife swapping, wild parties and fast cars, at least I don't think they did, it was just that they became more relaxed. Personally I put it down to 1979 and Maggie getting into power. This seemed to signal some kind of rescue to them, a sign that the bad old days had indeed gone, that what they'd been holding out for and perhaps even praying for, had come and things were going to be alright from then on; Maggie and her cronies became their new saviours.

Ironically, and I'm not sure I'll ever forgive them for this seeing how much I longed for it when I was growing up, they even stopped going to church. At first they seemed to miss the odd Sunday and then Dad retired from all his official duties, saying it was time for a younger man to take on the mantle, even though he wasn't really that old, he just began to consider himself old. Every other week seemed to stretch to once a month and then once hardly ever, and although they kept up the charade if by some chance I was at home, after a while they even gave up that pretence.

Nothing was said, no justification given, it just happened and I was left with the memories of the Mum and Dad I'd grown up with - uncommunicative, loving but distant, a reminder of times past rather than a role model for the future. That was why going home was always such a 'deep breath and jump' situation for me, something to be endured not enjoyed, but there was no getting away from the fact that at that particular moment home was where I had to go. Not only was this my 'official' return from university but I also had the job interview to report back on. After that there was the small matter of the rest of my life to sort out.

As I walked up the path and got my key ready I could hear the TV blaring from inside, turned up to what must have been pretty close to maximum volume. I imagined the scene, Dad on the sofa clutching his new toy - the remote control pad - drinking in the scenes of jubilation from Westminster and the BBC Studios. He'd be wearing a jacket and possibly even a tie in deference to the occasion but no hat to hide the bird's egg freckles that covered his bald pate, all in all, clean shaven and tidy, along with the rest of the house. Mum would be wearing her pinny, but this hardly qualified as an insight as she was rarely seen without it. Even if she hadn't done any cooking for hours she'd keep it on as generally the gaps between cooking were barely long enough to justify the effort. There would be smudges of flour down the front, evidence (supported by a sweet warm smell emanating from the kitchen) that cake or scones would be imminent.

Mum answered the door before I could get the key in the lock. She'd seen me coming down the drive - she'd always had a sixth sense for my arrival. As she opened the door wider to allow me and the rucksack in she gave me a peck on the cheek. She said how lovely it was to see me again in her usual ritualistic way which I know she meant, but somehow never seemed sincere. She had her usual 'other world' face on, like she was living in some kind of parallel universe, and said nothing about my appearance, smell or general state.

I plumped my stuff down on the floor and turned towards the living room to get it over with. Mum followed, as if in my slipstream. Entering the old familiar room, with its fading photos and souvenirs from barely remembered holidays, I sensed immediately that something was wrong. It came as a surprise to register that it was Dad. I was right about the jacket and being clean shaven but as he rose to greet me, hand outstretched for a handshake - none of that namby-pamby hugging stuff round here thank you very much - it became immediately clear that he was more than a little shaky on his pins.

I quickly took in the room for clues and immediately spotted a half empty glass on the coffee table, an amber film still draining down the side from the last time he'd tilted it down his neck. Next to it sat a bottle, its top off and label turned to one side, although the shape marked it out as Bells.

Spirits?! In this house? This was on a par with catching the pair of them at it on the floor - simply unthinkable. They'd known I was coming home surely, why hadn't they kept this from me? Why this brash in-my-face confidence all of a sudden, why the need to challenge my preconceptions?

We touched hands and he fell back into the settee like a stage drunk performing a pratfall, both legs together and bouncing slightly into the air when he hit the cushion and rebounded off the springs. I couldn't swear to it but I think he even repressed a giggle. Small red veins had risen at the top of his cheeks and what little hair he had left seemed to have turned a silver grey over the past year.

'Etch,' he said, swallowing his words before trying again, 'etch,' he repeated, taking a deep breath. Third time lucky. 'Etchelent newz don't you think eh?' he demanded, directing an unsteady finger at the TV screen where the Blessed Margaret was speaking to the press outside what I recognised as the front of Conservative Central Office.

I couldn't take my eyes off him.

My Dad.

Squiffy.

Drunk.

The sound on the TV had been turned up and this helped disguise the moment a little but the evidence was incontrovertible. He was as pissed as a newt. Rat arsed. Absolutely bloody bladdered. Incredible. I continued to stand before him, my mouth open but saying nothing, caught like a freeze frame in a home movie. Thankfully Mum came to the rescue.

'Colin dear, what's this on your nice new jacket?' she asked, having already rifled through my bags in the endless quest for fresh washing. Instinctively, she was holding the offending article out at arm's length.

'She'll sort the bloody unions out once and for all,' came the voice from the sofa as I turned to see that Mum had now

58

overcome her initial reaction and was holding my jacket up to the light for inspection. First the demon drink and now swearing, I'd begun to wonder if I was in the right house.

'Um, what's that Mum?' I responded.

'Your jacket dear.'

'It's just a bit of blood Mum. Oh, and before you ask, there's some sick on it too,' I gestured, in the interests of absolute clarity. 'Quite a lot actually.'

'Oh dear, dear,' she sighed, 'and on your best jacket too.'

'My only jacket Mum,' I reminded her. No 'Are you all right?' No 'What happened?' Just concern for the jacket.

'Stick it up the unions she will, hey hey!' uttered the voice we had started to ignore, the unfamiliar having become now strangely, very strangely, familiar. Maybe he could afford to indulge himself now? Perhaps my theory about the Tory victory in '79 freeing my parents up was entering a fresh chapter, a second victory somehow sending a message of reassurance that things could never turn back to how they were before, that they as a group, as a class if you like, were the chosen ones and now was the time to go for it, to really let rip and say and do all the things they'd kept repressed all these years.

'I'll send it to the dry cleaners,' Mum suggested, ever the pragmatist, and still stuck on the whole jacket thing, acting as if Dad's behaviour was perfectly normal.

'Thatcher,' the voice from below murmured, half in reverence as if addressing a saint. A look suspiciously like love filled his eyes, a look that clashed poorly with the red, raised veins at the top of his cheeks.

'Stuffed your lot anyway,' he offered, a comment I chose to ignore. Never argue with a drunk, a piece of good advice I'd been given once - by my Dad actually. Ironic. I didn't even know I had a 'lot,' but to Dad all students were raving lefties.

'Best get changed son,' Mum suggested, registering the fact that the clothes I was wearing were patently at least a size too big for me but foregoing the opportunity to ask why. A slight tilt of her head suggested a 'leave him to his pleasures' footnote to the previous bizarre exchange. I did as she suggested and climbed the stairs to my childhood bedroom where memories lingered, ready to be re-awakened, memories that had just been uncomfortably challenged.

Home?

It had finally become a place I didn't recognise anymore.

WORK?

6

'YOU CAN GAZE into my eyes as long as you like, but I'll stare back at you longer and I will not bend to your will. I will rebuff every attempt at affection and reject your wish to blackmail me into loving you. So long as we are alone in this room I will deny you. You know it. I know it. Let's face facts and bugger off, will you.'

The imploring face of Andrea's family bulldog continued to hold its glare, but I was as good as my word. We had this love-hate relationship. For some strange reason it seemed to love me. For reasons that were perfectly clear to me, I hated it. I hated its hairs, I hated its smell, I hated the way it left little pools of blood on the floor when it was on heat. I hated its odd little triangular ears and most of all I hated the way everyone seemed to dote on it, even Andrea's Dad, Frank. As far as I was concerned the only good thing about this mangy mutt was the fact that it regularly needed to be taken for walks down what I knew as Dog Shit Alley, or what Andrea's family more daintily called 'The Ginnel'. These walks got the pair of us out of the house and away from the surreal atmosphere that usually inhabited it.

I was standing in the kitchen at Andrea's family home. Outside, the sun had started to shine, burning off the mist that had hung around persistently since the morning and offering up the possibility of a reasonable afternoon. A massive mural of Snoopy lying on top of his kennel covered one wall. Painted a few years before by Andrea, it was probably destined to stay there for ever, this being the house it was. Being artistic and creative were two of Andrea's defining characteristics, features that I admired but was also slightly in awe of. A thought bubble coming out of the sleeping dog's head expressed how I was feeling: 'Zzzzzz'.

Frustrated noises were coming from the front room where Andrea was trying to master her Dad's new video recorder. She wanted to test it on an episode of the new Rowan Atkinson sitcom later that evening but the manual was clearly proving to be a bit of a challenge. I was going to have to go in and help her.

It was strange how quickly we had fallen back into old ways. After only a couple of weeks it was as if university had never happened, part of a parallel universe populated by dream-like creatures whose company we'd enjoyed for a while through different adventures but who had now dispersed and been somehow vaporised.

Andrea had followed me back home shortly after the end of her finals and we were hanging out together again in much the same way we had after 'A' Levels (although older, and perhaps a little bit wiser) as if we couldn't think of an alternative. I'd spent the intervening time constructively topping up my suntan in the garden and, if the sun was unwilling to play ball, digging the vegetable patch. I'd signed on for the dole, naturally, both for the money and for the chance to wind Groovy up down at the DHSS. With Mum and Dad seemingly prepared to continue feeding me and provide a roof over my head, and the government generously providing me with the necessary beer and music money, life was generally okay.

I wasn't stupid, I knew that I would have to get a job at some time, but I felt I'd earned the right to have a little break after the rush of the exams and I wasn't ready to start looking. I spent much of my time on the sun-lounger stockpiling excuses: I needed to know what kind of degree I was going to get. I wanted to wait until the degree ceremony itself was over in order to draw a line under the whole experience. I needed a suit.

Most basic of all though was the reason I didn't share: I needed some idea of what I wanted to do. Some friends at university had been thrown into a whirlwind of panic after Christmas during the final year, with most of them grabbing the first thing that was offered, even if it was accountancy, which two years before we'd all agreed to a man was the lowest of the low, a pact with the devil. Although I didn't know exactly what job I wanted, I knew what type of job I wanted - something which would elevate me, one where I could make a difference. I wanted to aim high, not settle for mediocrity. Like my football team, I wanted to at least try to reach for the stars, even if they turned out to be unattainable.

Andrea reckoned I was nuts, that in the current job climate you had to compromise your principles and get what you could. There would be time for all that job satisfaction stuff later she said, but I was unconvinced. Andrea was the only person I'd spoken to about this. Groovy wouldn't have understood and my parents, well we didn't really talk about anything any more - other than what type of cereals I wanted Mum to get. As a result whenever the subject came up I swung back on my standard excuse: why bother at all? With three million unemployed what hope was there for me? If that didn't work I resorted to impersonating Yosser Hughes from 'Boys From The Blackstuff', putting on my imploring face and mumbling 'Gis a job, gis a job', which tended to unnerve people enough to stop the badgering.

None of this stopped Dad from continuously suggesting that I give old Tim Grady a call though. Just the thought of Tim Grady's voice and the vision it conjured up of the rest of that

God-awful day was enough to make me turn green and start retching. I knew he'd never call me, but it was useful to maintain the fiction that he might, it gave Mum and Dad a modicum of hope.

Back in Andrea's family kitchen I stood up, reached into the food cupboard over the kettle and got the coffee out as I had countless times before. For long periods of my life I'd spent more time here than I had at my own home and I was grateful for the way that Andrea's parents had welcomed me unquestioningly, accepting me as their daughter's friend. I felt oddly comfortable here, almost (but never quite) part of the family unit. The only part of that unit that didn't work was the dog, and as if to underline the point I became aware of a terrible smell from her corner which she must have produced - as if in revenge - just before she'd gone to sleep. I exited as soon as the coffee was ready in case someone thought it was one of mine and was immediately thrust into a fresh combat zone, this one featuring an intelligent female graduate against a complex Japanese electronics manual.

'Just listen to this,' Andrea demanded as soon as I crossed the threshold, as if she'd been waiting for me to arrive. Her freshly shortened hair stood out at right-angles having picked up a static charge from the carpet where she'd been lying as she checked the connections at the back of the machine. Patiently, as if to emphasise her point, she ran her finger along the words in the manual as she read them out. 'Taking the red wire insert delicately in slot C nearing power cable.' She shrugged. 'I've tried every combination but nothing seems to do it.'

She may have been creative, but practicality was not one of Andrea's strong suits.

'Let me look,' I offered, holding out a hand for the booklet. She gave it to me with undisguised relief and before I'd even thought about it I realised that I'd assumed the dreadful mantle of male responsibility with no possibility of admitting defeat.

Cardboard and polystyrene lay scattered across the carpet, a tangible manifestation of her almost terminal untidiness. I ran my eyes over the instructions. 'What took you so long anyway?' she asked, but I gave her an impatient shush as I tried to get inside the manual writer's head. This was serious now.

'Have you put enough petrol in?' I asked in an attempt to buy time, but she just gave me one of her looks, like she didn't know why I even bothered. I decided to opt for action and assumed the prone position fiddling with the wires, not really sure what I was doing, but at least doing something.

With misplaced confidence in my ability Andrea wandered over to the sofa and started to flick through the Radio Times, making it clear that we weren't going to work together on this as a team and that I was expected to solve her problem for her. I swapped two of the cables round, the red one was definitely wrong, the power cable was on the side, which meant that slot C wasn't where she had it. After that it was a process of elimination. Slot B it seemed was destined to provide a home for the 'Audio In' wire whilst Slot A was happy to accommodate whatever was left. After that it was simply a question of plugging the thing in and tuning - the work of minutes.

'There. I think that'll work,' I announced.

'Work? Work?' Who dares to utter the dreaded 'W' word, heh heh heh?'

'Daddy!' Andrea screamed, and as her father introduced himself with his trademark chuckle she jumped up out of the sofa and gave him a big hug, lifting her left ankle as she did so as if she was squeezing a giant teddy bear and burying her chin in his hair. It seemed she hadn't yet got used to the novelty of seeing him every day again and I felt a twinge of envy: she'd never greeted me like that.

'Hello Colin,' he offered, levering his head past his taller daughter's shoulder and extending a hand to be shaken. I was happy to oblige, although my happiness at seeing him was genuine it didn't quite fall into the Andrea category.

'Frank,' I replied. Frank was the sort of person it was easy to like, and it was largely down to him that I felt so comfortable at Andrea's house. The previous Easter, perhaps in anticipation of the end of our student days and the onset of adulthood, he'd insisted I started to call him Frank after five years of awkwardly greeting him as Mr. Kendall-Jones. Medium height and build, with owlish eyes staring out of an oval face, Frank was the sort of bloke who could get lost easily in a crowd, a description he'd probably have taken as a compliment. Perhaps his greatest fault was his habit of wearing a tie around the house, not so bad in itself, but a crime when combined with a sleeveless sweater.

Frank seemed to inhabit a world of endless patience, a world that existed independently of everyone else's and one where the soundtrack was soft New Orleans jazz played at around volume level five - not too loud, but enough to infiltrate a room and provide mood music. Although you would never have guessed it from looking at him, Frank was a senior consultant surgeon at the Watford General, which was right next to the football stadium. As such, on the few occasions we were on our own, he could speak authoritatively on latest developments with the team and their progress using titbits he'd picked up from staff and patients, whose own knowledge was fed by a live feed from the football-crazy head of their Hospital Radio.

The reality was though that Frank was one of those people who could speak authoritatively on almost anything. His breadth of knowledge was impressive, ranging from horticulture (he was a keen gardener too) through music, rowing (he'd rowed for his college when younger) and politics to food - despite being the only man in the house, and the only person working, he also tended to do most of the cooking.

He had opinions on The Falklands, world hunger and the

66

last of the Star Wars trilogy. My parents hadn't even been to the cinema since people had stopped standing at the end when they played the national anthem, something they always mentioned if the idea was floated, as if to suggest that the whole idea of what they called 'the pictures' was somehow, to use one of their favourite words, 'common'. I hadn't had the heart to tell them that they didn't even play the national anthem any more. If Frank hadn't been so self-effacing and modest he would have made you sick. The only thing he didn't really talk about was his work and I wasn't even sure what his specialist area was.

Perhaps Frank's most endearing quality was that he seemed to find the whole world amusing, as if he was a spectator at a mildly risqué summer show at a seaside resort, and in fact I'd often wondered if his whole approach to life was to regard it as an entertainment put on for him to enjoy from the sidelines. His patience stretched beyond his daughter through the damned dog, which I always had the impression had simply been imposed upon him, to encompass his strange wife, of whom more in a moment.

Bang on cue he extricated himself from the loving embrace of his daughter and ambled purposefully over to his record deck. Without even pausing to look he pulled an LP out from the collection under the deck and casually slipped it out of the paper case and onto the turntable, lifting the needle and placing it on the edge of the disc. The sound of a melodious clarinet gently permeated the room.

'So, any idea what you're going to do now?' he asked.

I hated that question, but it was the one all adults seemed to feel they had the right to ask me at that time and one I really couldn't begin to put an answer to. What exactly were the prospects for someone with a reasonable Economics degree from a middling university? Of course, the fact that I never wanted to even hear the words 'Keynesianism' or 'Monetarism' again - let alone consider the price elasticity or otherwise of Mars Bars - didn't help, and as far as I was concerned the best use of M1, M2 and M3 were as motorways.

'It's a tough one, Frank,' I replied, I hadn't quite got the hang of this 'Frank' thing yet, I was finding that I couldn't stop saying it, almost daring myself to let it pass my lips one more time. 'I was thinking of trying something new. Just looking around at this stage. Marketing, that kind of thing, advertising maybe.' I wasn't even convincing myself with this line, so I decided to switch tactics. 'How are things at the hospital, Frank?'

'Ooooh! All right I suppose,' he replied. Given Frank's normally sunny disposition, his 'all right' equated to a normal person's 'pretty bloody awful actually.'

'There's talk of more cuts,' he added, 'and then there's another big review around the corner, heh heh heh.' Frank would probably have found Armageddon amusing.

At that point Andrea's Mum wandered in and aimed directly for her favourite armchair, which she duly eyed up and down as if she'd never seen it before in her life before letting it absorb itself around her. Still Mrs Kendall-Jones to me, Andrea's Mum was what can only be described as a large woman who patently didn't, and probably never had, subscribed to such soft notions as diets and watching what you eat. She consumed food with abandonment, if not enjoyment, often conducting it in parallel with her other favourite occupation of talking sheer gibberish.

Andrea called her Mummy and Frank called her either 'Mother' or, usually when he wanted to bring her into line, by her Christian name Irene, with the second 'e' always pronounced separately, as if for emphasis. I didn't know how or where the Kendall-Jones' had met, but it was my impression that Mrs Kendall-Jones had done rather well for herself, a product of the growing social mobility of the early 60s. I didn't know where Frank had actually picked her up, from somewhere outside Leeds I think.

She often talked about her childhood and where she grew up, and I had formed a probably unfair image of grimy back-to-backs with coal holes and flat-capped men coming home from a hard day down t'pit with half a sack of the black stuff under their arm instead of wages. In summary, Mrs Kendall-Jones was an embodiment of the saying that you could take the woman out of Yorkshire, but you couldn't take the Yorkshire out of the woman.

She also had that habit some middle-aged women seem to have of not really listening to the flow of conversation around her, instead she made announcements that drew attention to herself and a subject she had probably just become an expert on from her reading of the Daily Express that morning or from the previous night's news. The Kendall-Jones' had a TV in their bedroom - something people from my neck of the woods regarded as supremely decadent.

Still, her arrival offered a mix of relief - from the whole work topic - and dread - for what might be about to happen next. The one thing Mrs Kendall-Jones wasn't was predictable, as she duly showed by going against type and picking up on the thread she'd clearly heard being discussed as she was entering the room.

'You want to get a job in a bank, that's the only way of getting a mortgage these days.' She never did like me. Luckily, this proved to be a conversation stopper so she filled the silence in the time honoured way.

'Do you know what my Uncle George said just moments before he died?'

This was of course one of those questions that only had one answer, and even if you did know the unfortunate gentleman's famous last words, you were going to be told them again. In the circumstances, and I'd been in them more times than I cared to remember over the previous five years, I'd learned that no actual answer was required beyond providing a blank canvas for a response by offering an open face and maybe a smile. The story was there to be told.

'George and Auntie Elsa were at a small hotel in Bridlington and he'd just come down to breakfast. He sat down and announced: 'The bed was rock hard, that egg's too runny and that dress never suited you', and with that he just went, like someone had flicked a switch.' She clicked her fingers by way of a demonstration.

Frank of course was immune to this stuff and 'heh heh heh'd' as if on automatic pilot as he wandered around the room looking for something. Of course all of us knew what was coming next and each of us was keeping a low profile, our eyes to the carpet, to avoid being its target. After a silent countdown of five it duly arrived, delivered in a curiously challenging way: 'Well, what do you think of that then?'

It was me, it had to be me, at the end of the extended neck stare. I took a stab in the dark - I think my willingness to even attempt an answer was one of the reasons I'd been welcomed in this household, the rest of the family had given up years ago and were virtually immune. 'I suppose we're all entitled to our opinions,' I ventured.

'Eh! You're not wrong there,' she harrumphed. It looked like I'd got away with it as she went quiet, a sure sign that she'd begun to dredge her memory and imagination for her next effort, which on past form was a process that took between six to eight minutes to gestate - my window of opportunity to leave.

Out on the doorstep Andrea and I kissed and we promised to call each other, although no time or day was set. Just as I got ready to leave she stopped me in my tracks.

'Colin?'

'Um,' I replied, bending over to tuck the bottom of my trousers into my socks.

'You weren't serious about advertising, were you?'

I looked up. Andrea has a concerned look about her. 'Hell no, do me a favour. It was just something that popped into my head that sounded vaguely respectable, I wouldn't be seen dead in advertising.'

'Okay, good,' she confirmed, and began looking beyond my shoulder as if seeking her next distraction.

With that sorted, I checked the tyres on my bike and threw a leg over the frame. We waved and I was gone, head down, on my own down a road I must have been down a thousand times before. So ended another unsatisfactory encounter. It had been typical of our recent meetings, as if we were both avoiding the Great Unanswered Question - where did we go from here, both as individuals and as a couple?

Getting engaged was out of the question, both of us knew it but neither of us dared to admit it, so nothing was said. How did we know it? We just did. We were mates with a bit of serious fondling thrown in for fun, not even lovers, even after all these years, not that I'd yet given up hope - and certainly not life partners. Did we want to make the effort to see if we could be? Not really, we'd been together too long, knew each other too well, we'd skipped the exciting can't-bear-to-be-parted bit and slipped straight into comfortable mode.

The truth was though, I wasn't even sure there'd ever even been a can't-bear-to-be-parted bit, I think we may have started at the comfortable stage. We both enjoyed having a partner to go around with, enabling us to avoid the mayhem of dating others. That had been fine for our teens, however neither of us had planned for it to continue beyond school but UCCA's clearing system had decided otherwise - just for fun.

The sensible thing at that point of course would have been to call a truce, but faced with our new uncertain adventure we'd bottled it, and by then the die had been cast. We started university as an official 'couple' - off limits to all the other eighteen year old sexually-primed late adolescents let off the leash (with their own private rooms thrown in for good measure - what a wasted opportunity!). Was it ever love? Well, let me put it this way, I thought I understood what love must feel like, but I wasn't sure I'd ever actually felt it.

It felt good to be pumping the pedals as these thoughts

span around my head, feeling a slight burn in the back of my calves, a numbness in the bum, and a sense of unadulterated freedom. It was only as I reached the crossroads that I realised that I didn't really know where I was going. I didn't fancy going back to Groovy's, he'd be out and although I knew where he hid the spare key there wouldn't be anything to do there except watch TV or listen to music, even if I did own half the collection. Home was out of the question, I couldn't stand the prospect of another 'adult' conversation like the one Frank had just tried, well-meaning enough but they didn't half get right on your tits. What was the problem with accepting that I didn't know what I wanted to do? By way of confirmation, I shouted that very phrase at the top of my voice as I spun down a hill at full-whack, and felt a little better for it.

What I really wanted was my old life back. Not university, but those innocent, optimistic days from the Sixth Form. The days when anything was possible, when even lowly, 'unfashionable', as it had become fashionable to call us, Watford could force our way through the ranks and into the First Division. I wanted to be approaching the edge not peering over it, when the future was something sufficiently far away to be exciting, not staring you in the face and challenging you to meet it.

Perhaps it was this mood of nostalgia that watered the seed of an idea and allowed it to spring forth from the mud of my mind. Of course - the golf club, where I'd worked during my second summer at university and earned enough to pay for an Interrail ticket around Europe before going back for my final year. Somewhere I looked back on with pleasant nostalgia and, more importantly, somewhere where I could rewind the clock.

It was still early enough to steal a march on the other students, I might just stand a chance, after all I knew the ropes and I'd got on well with everyone there. I turned the handlebars to the left and stood up in the pedals, as I started to work my way steadily back up the hill.

THE CLUB

7

THE ABSOLUTE BRILLIANT BEAUTY of the golf course in
the summer was that it was like painting the Forth Bridge, the
work just never dried up. The previous year I'd spent a hard
but satisfying summer 'on the mowers' before disappearing to
Europe in September. Along with another student, Dennis, we
started at the first hole and worked our way round, two or
three holes a day until we'd done the whole course, by which
time the grass was about ready to be cut again.

It wasn't just a case of mowing either, oh no, there were
gradations of skill involved, the pinnacle of which was the fine
manicuring of the greens, something which took place every
day using an old Atco with a huge engine mounted on its top
alongside a massive clippings box the size of a small dustbin.

This wasn't a task for causal labour, it was performed
instead by Harry, who'd been with the Council for fifteen years
and had worked his way up during that time to become an
Assistant Greensman. Harry sported a long salt and pepper
beard out of which a roll up usually poked, like a smouldering
twig hanging out the side of a dried up hedge. This matched
his unruly hair which fell down the back of the oily boiler suit
he donned each morning, whatever the weather. Harry lived
alone.

Assistant he may have been, but the greens were his bailiwick. He started the day 'swishing' them with a yard-long strip of nylon attached to a long bamboo pole, a job that required a wide scythe-like action and was required to get the dew off the hallowed carpet-like turf before it could be cut.

After a week or so I'd realised that, contrary to council practice, Harry always started at the fifth hole for this task, his quarry being less the greens themselves than the cause of the mystery footprints left in the early morning dew and the tell-tale lines that said that someone from the nearby housing estate had grabbed themselves three free holes at dawn - the fifth, sixth and seventh. Like Tom chasing Jerry, he'd never caught the miscreant, but he took his bag of tickets with him anyway, determined one day to charge back-fees.

After swishing, Harry lovingly sharpened the blades of the Atco with a file and set off for the morning, swinging his monster around the greens with a deftness of touch that wouldn't have disgraced a ballerina. He returned to the sheds for lunch of course, we all did, but by then Dennis and I would have spent the first half of the day on the more rudimentary mowing of the bits the gang mower couldn't reach between the trees and amongst the rough.

The gang mower was pulled along by the golf course's tractor and was the responsibility of Ted, the Head Greensman - he reckoned his higher perch allowed him to gaze out over his domain more easily, although we all knew the truth, that he was past it; an irreconcilable truth rammed home by the fact that an earlier incident with the Atco had left him deficient in the finger department on his right hand, which made operating the complicated clutch system impossible, even if he ever wanted to be near the beast again. Ted was all right, a classic old geezer who enjoyed a few pints at the pub and some mucky videos on his VCR, for which he'd amassed an impressive library in a short space of time. Ted also lived alone.

The job had other compensations too, which were worth

keeping in mind through the long days of pulling and pushing a barely-motorised bottom of the range rotary mower through long and often sodden grass, with the added attraction of brambles to leave bear-like scratches across your legs.

Every now and then the tedium was enlivened by the sound of a clunk underneath the plate signifying that the blades had located a lost ball. This was the signal for two actions: first a leap into the air in order to avoid the possibility of a nasty bruise on the shin, and second a pushing back of the throttle in order to cut the engine. In the time this took, the blades would have found the ball, flung it around a few times and ejected it like a manic pinball through the gap in the side of the mower where the clippings were normally discharged. With practice you got good at watching where the ball flew and if you were quick you could find it and liberate it. If the blades hadn't done too much damage good balls could be sprayed back to life with some white paint and flogged on as practice balls, at another course naturally; all in all a pretty useful tax-free perk.

It was nearly packing up time when I reached the course and found Brian out the back in one of the greenhouses, the first place I'd looked. Stumpy, with legs that looked too short to carry him, Brian was the site manager who also supervised the putting green, tennis courts and gardens which made up the rest of the complex. He was most at home in the long wooden greenhouse, where he raised a steady flow of geraniums and begonias each of which found a home on one of the town's many roundabouts. No one knew if Brian lived alone.

He looked content, which was good. My luck continued as he listened to my proposition. It seemed I hadn't been so quick off the mark but one of the students he'd had lined up had pulled out at the last minute, he'd been offered a Camp America placing apparently and, for some reason Brian couldn't fathom, had favoured this over a summer at 'the club'. Could I start the day after next, only the recent rain had brought the grass on and Ted was getting restless?

We shook hands on it and I made plans on the ride home. I'd made a strike for independence. No more living at home, Groovy would see me right, I'd kip in his spare room, if he was lucky I might even slip him some rent. Hours spent cutting grass would allow me to get my head together. Things were looking up at last.

'Ever done it with a black girl?'

'What, all the way?'

'Of course all the way, you bollocking wally.'

Paully paused to consider, as if answering this question required a detailed consultation of the card index file he maintained inside his head. While he waited for his answer Groovy was crouched on the floor, flipping through an overflow of his record collection he kept in a decrepit cardboard box.

'I had my hands on a black girl's tits once, Christ they were massive. A party it was, Hemel somewhere; but if I'm being perfectly honest, I can't remember a full scale rogering, not even in the interests of racial harmony.'

'Well, let me recommend it,' Groovy advised. 'There's this girl in our office and last Christmas she got totally out of her head and practically dragged me up to the top floor where we ...'

At that moment the sound of a key in the door broke the mood and a four way chorus of 'You 'Orns!' went up, only to trail off when we all realised that it was only Sarah.

'And good afternoon to you too,' she responded, kicking her working shoes off into a corner of the room and automatically donning a pair of fluffy slippers she kept by the door before waltzing over to the kitchen where she promptly put the kettle on, the whole sequence executed with an effortless ease.

'Coffee please,' yelled Groovy, his head still down in his records.

'Anyone else?'

'I'll have a tea,' I shouted, adding 'make that three' as both Paully and Trev made the letter 'T' with their forearms.

In two weeks of living with Groovy I'd come to appreciate quite what an open house he ran. No one had commented on my being there all the time, it didn't seem to be an extraordinary set of affairs, and for the first time since coming back I'd felt like I'd drifted into some kind of equilibrium. The conversations had been enlightening too. Clearly while I'd been getting to grips with the finer points of John Maynard Keynes, they'd been getting on with their lives. Or their sex lives to be more accurate. Sex had metamorphosed from something we'd only ever considered in the abstract when at school to an everyday topic, the sort of lowest common denominator for all conversation - unless, of course, a girl was present; and especially if that girl was Sarah.

The only problem I had with this was that for me the subject still remained in the abstract. Ironically I should have been spending the last three years shagging for England. I had the girl, the time and even the private space to do it in, but that wasn't the way it had turned out. Andrea and I had had one of those unwritten contracts to do 'everything but', a phrase that seemed to demand three full stops at the end. Within these confines I have to say we were pretty adventurous but I'd come to the conclusion that this arrangement was significant, as if we were using each other to educate ourselves as to the art of the possible, without actually feeling the need to actually consummate anything.

Then there was the spectre of AIDS, although clearly once we understood exactly how it was transmitted this had become something of a red herring, after all if neither of us had had sex, then neither of us could have had the virus. The damage had been done though. The whole thing, with its accent on bodily fluids and flimsy rubber condoms, seemed to taint the idea of sexual congress somehow, to make it something to be avoided rather than enjoyed, something to be imagined, not indulged in. Sex seemed to suffer guilt by association, if not AIDS then STDs, and if not STDs then there was of course the whole risk of pregnancy thing. All in all, it had seemed safer all round to avoid it - too many problems.

Don't get me wrong, we were as red blooded as anyone else. The early days of our relationship had been marked by frantic fumblings and a race to see how much could be achieved in twenty minutes, the time it took for a side of an LP to play, the automatic lifting of the needle usually acting as a signal for Andrea to sit up and do up some buttons - a constant case of two steps forward and one step back. The music acted as a mask, with 'just going upstairs to listen to some music' becoming as useful a euphemism as others found 'would you like to come in for a coffee'?

During those days we got as far as was possible, but the problem was that just as the green light came into view we seemed to stall at the lights just as we might have expected to put our foot down. I won't pretend it hadn't been frustrating. She'd had a habit in those days of wearing jeans that were just too big for her, and whilst this didn't do her any favours (the sagging seat made her bum look a lot bigger than its actual pert self), it did make 'access' to the important areas much easier. So near yet so far. Four days a month the jeans were replaced by a skirt - the only time she ever wore one, and it sent a pretty clear signal.

Naked, she had the body not of a teenage girl, but not of a woman either. There were still pockets of puppy fat and her thighs were still a little thick. Her breasts however were perfect. Good-sized little pyramids that stood up to play and fitted her bra perfectly, as if it was custom made for them. In short, the whole no-sex thing had become somehow normal for us. The subject did raise its purple head occasionally, but she would always boot it out of play with some curt phrase like 'I'd really rather not', or 'You know my view on that', and I could never find just the right words to convince her otherwise.

Of course it went much deeper, ours wasn't exactly what you'd call a nurturing relationship, it had more ups and downs than the mountain stage of the Tour de France and was as straightforward as a civil war, with periods of truce and periods of intense anger and frustration bookending phases of normality. Every term was an adventure, but somehow we always ended the ten week period travelling home together, either by train or with one of our sets of parents. It made logistical sense and represented sheer good manners, to do otherwise would have been to prompt questions neither of us was ready to address.

Our history was made to look ridiculous when cast against the antics of all and sundry while we'd been away. They were all at it like rabbits, with Paully apparently managing a different girl almost every weekend, the lucky sod. I had no reason to doubt their stories, incredible though some of them seemed, it was a regular occurrence to see my mates acknowledge some girl they'd met in the street or meet with them in a pub, the temporary nature of these dalliances reinforced by the fact that none of these girls ever seemed to make it into the inner core of those who hung around in Groovy's flat.

Quite naturally, everyone else assumed that Andrea and I had had three years of unbridled lust, and as such I felt something of a fraud when I was accepted as a fully signed up member of the club without having to show a card. Faced with this reality it dawned on me that I really should do something about it, but in the meantime I had more pressing worries: the unfinished business of Graduation Day.

Thankfully, I'd remembered to mention to Brian that I'd need a day off for my graduation when asking for the job. He'd agreed, but made it clear he wasn't best chuffed and I shouldn't expect to be paid. Somehow the whole idea of me being a university kid broke an unwritten pact shared between us that I didn't remind him how immensely more qualified I was than him, for which, in return, he graciously assented to treating me as just another one of the lads. As the day approached I felt like I was carrying a guilty secret, that I had an appointment at the VD clinic or something. Either way no one mentioned it and wishes of good luck were noticeable by their absence.

As such, I had little opportunity to work myself up into a state of anticipation before the big day. The grass kept on growing and I kept on cutting it. Not that there had been much of a glow of expectation to kindle in the first place, more a sense of dread for a ritual that had to be got through. Already university had seemed to have drifted into part of a separate era, one which I'd passed through, but I saw the benefit of marking it with some kind of ceremony even if it was just as a way of underlining the fact that it was over.

If I'd taken more interest I might have caught wind earlier to the fact that Andrea's parents had got together with mine and come up with the petrol-saving wheeze of sharing a car, and naturally the car in question had to be theirs, a Volvo Estate, as it was the only one big enough to take all of us, even if, as I could hear her Dad say, 'it might be a bit of a squeeze, heh heh'. It was all right for him, he'd be driving.

So it was that we became a party, wandering round campus in a pack as we negotiated our way around a choreographed afternoon where we were herded around like cattle through a series of pre-set pens. The most bizarre of these was probably the one where we grabbed a graduation gown out of a random pile left thrown on a trestle table and tried to find a mortar board that fit before heading off to have our photograph taken holding a rolled up piece of wallpaper with a red ribbon tied around its middle which was supposed to represent our degree and probably held an equivalent value.

After the photo we hung around in the unventilated Main Hall for what seemed like hours, the modern glass ceiling making us feel like tomato seeds in a greenhouse. All this to have our fifteen seconds of fame as our name was read out, we bowed to the Chancellor, a little known minor retired academic who'd once written a seminal biography of Keats, and buggered off for good with a slap on the back and little else.

In the end I'd managed to scrape a 2:1, the same as Andrea, which was good on two counts. Firstly, it proved what I'd always suspected, that I was her intellectual equal despite her fancy convent education, and secondly a 2:2 just sounded wrong, like an unsatisfactory draw when you were expecting a win. After the ceremony Mum dabbed her eyes with a hankie and Dad shook my hand and told me they were both proud of me. It was all I could do to choke back the tears myself. He'd only ever said that twice before, once when I'd passed the eleven plus and once when I'd came first in the egg and spoon race in my last but one year at primary school. This handshake had felt special, firmer than ever before, almost Masonic, as if he was welcoming me into the world of grown ups.

After tea and biscuits Frank took the wheel and pointed the specially-washed Volvo towards the main entrance. A tired silence fell on the car as we all seemed to contemplate what had just happened. Then, from nowhere, and bang on the cue inside only her head, Andrea's Mum had piped up. It was probably seeing a group of two openly gay men holding hands at the ceremony that did it, but just as we were getting going she turned round to look at my Mum and announced:

'You know, I didn't know what a homosexual was until I met Frank.'

'Mum!' Andrea screamed. This wasn't the sort of conversation you expected from your parents, although I was trying desperately not to laugh.

'Heh heh heh,' Frank announced, remembering something. 'You know when I was in the army we called them all Carruthers.'

'Not like the others!' my Dad piped up, and the two men chuckled away to themselves, enjoying a rare shared moment which probably dated back to National Service.

Luckily this wasn't to be the beginning of a general gay-bashing session (my Dad still preferred the word 'queer'), as in the short time this had been going on Mrs Kendall-Jones fell asleep before she had the opportunity to deliver her usual punchline. Her mouth had formed into a small 'O' and out of it she wheezed a chorus of teeth-rattling snores all the way home. By unspoken consensus it was agreed that we wouldn't wake her.

Andrea and I sat together in the back. She gave me a forced smile and surreptitiously took my hand, resting her head on my shoulder, although this was probably as much through lack of room than affection, but it felt reassuring all the same after a strangely confusing day. In my silence I reflected that, putting aside the most recent incident, the day had had the advantage of having gone without any of the sorts of embarrassing incidents of the kind our parents still seemed to have the power to inflict on us almost at will. This seemed to fit a general emotion of what could only be described as relief.

As we left and passed through the gates for what I knew was the last time, it felt like we'd just been ejected from a none too exclusive club, asked, ever so politely, to leave and never come back. Whatever happened behind those gates would continue to happen, but from that moment on it wouldn't be our concern any more. Even though there were still people I knew there who I wouldn't mind seeing again, I knew at that instant that I'd 'done' university. It had been a good, but not great, experience, but one that was over, like a holiday with indifferent weather and not enough to see.

The analogy worked. University friends were like holiday friends. We had no shared back story. Instead our conversations tended to involve neutral topics, others peoples' thoughts and views, not shared experiences, and even then on a fairly superficial level, with cheap cider the lubricant and kebabs from the van outside the Student's Union the fuel.

As we headed closer to Watford I began to look forward to the next day and the familiar smell of fresh cut grass.

SUMMER

8

'WE COULD GO OUT OF TOWN, St. Albans maybe, one of those bed and breakfast places down by the station perhaps?'

'Ugh!' she'd shivered, 'that's so tacky. You just don't understand do you?' I hadn't. 'I want it to be special, I want ...,' and here she hesitated, as if she was also having difficulty articulating what this nebulous thing she wanted was '...to be seduced, to be cherished, not just 'do it' in some seedy little back bedroom.'

She was back in that fantasy world again, the one where the real world was an inconvenience, although in reality we were actually back on the sofa in her parents' front room, tucked away in a convenient recess at right angles to the door. It felt nostalgic to be there, like revisiting somewhere special from childhood, which in a way I guessed we were. This was the place where we'd served our fumbling and groping apprenticeship watching the late night Hammer Horrors on BBC2 on a Saturday night after her parents had gone to bed.

The whole discussion had been confusing from the start. After three years of having the location but not the inclination, I'd begun to pick up signals that she too was ready to break her duck, only now of course, and this was typical of our

84

relationship, we lacked the opportunity. Her house was clearly out and Groovy had made it a condition of my tenancy that using his flat as a knocking shop was off the cards - not that a single mattress on the floor was likely to meet her demanding specifications anyway. She hadn't exactly said she was ready to go for it, but I'd taken the fact that we were talking about 'where' and not 'if' as a good sign. Andrea had seemed to have passed through a door since graduation and gave out the appearance of someone eager to embrace the next stage of her life. Losing her virginity was, I guessed, part of that: a rite of passage. Of course, it was possible she could just be teasing, but that wasn't really her style. It was enough of a crack for me to chip away at anyway.

'How about getting a cottage somewhere? On the coast, Norfolk maybe, romantic swirling sea mists that sort of thing?' I suggested. She'd gone silent, I sensed a spark of interest, followed by a strange triumphant smile as she found a way of dousing it.

'And how will we pay for it exactly?'

She'd known, of course, that that was always going to be the killer blow.

Summer. The annual purgatory that every football fan is sentenced to suffer. To make things worse, this wasn't even one of those years with a European or World Cup to get us though the early stages. As the weather heated up people slowed down, and unaccountably as a nation we seemed content to swap ninety minutes of pulsating action for five day cricket matches in which very little happened. Not for nothing were they called Test Matches: a test of patience.

For me summer was a time of renewal, when broken legs mended and niggling injuries that had plagued players all season finally got a chance to mend. It was also a time to dream, to anticipate future success and the promise of late August when all the slates would be wiped clean and anything could happen. Summer was the pause button on football, which, when released, would unleash our players back onto the field like so many regenerated Dr. Whos.

A sign that summer was ending, the return of the football season allowed an opportunity to re-establish our territorial rights on the terraces, although even if the sun was shining we still wore our scarves, a sign of allegiance both to our team and to the season in which most of the work would take place: the long, cold and often grey, time of winter.

Winter. Standing in bitter winds, breathing in icy air so cold it sears your lungs and slowly freezing both your toes and your nuts off until the sound of bits falling off all around becomes deafening. By the time the first hints of the following summer arrived your team's fate would either be clear or you'd be locked in a fight for glory or survival.

That was the tempo I'd grown used to living to, and for me summer marked not the middle of the year but some indeterminate neutral and ultimately flat period between seasons. As any fan knew, the year proper started with that glorious August day and ended in May at the one party that really mattered: the FA Cup Final. Three pm on a Saturday with the whole world watching - that was pure football. Of course it was a party I'd never been invited to, in fact I'd never even been to Wembley Stadium, vowing like an obstinate donkey never to go until my team took me there.

Past experience had told me that as the evenings drew out I had to create diversions, fresh challenges to take my mind off things until August came around again. The previous year it had been the tour around Europe, this year it would be losing my virginity. I knew Andrea well enough to know that just waiting for serendipity wasn't going to work - this was a project that was going to need detailed planning. It had to be pre-meditated, but it couldn't appear so. Taking first things first, simply dropping into conversation to Andrea the idea that she might like to go on the pill clearly wasn't going to work. I was going to have to taken the initiative, and that meant getting some rubber johnnies, or RJs as we knew them. The one good thing to have come out of the whole AIDS scare was that people were much more open about the subject of what we were learning to call condoms. Whereas once your only option for getting them had been to visit the barber or wait until the chemist cleared of customers and praying that there wasn't a woman behind the counter, they had now become available in petrol stations, supermarkets and for all I knew from the local Women's Institute.

All these options carried a fatal flaw however: the need to interact with another human being. I wasn't quite ready for this so my grand strategy revolved around getting a packet from a machine in a pub. This in turn carried two drawbacks. First, the machine had to carry a national brand, really it was Durex or nothing as I could see Andrea baulking at anything she hadn't heard of. Second, I'd heard that the RJs in pub machines could sometimes linger there for a while and I didn't want to take the risk of having an old one that tore on me. I therefore needed to wait for a fresh batch to come in.

It followed that the next part of the plan was to stake out the machine in my local pub, which I knew carried Durex. The moment it was refilled I had to be ready to strike. In the meantime I made sure I always had the required change on me and conducted some research on which type I wanted. Given that I was supposed to be an old hand at the whole sex thing this wasn't something I could ask anyone about. I doubted one of the new flavoured ones would be regarded with favour and knew that RJs was an area where advertisers' copy writers' euphemisms were almost as notorious as those of estate agents. 'Maximum sensitivity for your partner' meant you wouldn't feel a thing. Likewise 'ultimate protection', meant there would be enough rubber to act as a spare tyre.

It was a midweek lunchtime when I finally hit pay dirt. The man who replenished the machines was as discrete as his product required him to be. No overalls with 'Johnny Man' embroidered on the back, no samples dropping out of his pockets (unfortunately), no suitcase in the shape of a packet of three. No giant rubber teat instead of a hat. I knew his game though, and even feigned the need for a slash to go into the Gents to make sure he was who I thought he was. He took around ten minutes to complete his work, during which time I managed another pint to pass the time and, if I'm honest here, to build up a bit of Dutch courage. I watched him leave, with a barely noticeable wave to the landlord, who I swear touched his crotch in some kind of secret signal by way of return, and waited a further five minutes. The bar was pretty empty, so I decided to strike.

No one was in the Gents when I got there a second time so I decided to get it over with straight away, even though the pint I'd thrown down my neck had filtered straight down to my bladder and I was desperate to go again. The white metal box was there on the wall waiting for me, looking slightly the worse for wear with golden flakes of rust on its corners. Innocent looking pictures on the front of romantic couples frolicking in spring meadows belied the more base needs the machine was there to help satisfy.

Kids had scrawled the usual graffiti into the metal with their penknives - 'Buy me and stop one' and 'This is the worst chewing gum I've ever tasted', and I marvelled momentarily at the nerve it must have taken to stand there and etch the letters into the paintwork. I fished the coins out of my pocket with ridiculous nervousness, and fed them one by one into the slot. Each one dropped on a tray inside with a discrete and almost polite clatter. Once all the coins were in I pulled the requisite knob to pull out the tray which would deliver up to me the blessed packet.

As I tugged, the money fell from its tray, which I immediately realised was a mere holding mechanism, and fell eighteen inches down to the, of course by then empty, metal container. They exploded with a deafening, echoing racket, as they hit the bottom, not unlike a metal dustbin with a loose lid being thrown down a lift shaft, a noise I was sure would be heard from the bar. I could imagine the stares if I went back in and voted instead to take the exit at the back of the pub leading into the car park. I lifted the sacred packet out from its tray and pushed the drawer back in, as decorum dictated, and exited hurriedly, ignoring for the moment my desperate desire for a slash. The unfamiliar, squishy feeling packet that carried so much latex promise inhabited my pocket at last, although the truth was it felt more like I was carrying a radioactive component, and I was sure I was attracting funny looks. The whole episode had been over in seconds but left me feeling rather sordid, and I hoped this wasn't a portent for things to come. The important thing though was that I had my RJs - the first hurdle of my quest had been cleared: I was armed and ready for the next round.

Meanwhile there was the sheer relentless reality of life to be getting on with. As well as its inherent tedium, the other downside of the summer of course was the bloody grass, which simply refused to stop growing. Due to financial cut backs the council had only taken me on as casual labour and they were working me hard. Every morning I'd get to the golf course for eight when Brian would turn up and release the padlock that secured the two large green doors on the front of the main shed. Both the size of our garage door at home, these sat on small pram-sized wheels which allowed them to slide back. Made of wood which had begun to rot from the bottom, they both looked like a decent kick could fell them. Once the doors were open Brian would cast his eyes heavenwards and give a weather forecast before going in. Seeing as we were undergoing a heat wave at the time it didn't take too much to guess what was going to happen, but it was his little ritual and the three of us indulged him in it.

Next up, Harry would wander over to the bench at the back of the shed, pick up the kettle and fill it up from the outside hose before putting it on to boil. Meanwhile we carried out routine maintenance on our designated pieces of kit. For me this meant checking that the blades on my rotary mower were both sharp and secure - there was nothing worse than having to traipse all the way over from the eighth or ninth fairway to get a fresh blade, and the ground was stony enough for them to take a fair bit of punishment.

After this it was simply a case of picking up where I'd left off from the day before. It was a lonely existence, but strangely satisfying. I'd considered getting a Walkman, but the damned mower was too noisy and it was useful to be able to hear the golfers' cries of 'Fore!' when they sent a loose ball flying, so I had no choice but to be content with my own thoughts. Some features of the job had survived from the previous year however, including the golf ball scam. I'd already amassed a reasonable collection and was looking to trade them in at a club to the south of town at some point. Another was the on-going battle with the enemy, the tartan-trousered brigade, a game of cat and mouse that gave a little added spice to the day.

In getting on with the job it was impossible to keep an eye on everything going on around you and as I was usually working in one of the copses surrounding the course I tended not to take too much notice of the actual golfers. It was difficult to avoid them when they played such a crap shot that it came towards you however, and when this happened, if the ball was near enough and looked good enough to add to the collection, I'd saunter over to it, cutting the engine on the mower as I went, and do what I called an 'Oddjob', treading it into the ground like the bald fat bloke in 'Goldfinger.'

Then I'd gently slide the mower plate over the ball and wait. They'd always come over and ask if you'd seen the ball and once they'd handed you the initiative like that it was a piece of piss to point them in the wrong direction. If I was feeling particularly bored I'd even walk over and help them look for it, sometimes earning a tip in the process. With that and a new ball to sell these were without doubt the most profitable, and most oddly satisfying, parts of my day.

Then there were the standard random lost balls left in the grass which the mower picked up. One ball was okay, it was when they came at you in packs that you had to worry. All was going swimmingly one Wednesday about a month into the job when the unmistakeably familiar sound of something ricocheting around the underside of the plate had alerted me to a fresh catch. I'd already got ready to leap in the air when a nanosecond later I heard a second and then a third clang.

That wasn't a good sign. One ball you could track, two maybe, but three certainly not. All I could do was follow the action by the sounds that were made. I'd managed to cut the throttle and in the silence that followed I heard two deep hollow knocks as balls bounced off the trees. These were followed by a whishing noise, like you'd imagine a bullet to sound like, and then an ugly, vicious crack as one of the bastards caught me on the wrist. Even before I had time to yell I felt the next bang me hard on the shin, like a hammer missing a nail, and the third entering my peripheral vision a mere instant before slamming right on the edge of my temple, felling me like a tree.

It was a sheer fluke that Ted was nearby. What was less lucky was the fact that he only had scraps of cloth on him, including his handkerchief, all deeply encrusted with black ingrained dirt and grease, because all of a sudden I was a blood fountain.

That Ted wasn't a man to have near you in a crisis was confirmed when he suggested I get up. Two things happened as I followed his advice. First, I fell down again on account of the fact that my brain had had enough and had decided to rest its consciousness for a bit, sending a sheet of black over my eyes and turning off the volume button in my ears. As I fell the second thing happened. About a dozen golf balls were instantly liberated from my pockets and bounced onto the uncut grass below.

9

THERE'S ONLY ONE THING worse than one of those dreams where you feel like your body is a ten ton weight and every movement is a concerted act of will, and that's to wake up and find out that it isn't a dream.

I knew I was lying down but decided to keep my eyes closed while I struggled to get my thoughts together. I could sense I was indoors and that the room was full of different noises all competing with each other: the swish of curtains on a rail, metallic clatters and a backbeat of mumbling male voices interspersed with the occasional suppressed moan. Then a drift of a scent took me right back to childhood, to days off school with a cold, tucked up between warm sheets with a comic and a glass of Lucozade on my bedside table.

Dettol. A smell that positively defined cleanliness and the constant fight against germs and all that is unrighteous, a fight symbolised by the sword that decorated the front of the bottle. Thick, cloying and astringent the antiseptic's smell was underscored by a sweeter counterpoint, the unmistakeable odour of Plaster of Paris. I opened my eyes to find my right wrist encased in the stuff and suspended vertically in a sling-like contraption, as if I'd been holding a balloon and hadn't noticed I'd let go of it. My eyes confirmed what my senses had already told me - I was in hospital.

I was the youngest in the ward by some distance, the beds around me all apparently occupied by old men with thin grey hair and striped pyjamas each of whom seemed to be preparing for death by practicing the pose they were going to adopt in their coffin. Each breath they took seemed to carry the possibility that it may be their last and the skin on their faces was stretched taut and shiny, reflecting little islands of light from the bulbs overhead. All in all the ward had all the appearance not so much a place where people came to get better but a rehearsal room for the hereafter.

A clip-clop of heavy shoes echoed down the ward, a healthy sounding pace, and I just knew they were working their inexorable way towards me. They stopped and I looked up.

'So, how are we feeling, heh, heh, heh?'

Of course.

'Hello Frank. I don't know about you, but personally I'm feeling pretty bashed about, actually.'

'Heh, heh, heh. Well, you will, heh heh. Pretty nasty accident you suffered there, probably put you off golf for life, which would be a shame.'

'You're not wrong there, Frank,' I agreed. A silence retreated away from us like a wave that had bounced off a sea wall. 'Was it you that patched me up?' I asked eventually.

'Yes,' he confirmed, before adding 'yes' and 'yes', again, as if he had to remind and then convince himself, in that order. He then slipped into professional mode and gave me a good old prodding about whilst at the same time giving me a run down of my injuries, which if they'd been anyone else's other than my own would have sounded pretty impressive. As they were mine however their significance was more as a list of potential sources of pain and inconvenience. Three to four weeks for the plaster on my broken wrist and a watching brief on the concussion - no operating heavy machinery apparently, which was just as well as I wouldn't have known where to start with any heavy machinery.

There was some good news however. The shin was just badly bruised and the discolouration would more or less disappear after ten days or so All in all then, and to summarise, it seemed my plans for the summer had just been well and truly kyboshed.

Just as Frank was finishing I noticed through the haze that my parents had wafted up behind him like extras in a crowd scene. In a show of awkwardness, they approached and requested permission to 'see the patient'. My folks had never felt comfortable around Andrea's parents and this particular situation offered the additional complication of being both social and professional at the same time which made finding the correct etiquette nearly impossible, with things made terminally difficult by the fact that they had a barely disguised reverence for the medical profession.

'Of course, of course, welcome, welcome,' Frank declared, waving them into the gap where he'd been standing. They approached warily, not sure that they were actually worthy of occupying his recently vacated space. 'I think he'll live,' Frank announced, artfully avoiding the need to call my parents by their first names, which he never could remember, before adding his customary chuckle. The look on both my parents' faces betrayed neither delight nor disappointment at this news. Thanks a lot.

'Well, I'm sure you've got lots to talk about,' Frank declared and, much to my father's surprise, thrust out his arm for a valedictory handshake. 'I'll catch up with you later young man,' he added from over his shoulder as he dashed off to his next appointment, throwing in the announcement that he thought Andrea was going to pop in later as an afterthought just before he disappeared around a curtain. I tried to raise a hand in acknowledgement and thanks, but found my arm had beaten me to it.

Mum sat down next to me while Dad borrowed a chair

from the adjacent bed with a nod of thanks to the occupant who, being asleep, hadn't nodded back.

'We thought you'd like these,' she announced, handing me a brown paper bag full of grapes, a damp patch at the bottom of the bag revealing that at least one had already been squashed. Ten out of ten for imagination then.

The conversation that followed was equally predictable, but I was knackered and I had no option but to fall in with their plans. It was like being their little boy all over again, being told what was going to take place rather than being asked what I'd like to happen. The hospital wanted to keep me in for observation, but after that I was to go home to recuperate. Home, with its routines, long silences and over-cooked meals. Sinking into my hospital bed I could just imagine it: waiting around for Dad to come home from work before we could eat, and no trays round the TV, no, it would be all sitting down round the table pretending to be a happy family. Dad would ask what kind of day I'd had and I would have to think of something to say. Mum would hover with the teapot and pop out to refill it with hot water, with no meal being complete without at least one refill. If I went out I'd have to be quiet when I got back as they went to bed by ten, and there'd be no chance of a lie-in in the morning as Mum would make enough racket in the kitchen with hot baking trays to wake the dead from eight o'clock onwards.

Home was clearly the 'big announcement' they'd come to deliver and after it had been served, like a court notice, conversation became awkward and cold, offering a portent of what I imagined I could look forward to over the following weeks. Thankfully the situation was rescued by the promised arrival of Andrea just as the visiting time clock, already slow, threatened to stop completely. After some more uncomfortable moments, during which Mum insisted on repeatedly calling Andrea 'Dear', they left, promising to return after teatime with some fresh clothes and 'things', the 'things' in question presumably being pyjamas and underwear, neither of which Mum would have deemed to be fitting items to mention in front of an unmarried girl.

'Oh grapes, scrummy,' Andrea announced as soon as they'd gone, and proceeded to help herself from the now more than damp brown paper bag. One of her most endearing qualities was an understanding that the world and all its accoutrements had been laid on for her benefit, including grapes. It was all part of her general philosophy of being positive about everything and who could blame her? Things always seemed to work out her way.

Her Dad had given her a run down on my injuries and after a fairly routine exchange of pleasantries she changed the subject with an announcement of her own. I began to feel that being in hospital gave people an inalienable right to tell you things rather than discuss them, as if sitting in bed made you incapable of rational thought. I was beginning to appreciate how a priest must feel in the confessional. Any lingering hope that she might pull the curtains round and jump on me flew out the window. So much for the sympathy vote.

'You know how I've always wanted to visit Firenze,' she asked - she was one of those people who could get away with calling Florence 'Firenze' without it coming across as pretentious. I wondered where this was going, and dared to wonder if she'd come up with a solution to our 'little problem'?

'Um,' I affirmed, cautious, but positive.

'Well, guess what? Jacqui's parents have got a villa in the Tuscan Hills and Jacqui has suggested that I should go too, to keep her company. Isn't it just fabulous news?'

'Um,' I agreed, a clear downward tone in the note in which this second 'Um' was delivered would have been discernable to anyone else who might have been listening. Although the delight on her face was transparent, selfishly, once having dismissed the possibility of going myself, the next thought that came into my head was that this trip was going to make achieving my quest by the end of the summer nigh on impossible. I hurriedly revised the deadline to the end of year and tried to show my happiness for her more genuinely. Positive thinking in action.

Jacqui was one of the stuck up, horse-riding and lacrosse stick wielding little madams from Andrea's convent school who had given the place such a bad name amongst my mates. Just thinking of her rekindled memories of the Hooray Henries I'd met on the train that fateful day earlier in the summer. I was a little surprised that Andrea had gone for this idea, I thought I'd weaned her away from that set, but there it was, it seemed the allure of the Uffizi and the Ponte Vecchio was all that had been needed for her fickle allegiance to revert.

She seemed to need my permission, or not permission so much as acquiescence, there wasn't any question of her not going if I hadn't have been happy about it, and it seemed churlish to be petty about it; so I told her to have a good time, that I wasn't going to be much fun for a while anyway, and that she was doing the right thing. She knew all this of course, but seemed grateful to have it confirmed. My frustration was soon compounded by the realisation that Andrea was about the only one of my friends who was vaguely welcome at my parents' house. All the others had been put off during the evangelical years, and having friends back hadn't been something either I, or they, had encouraged; but for Andrea all the churchy side of things had been as natural as Spring following Winter, what with all those nuns at her school. I lay in my bed contemplating some lonely times ahead.

To make things worse, ever since I'd resolved to consummate our relationship I'd found I'd been having erotic dreams featuring the two of us, a sort of sex by proxy, or if I was lucky a rehearsal, which meant I woke most mornings quite literally up for it. Somehow I didn't see having a plaster cast on my wrist as improving matters.

Andrea had somewhere to go, so after a lingering kiss, which seemed to carry an undercurrent of tenderness, although that could just have been because - as usual - she'd got her own way, she dashed off. There was no peace to be had however for as soon as she passed the corner at the top of the ward she was replaced by Brian from the club, who was heading towards me with determined strides, or as determined as he could make them. Maybe I'd missed it, but it felt as if people were running to some kind of appointment system, and I wondered if they passed an invisible baton as soon as they went round the corner?

Brian looked concerned, as if he too was carrying a message, or maybe a secret. He was also clearly uncomfortable around hospitals. It suddenly occurred to me that he might be worried I was contemplating suing the council - I happened to know that something similar had happened before - and Brian was not a man for enquiries or paperwork, his natural milieu being the greenhouse and herbaceous border that ran behind the tennis courts. In other words, somewhere he could hide.

Our meeting didn't start well as he made ready to shake my hand before realising that this probably wasn't such a good idea. He was carrying a geranium in a brown plastic pot, one he'd no doubt raised himself from a cutting, and with an embarrassed mumble he made it clear that it was a gift, although his reluctance to hand it over suggested that as far as he was concerned he could have been offering me one of his children.

'The lads send their best,' he announced, shuffling in his chair as if a low voltage electric current was passing through it. 'How are you coping?' For once I was able to run through my injuries to someone who hadn't already got the low down from someone else, but Brian didn't seem to be listening too closely as he continued to wriggle awkwardly in his chair like a small child desperate for the toilet. Exercising charity, I gave him the space to speak.

He edged a little closer to me, scraping his chair across the lino as he did so, thereby drawing to himself the very attention he had been hoping to avoid.

'There's a rather delicate matter I need to discuss with you,' he began.

'Yes?'

'It's about your balls.' There was a perceptible lull in the general hub-bub the second he said this, but not enough to suggest that it was related to this frankly distressing announcement. Having started, Brian clearly decided to go for the tape. 'We picked them up after the accident and have hung on to them.' At this point a surreptitious grope under the sheets with my good hand was unavoidable. Everything seemed to be as it should be. At the same time, Brian was rummaging in a carrier bag he'd brought with him as if he was going to produce the offending articles.

'Only there seemed to be rather a lot of them.' I raised my eyebrows in horror. 'One of them even spilled out onto the fairway, but Ted managed to rescue it before one of the customers belted it with an eight iron.'

'Phew!' I declared.

'Indeed.' Brian leant forward, distancing himself a little from the seat of the chair. 'Thing is, we were wondering where they all came from?'

By that point I'd realised he was talking about my little sideline and a few moments thought seemed in order before giving him an answer. A few further moments might not have been such a bad idea though as I found myself launching into a story that concerned a cache of balls under a tree and a sighting of a squirrel with a ball between his paws, but it wasn't to be.

It was enough though. All Brian needed was an explanation it seemed, plausibility was an added bonus and one I wasn't in a position to supply. He then launched into phase two of his rehearsed discussion, the deal he was prepared to offer me to keep me sweet. As a casual it seemed I wasn't entitled to any sick pay, but they could offer me a spell in what he called 'the hoot'.

At first I wasn't sure I'd heard him correctly and wondered if I was to be made the temporary custodian of a piece of treasured headgear or charged to look after an injured owl. Even when I realised he meant 'hut' not 'hat' I wasn't that much clearer. Was this some kind of secret groundsman's punishment I wondered, like the solitary confinement pit in a Japanese prisoner of war camp? Brian took my shocked silence as relieved acceptance and went on to explain my duties.

As it happened 'the hut' turned out to be my saviour - a reason to escape the bounds of home and continue to earn money. The hut in question was an old five by seven shed with a picnic table, a chair and a cash box, along with a small blackboard on the top half of a stable door. This was for writing down the time the last round could go out each night on the municipal pitch and putt course that I had now become the guardian of, the closing time being a shifting target due to the increasingly shorter evenings.

My duties were classed as 'light' and involved taking money, handing out a seven iron and a putter, along with a ball and a spare and a handful of tees to each paying customer. At the end of every night I had to walk round the course and check for damage while collecting all the flags and filling in a sheet recording the number of the last ticket sold and loading the cash bag into the safe. It was a position of authority, one granted me by virtue of the fact that I was reliable, was prepared to work odd hours and could count - three attributes none of my other colleagues could muster apparently.

With my wrist slowly healing and the bruises on my shin going down, I whittled away what remained of the summer. I seemed to exist in a semi-catatonic state, drifting through the days rather than living them. It was around this time that I realised that in contrast to previous years, when I'd rushed out to get a Watford Observer the day they were published, I'd missed the publication of next season's fixture list, that annual ritual during the cricket season that gave some hope for the months ahead.

Groovy popped by on his way home from work one day and dropped a copy of the list in. It felt more like a work of fiction than a manifesto. The names listed on it still seemed to belong to another world: Arsenal, Liverpool, Nottingham Forest, all presented as our peers, not a distant prospect for a possible one off cup game. Yes, we'd done it last season, but it still felt like we were a guest at someone else's party, gatecrashers, not someone with a genuine invitation in our hands.

Crazy. One season yes, as if we'd been granted the footballing equivalent of a 'Jim'll Fix It' wish. To do it all again seemed incongruous, like a magician who had just performed his best trick being asked to repeat it to prove he wasn't cheating.

Sitting in my wooden hut, doodling absentmindedly on my plaster, I was surprised one day by the sound of a polite knocking on the bottom half of the stable door. When I looked up it was Andrea, her face tanned and glowing, an Alice band holding back her hair. I emerged from my deck chair and gave her a hug and a kiss. It was good to see her again. I held her out at arms length and drank in her femininity, realising for the first time in days how much I'd actually missed it, and her.

'You look great,' I told her. It was only the truth. She accepted the compliment as if this was something she already knew and asked how I was feeling.

'Oh, you know, suicidal, the usual,' I'd responded. 'Welcome to my world,' I offered, sweeping a hand before the entrance to the hut. She stepped in and took a deep breath.

'Um,' she announced, 'it smells all woody, with a dash of resin thrown in.' Andrea could see the good in anything.

'Hey, guess what?' she shrieked, changing the tone. Clearly we'd done enough on my world and had re-entered hers.

'They've discovered that Nigel Lawson is from another planet after all?'

Andrea gave me a look. She didn't like it when I went political.

'No, I've been offered a job!'

This was a surprise. I didn't even know she'd been applying for anything. It took me a moment to recover. Perhaps she meant something local, or at the hospital working with her Dad.

'Well done!' I exclaimed. 'Where?'

'Oh, it's some company with lots of names in the title,' she offered, adding 'advertising' almost as an afterthought.

'Advertising?' I was confused.

'Yes, you gave me the idea, that time you were chatting with Dad at our house. I thought it sounded like fun and saw an advert in one of the papers and they saw me just before I went off to Italy and hey presto, what do you know, they want me to join in two weeks time. There was a letter waiting for me when I got back. Isn't it just fab-u-loso?'

It took me a moment to get my head around this. First, it wasn't even her idea. Second, it was the only job she'd tried for. Third, I distinctly remembered her asking if I was interested in advertising and being relieved when I said no.

Was she deliberately trying to get away from me? Perhaps she was trying to avoid the risk of us being thrown together again, like we were at university? Whilst all this processing went on I remembered my manners and offered my congratulations once again. We agreed to meet that night in the pub to celebrate.

I got there early and had arranged for Groovy to be there too. I needed to talk this development through with someone.

'It just doesn't seem fair somehow,' I complained as we stood at the bar and I got another round in. It was only half past six and this was going to be our third. The tone of the conversation had already been set however and lack of fairness was its theme. Groovy listened patiently as I ranted on, through a fourth and then a fifth pint. By then the clock was ticking its way towards eight, the anointed time when Andrea said she'd arrive, although she was always late.

Perhaps it was this, or perhaps Groovy had just had enough, either way he took me outside and parked me on one of the picnic tables in the small garden out the back.

'Listen mate,' he began, 'you've got to calm down, you're half cut and I can see, with my special Groovy eyes, that there's going to be trouble if you carry on like this.'

'But it's not fair,' I repeated. 'Her first application, her first bleeding application.'

'Yeah,' Groovy agreed, saving his sting in the tail for the end. 'But at least she applied for something. How many jobs have you applied for?' We both knew the answer to that one.

It was like being told by your best friend that you have BO. What Groovy had had the guts to tell me was only what everyone else was only thinking. It was also extremely effective at shutting me up.

'Need a piss,' I announced and staggered my way to the Gents, where the RJ machine on the wall was ready to mock my empty ambition. As I stood, swaying from side to side and watching the lemon coloured liquid ease its way past the disinfectant block in the urinal, I realised that something had to change.

It was time to get real.

BEGINNINGS

10

IT'S STARTED AGAIN. The clicking of the turnstile, the grunt from the gateman, the first sight of the immaculate green sward below with its alternating light and dark green stripes. The coppers patrolling the old dogtrack, the wind catching the corner flag, the nods to recognised faces nearby, the lone cameraman in his gantry. The referee finally blowing his whistle. It's started again.

Across the country middle aged men dressed all in black were re-starting my world. 'The big kick-off' the papers always call it, and for once they weren't lying. You waited all summer for it to come along, the Saturday of the August Bank Holiday weekend, summer may still be in full flow, but in reality this was where the year began. Wearing scarves proudly in the summer sunshine we met as usual at the One Bell in the heart of town. We were a breed apart, separate from the shoppers who normally occupied the High Street, we were a community with a shared aim. Optimism was the glue that bound us together, that and a love for our club and our team.

The pub was our watering hole, but we weren't there to get tanked up. We may have been young with strong bladders, but we didn't want to miss any of the action standing in the pisser inside the ground. We had just enough to feel good, then out into bright mid-afternoon daylight and a stroll up through the graveyard and a mad laughing dash over the ring-road. We joined the gathering crowd, walking with determination, and even though there was still half an hour to kick off, adrenaline was pumping through our veins.

Closer to the ground the programme sellers were barking out their wares and I fished out a fifty pence piece to keep my collection going and to catch up on the season's opening words of wisdom from our manager. The sausage and burger vans added their smell and sizzle to the general air of anticipation. A crowd of drinkers had spilled over from the Red Lion on the corner and a line of hoardings let us know which journalists from which rags would be covering the game the next day in the Sundays.

The national journalists never were our favourite people, always ready to put us down, but it was good to see that they were having to take us seriously. To us they were merely the butlers to the football aristocracy, there to do the establishment's dirty work for them, making it clear who was and who was not welcome at the top table and ever ready to point out when we might make a social faux pas or fail to conform to their social rules. They'd learn, we told ourselves, in time they'd learn to accept us as one of them and that times had changed, forever. Groovy, Paully and Trev were with me as we picked up where we'd left off, nicking Paully's hat and trying to toss it up onto the top of road signs. It was like we were in our first long trousers except the beer was kicking in by then, making us more adventurous, more daring.

The opposition that first day was Coventry and there was a smattering of sky blue shirts heading the same way as us, although we chose to ignore them. This was our patch, our turf, our Vicarage Road. After the previous season we feared no one here. Then we arrived, the tall floodlights gazing down onto the pitch hidden behind a high wall, unlit and redundant in the bright summer sunshine - their time would come. A background chatter of noise on the outside and a deep resonant rumble from within. Mums and Dads with their kids, lads like us in their gangs, policemen with their dogs and one or two perched on top of horses. We headed for the far corner and stood dutifully in line and after what seemed like an age we finally got to the front of the queue and handed over our money. The man behind the grille in the gate pushed his foot down and the cold metal of the turnstile squeaked and turned, admitting us to the open space inside.

At last, for reasons lost in the mists of time, the familiar opening bars of the Z-Cars theme tune started up, and the teams came out to a crescendo of cheers and a rain of torn up Yellow Pages, one inch squares that fluttered down like sycamore seeds and carpeted the concrete terraces. Our boys, our golden boys. The players ran into their respective halves and immediately started kicking balls to vent off some of the pent up energy they too must have been feeling, a summer's worth of frustration, whilst the managers slinked towards their dug outs and hid.

There was no great ceremony, no pom poms or brass bands, this wasn't American football, there was no need for a great fuss, it was a simple game after all, the only cameras there were from Match of the Day and even they were there only to record the highlights. It was all terribly restrained, and although individual players might choose to raise their hands above their heads if the cheer when their name was announced was loud enough, this was their only acknowledgement. Otherwise, it was as if we didn't exist, watching through a one way mirror, observers at the feast.

Standing on the terraces created an almost natural phenomenon as all of us fans morphed together into a single mass, swaying from side to side like a field of wheat caught in the wind as we all strived to follow the action. If sheer willpower were enough on its own the ball would never have left the opposition's half as we pushed our boys forward and pulled theirs back with shouts and hand gestures, both of encouragement and abuse. The players on the pitch were our playthings, a giant Subbuteo set, not human beings until they did something special with the ball, rising to heroes for a few vital seconds if they delivered the ultimate: a goal.

We were close enough to hear the players shout at each other, to see the sweat fly off their faces like salty rain as they raced around the pitch using every ounce of energy in their finely tuned athletes' bodies, to almost smell the fear they generated as they advanced on the opposition defenders and headed for goal. We could hear the tackles as studs met bone, not just watch them, and we knew they could hear us back; and as the slanted sunlight began to disappear behind the west stand it reflected off their shirts, at times making them seem as if they were truly made of gold.

When a goal was scored, the ordered swaying of the crowd became anarchy. Some leaped up and down, others merely clapped politely. The more experienced celebrated briefly and then watched where the surge of humanity behind them was headed as we were all pushed forward involuntarily towards the crush bars. Get one of those in your ribs with the weight of a few dozen yellow and red scarved fans behind you and you'd know about it until the following Saturday.

It was for this reason that we invariably stationed ourselves just after a bar, leaving ourselves room to become absorbed in the moment without fear. If the goal was against us a great collective sigh would follow, with a few of the crowd burying their faces in their hands, a few more appealing for offside and a few others berating the defenders. Then came a dissection of where it had all gone wrong, who we needed to blame. That was the routine.

For nearly ten years Groovy and I had stood in the same place and those that joined later had adopted the location as their own. Almost instinctively we homed in on a spot two thirds the way up to the right of the goal. Our end was uncovered, unlike the die-hard fans at the Rookery end directly opposite us. These were the true hard nuts, the ones who started most of the chants and had the advantage of a corrugated iron sides to bang on to get the noise levels up. Having a roof also amplified them of course, and they had the further advantage of the visiting fans to their left to taunt and respond to, the two factions divided by a thin line of men in blue.

Behind us was the electronic scoreboard, another Taylor innovation. State of the art stuff this was, with the capacity to run short pin man type cartoons or flash up words of encouragement. Our favourite used to be when it brought up the two words 'Black Magic' whenever Luther Blissett scored, which was often. Sadly we suspected this has been retired with the loss of our talisman to Italy, despite the fact that our new main man, John Barnes, or Barnesy, was also black. It was all a long way from the fourth division.

We'd waited all summer for it to come along, the Saturday of the August Bank Holiday weekend, but by the time the final whistle blew we wished it hadn't bothered. We'd celebrated goals from Barnes and the substitute Jobson, but it wasn't enough. We'd lost 3-2. There would be no unbeaten record that season, no fortress Watford, just an agonising three day wait until the following Tuesday for another home match, this time against Ipswich, and an hollow feeling in the pit of our stomachs.

A sense of anti-climax descended like a fog, a confusion of 'ifs' and 'buts' rattling around our heads, and a frustration it was impossible to vent in any way that didn't involve either violence or screaming - we could have won, should have won; but we didn't and we hadn't and there was no reversing the fact. The scores would appear in green on the Teletext and in black and white in the Sunday papers and the journalists would have their way after all. We left the ground and headed back into town, radios pressed against our ears.

'It's 5 o'clock and time for Sports Report,' and then the familiar marching music, a brass band given its head and told to enjoy itself, a tune that sounded as if it should have been backing a fairground sequence on a silent film, a sequence of notes that triggered an almost Pavlovian response of silence across the streets so we can hear the honeyed tones of James Alexander Gordon as he read out the results starting, as always, with 'English League Division One'. What had happened elsewhere and please, please God, we pleaded, make Luton lose too.

Sunday, also known as Bloody Sunday, especially when spent at home. A day comprised of elastic hours and ear-ringing silences. The first Sunday of the season had started with that half-forgotten feeling of emptiness, as if someone had drained the blood of hope out of your system and replaced it with distilled frustration. The morning after a defeat, there was nothing else that felt quite like it.

The one advantage of Sunday though was that it gave me time to fill and the single advantage of living at home was that it gave me access to my Dad's typewriter. It also provided the Sunday papers and their classified sections. There was no putting it off any longer: it was time to start applying for jobs. If Andrea could do it so could I, maybe the big bad world wasn't quite as big and bad as I'd made it out. A fresh season and a fresh start. I'd also heard from Brian that my remaining days in the hut were limited, once the kids had gone back to school my time would be up. The world of work was calling. Only two questions remained: what to apply for, and how?

Although I didn't know what I wanted, I did have the advantage of knowing what I didn't want. Accountancy was out, obviously, as was advertising, apparently. Anything to do with manufacturing wasn't a good idea, everyone knew that British manufacturing was dead on its feet, and I didn't know the first thing about science, so that was all the research and development jobs condemned. Publishing was just too snooty and marketing was full of air heads. I felt ambivalent about the public sector, the constant cuts hardly made it attractive, it didn't really come across as dynamic and on top of all this I really wanted to stay within striking distance of Watford, although graciously I was prepared to commute into London. In the end I spotted two opportunities that looked like they were worth going for. The first was as an Economic Forecaster with the Midland Bank. This played to my degree and involved a good solid employer where I could hope to get a foothold on a career without having to worry too much about cuts and takeovers. The other was more of a punt, a Statistics Compiler for The Economist, which kind of played to my degree but was attractive mainly because it was my favourite magazine and I quite fancied the idea of being part of their team.

The next challenge I faced was to make myself attractive to them. I'd done a CV writing session at the Careers Office at Reading and had had some copies of the finished article photocopied there as it was free. What I needed was a letter to go with it. After a couple of agonising hours and countless sheets of spoiled paper I finally crafted what I thought was a reasonable pair of applications.

Of course the central problem was that I wasn't really qualified for anything. Anyone taking me on was really taking a chance on my potential - which hardly separated me from the herd. It was an afternoon of 'if onlys'. If only I'd taken different modules at university. If only I'd taken some more relevant vacation jobs rather than cutting grass. If only I actually liked cutting grass I would have been well placed to make a career in golf course maintenance. Still, as Andrea no doubt would have said, there was no point focusing on the past, I had to look forward.

With a brace of applications safely posted, my next challenge was getting a job to keep me in beer money, but one thing at a time I told myself as I noticed there was a good film on the TV that afternoon. As it happened, fate stepped in. The following week it absolutely tipped it down, and sitting in my shed staring out at the course through the murky window I watched as puddles slowly formed on the first green, merging over time into a small lake, the flag in the middle seemingly offering surrender. My hours were dominated by the sound of constant hard rain falling on the felted roof above, that and trying to spot places where the rain was beginning to seep through the cracks in the wood.

Eventually, on the Wednesday, Brian came to my rescue. There'd been no punters all week and it was time to shut up shop. We had a summit meeting in the greenhouse, which I noticed was equipped with a heater, and he offered to pay me to the end of the following week in return for my P45. I saw this as a result, I was keen to move onto pastures new and this way I walked away with a couple of extra tenners in my pocket. With my wrist by then free of its plaster we shook hands and I left the club, hopefully for ever, but not without some memories, both fond and painful.

Knowing there was no time like the present, I called in on Betta Staff, a temp agency I'd spotted the previous week in town. Tucked away down one of the side roads off the High Street, the outside of the building had electronic displays advertising positions they currently had available, sending out a message that these were changing all the time and that Betta Staff was clearly a dynamic, happening sort of place.

The reality inside was rather different. The reception area was up a set of stairs lined on one side with a wall displaying rather tatty posters of busy secretaries and men working on what I assumed was heavy machinery - that was what it looked like. On the other side was a rickety banister which I didn't fancy placing any weight on and breaking anything else, and where the walls met the skirting boards the plaster was crumbling, leaving a thin layer of dust on the carpet below. The whole place smelled of a mixture of fresh chips and stale tobacco.

On reaching the top of the stairs I was told to sit down, fill in a card and wait for an interview, I assumed in that order. There were two other people waiting, although both had a look around their eyes and mouth that said that they'd been there for a while and it wasn't completely clear whether they were even alive. They were virtually ignored by the receptionist, as if she was used to her area being used as some kind of day care centre for the dispossessed. Both had the look of the desperate and offered a clear warning of what might happen to you if you stayed too long in this place.

Luckily I wasn't made to linger. The coffee I'd helped myself to was still only at sipping point when a woman not much older than me appeared from behind a door complete with a frosted glass panel and called me in, her eyes directed downwards at my card as she did so. When she did eventually glance up her eyes carried a look of curiosity, as if I represented a breed of animal she hadn't come across before and she was trying to place what I was called. A half-smoked cigarette dangled from her hand, the ash at its end precariously balanced.

'Mr. Westlake. Welcome to Betta Staff. My name is Karen. How can we help you?'

I outlined my situation, that I was looking for temporary work to tide me over and that I was prepared to contemplate pretty much anything - although I expressed a preference to avoid heavy machinery, now I knew what it looked like. This seemed like a perfectly reasonable proposition to Karen and we moved on to the next stage of the process, which involved her completing a much longer form and me answering questions. I guessed Karen was probably more used to dealing with people unable to write for themselves.

'Let's start with your name shall we?' she asked, reading it off the card. 'Col-in, West-Lake,' she mumbled, breaking each word down into its constituent syllables as she wrote.

'BSc,' I added, hoping this would sound more impressive, but Karen dismissed this addition impatiently.

113

'We'll come to that.' Suitably reprimanded, I went with the flow, giving her my address - which she liked because it was local - age and school, with relevant exams taken and passed. This seemed to do the job I'd intended with the BSc comment and, suitably satisfied, Karen looked up and took the opportunity to light up a fresh cigarette. The look on her prematurely lined and somewhat tarred face seemed to say 'what are you doing here?' before returning to her form and the metronomic process of completing it.

'Religion, you've told me that. Any other qualifications?'

'BSc,' I offered again.

'Qualifications please, I've done that bit,' she repeated, cranking up what appeared to be her low impatience threshold a notch.

'BSc,' I said, for the third time. This brought Karen to the point where she was forced to lift her head again, making out that the effort involved was roughly equivalent to lifting a bowling ball. She was probably used to dealing with simple souls, but it seemed I was beginning to push it a bit.

'No, not your religion,' she insisted, 'your qualifications.'

'My religion is C of E,' I replied, equally firmly, 'my qualification is Batchelor of Science - BSc.'

This was clearly a first for Betta Staff. The truck drivers, washers-up and office clerks they usually had through their doors clearly didn't tend to have degrees. Karen looked at me in a new light, a cross between a novelty (was she being filmed for Candid Camera?) and a challenge (what in hell's name could she do with this one?).

Eventually she repeated the three magic letters and wrote them on the form as if they were agency shorthand for blind, stupid and careless. I added that the degree was in Economics if that helped, but she gave me a look that said she doubted it, and although it may have been my imagination I thought I sensed a hint of sympathy too. At this point I went through my story once again, emphasising that I didn't expect her to get

114

me a job using my qualifications, just something to keep me going. She seemed relieved by this.

'Experience?' This was where the grass cutting and pitch and putt came in handy, and I confirmed that Brian would probably be happy to provide a reference. 'Anything else?' she asked, her pen poised over the form. Like what, I wondered? Did she want to know if I had any identifying marks or hereditary diseases? 'Any other experience?' she reiterated, for the first time looking me straight in the eye.

I thought hard, flicking through anything I'd ever done. I suspected school prefect wouldn't be relevant, and I doubted she was after my travel stories.

'No,' I told her, opting for the truth and even sounding disappointed on her behalf. Even here, it seemed, this was the gaping chasm in my prospects for employment, the black hole into which my chances of ever getting a job were inexorably sucked. My lack of experience.

'Um. Well thank you Mr Westlake, we'll be in touch,' she concluded, rising out of her chair and walking towards the door to open it. I rose, doubting her severely.

The extra ten days pay turned out to be nowhere near enough to tide me over and I was forced to visit Groovy once again at the DHSS. He treated me like a long lost brother and suggested I might want to get my name down for their Christmas Party, which didn't exactly lift my spirits. And they needed lifting. No jobs were coming my way and Watford had had a miserable start to the season, starting with two losses and two draws, two pathetic points out of a possible twelve. On all fronts, it was beginning to look as if the next few months were going to be a long hard slog.

In mid-September we finally managed a home win, but any uplift from this result was short lived as the following Monday two letters arrived together in that day's post. Both were in identical long brown envelopes, each franked rather than stamped, and each containing letters with almost exactly the same wording: 'Thank you for your interest. We are sorry to inform you we shall not be proceeding any further with your application. We would like to take this opportunity to wish you the best of luck in your future career.'

What career was that exactly?

I went back to my room and listened to some music. This was a situation which demanded the nihilism and anger of The Who's 'Quadrophenia'. Dad was out at work and Mum had set to with a duster and some Pledge. Monday was cleaning day and later on the house would be alive to the sound of the washing machine, a device almost as old as I was which had a tendency to walk across the kitchen floor like a drunk, rolling from side to side, until its hose was stretched to breaking point. I was just turning the first tape over when Mum interrupted me with a knock on the door. She seemed in a hurry and it turned out she'd been shouting up the stairs to attract my attention but I hadn't heard her.

'There's someone on the phone for you,' she panted, clearly eager to reach me before they rang off, 'something about a job.'

EUROPE

11

MY FIRST REACTION after seeing the draw on the Teletext was to reach for my old Philips' Modern School atlas. I'd never heard of Kaiserslautern, and even though it sounded German there was no way of knowing whether it was in the east or west, or even whether it was, in fact, in Germany. It was. Just. What was more they were known by the unfortunate initials FCK.

The news got better, the town lay in feint ink about fifty miles south west of Frankfurt, not that far from Luxembourg. Do-able in other words, maybe Paully would drive it? His Dad had finally had enough of his old Capri after the nearside wing began to sprout daises in the summer and had got him a brand new Astra hatchback, in theory it was a company car but he seemed to be able to use it whenever he wanted.

Playing in Europe, something none of us 'Orns could have reasonably expected to ever happen, but the blinking green script on the TV didn't lie. Then the phone went. It was Groovy.

'Seen the draw?' he asked, his voice reflecting the excitement I was feeling.

'Yeah, 'course,' I replied. 'It looks driveable,' I suggested, half hoping, half expecting he'd agree. My hopes were pricked the second after they left my mouth.

'Drive? Don't be bloody mad, you stupid git, it's on a Wednesday you know, we're not all dossers with nothing better to do like you.' The truth hurt, but not as much as the knowledge that he was still going to go. 'I've asked around and apparently there's a flight out of an airport in a certain small town in Bedfordshire, leaves at midday, gets you into Frankfurt for three local time, then it's a coach up to the ground. Back the same night and into work the next day, no doubt knackered, but it'll be worth it, only have to miss one day. He paused for breath before adding 'Piece of the proverbial,' concluding with the coup de grace, 'Mum's even said she'll pay for Freddie to come too, she's calling it his birthday present.'

It was the moment the subject of money came up that I knew I wasn't going to make it. Freddie, Groovy's twelve year old kid brother who'd been to barely a handful of games was going to make it, but not yours bloody truly, someone who'd followed the team all the way up from the fourth division, gone to miserable rain-swept nights in godforsaken holes like Cambridge and Lincoln, he wasn't going to make it.

Money. I was earning it, but it never seemed to hang around for very long in my wallet. Just surviving seemed to take all I could gather in and there was no question of money lingering in my bank account. The old piggy bank had been slaughtered, smoked and fried up to make a breakfast bacon butty, long ago.

'You want me to get yours too? They're selling them from the Ticket Office from Friday'. Groovy again. It hadn't even occurred to him that I wouldn't go.

'Thanks,' I mumbled, 'but I don't think it's a runner.'

To call me a dosser wasn't really fair, I had started doing applications and the temp agency had come up trumps with a job working as a picking clerk in a bonded warehouse out Rickmansworth way, all in all I was actually quite busy.

Everyone at the warehouse was a bit coy about what had happened to the person whose job I'd taken, only to say that they weren't expected back for a while, something about a pallet of whisky falling off the top of a fork lift just as he was walking beneath it, and as it happened I had detected a semi-permanent smell of booze about the place.

The warehouse had a bond, a great caged area where lorry loads of different types of alcohol would be stored while their customs duty was being paid. Once passed, the bottles would be loaded up onto different lorries, often from all points of the continent with each sporting a variety of European plates, all of it for export. The whole operation seemed to me like some giant B&B for booze involving a lot of to-ing and fro-ing, but it wasn't my job to question the system, just to receive and hand out the fork-lift driver's 'picking sheets', listing what they had to pick out of the shelves and where to take it, like giving them their shopping lists and setting them off on a trolley dash.

As well as booze, the warehouse also specialised in women's sanitary products, euphemistically known as 'towels', and I guessed it was my predecessor's misfortune that he hadn't been hit by a pallet load of these rather than bottles. Because of their bulk these took up a lot of the actual warehouse, but it was visits into the bond that the drivers really wanted, and after a week or so I started to pick up on hints that there might be something in it for me if I could allocate the workloads in certain ways.

Quite what the scam was I wasn't sure, but at the same time I didn't fancy a few cases of Famous Grouse landing on my head next time I visited the loo, so I played along, keeping my options open. I finally learned what was going on one lunch break towards the end of my first week when I heard something that sounded like a bomb exploding just outside the bond, sending out a deafening boom which echoed around the empty spaces of the warehouse, followed half a second later by a tinkling of broken glass. As we left the Portacabin to see what had happened, a mocking 'glug glug' sound provided a backing track as vodka seeped out of what remained of a cardboard case. 'Bastards!' my boss yelled. 'Quick, ring it off.' Men were running everywhere in a kind of comic battle, the suits against the overalls, with the overalls quite clearly better organised and getting in the way, using their advantage of surprise to great effect. Steel crowd control barriers kept to one side of the warehouse were grabbed and placed around the mess below one of the fork lifts with small A4 signs dangling from them by metal chains declaring that this was a protected area that no one could enter. Meanwhile sirens were going off and the metal gates over the loading zones were coming down. The whole thing was like being in the middle of a James Bond film.

'Shit, that's my afternoon buggered,' muttered the bloke who signed my timesheet, clearly annoyed. 'Bloody paperwork and officials. There'll have to be an investigation.' I asked him what was going on and he explained that this was a fairly regular occurrence. The whole pallet would have to be written off, the problem was no one could prove just how many bottles were on the pallet before it fell, and it was almost certain that a good couple of cases had been, quite literally, spirited away. In all likelihood they had been off the premises for a while, but a full search would have to be carried out and any evidence of box tampering looked for.

'It's a bloody waste of time of course. We know it, the men know it, the Customs guys know it, but it's the procedure and we can't afford to lose the bonded work, not with Sainsbury's pulling out.' I'd heard that the warehouse had lost the big supermarket's contract the week before, and that the resulting uncertainty had led to an immediate freeze on permanent recruitment, which explained why I was there.

The work wasn't exactly taxing, but at least it was adding something to my 'experience' column and was certainly an eye opener. It also gave me the opportunity to leaf through the job pages in the papers every lunchtime as we were too far out on an industrial estate to make it worthwhile going anywhere in the forty minutes I was given to eat, and I even managed to draft a few applications.

Getting them typed up was another matter as I found I was knackered every night when I got home, the bike ride there and back being much more than I was used to. What was more, the hours were stretched as soon as I joined, which put me in the classic bind of earning more cash, which was great, but having even less time to get out of the hole I was creating for myself. The longer hours also made it impossible for me to make evening games, which was, of course, a bummer.

And so it was that I had to follow our first ever European game on local radio sitting in a freezing cold cabin handing out chits to thieving fork-lift drivers. I had mixed feelings about not going. Ours was not a team in form and the feeling was that without a recognised strike force the best we could reasonably hope for was probably damage limitation. To rub salt into the wound Groovy and the others, including his brother, had ended up going by coach, the talk of a flight being just that, talk. I could have made it, but it would have meant jacking in the job and severely hacking off Karen at Betta Staff. All the same, it would have been nice to have been considered, but as it turned out no one had thought to ask, with everyone just assuming I couldn't afford it.

The evening itself was unusually quiet and I got away with having a small transistor radio on. I wasn't the only one there with an interest and soon a small crowd had gathered around the window where I handed out my tickets. All the papers said we were going to be found out by Europe, the journos still taking every opportunity to put the boot in, and they were probably rubbing their hands and sharpening their pencils when we went 1-0 down. Ours was a young team, but at the same time they seemed to be holding their own. More goals seemed inevitable, but when the next one came our little group went mental.

The dream was suddenly re-ignited. Little Jimmy Gilligan, little unknown quantity Jimmy Gilligan, his first time in the starting line up, only managed to equalise. Our first goal in Europe, a mountain climbed, a rite of passage passed. The euphoria didn't last, we ended up losing 3-1, but we weren't completely dead and had achieved that precious away goal all teams playing away in Europe prayed for.

Not being able to make evening games wasn't a problem by the time of the return leg. Half way through my third week there was a big meeting and it was announced that the warehouse was going to close down. I doubted this was a direct result of a single pallet of lost vodka, but it couldn't have helped. I immediately ran to a public phone and told Groovy to get round to the ticket office in his lunchtime and get me two tickets.

Two tickets because something inside of me had said that this was an evening I wanted to share with Andrea. I didn't know why, it just seemed that this game seemed to bring out the sentimentalist in me. She had shared me with the club for some time now, had been one half of a split loyalty, and it seemed only fair that these two halves came together on this special occasion.

On the night itself I cycled to her house via Betta Staff where I dropped in my timesheet, showing my face again to Karen just to make sure I was still on her radar, and to let her know that the reason the warehouse assignment had come to a sudden halt was nothing to do with anything I'd done. She was friendly and seemed to understand, there was even a danger that some kind of bond was building up between us, I had a lingering suspicion she saw me as her pet project.

Talking of projects, I had another reason to connect with Andrea that evening. My own project, even with its extended deadline, had completely lost momentum. The pair of us had hardly seen each other since her holiday, mostly because we'd both been so busy, with Andrea, in particular, having to take the Metropolitan Line into London every day.

I got to her house slightly early and was allowed to go up to her room to change. The plan was to grab a quick sandwich and join everyone else in the One Bell for a couple of jars. Andrea had promised to do her best to get off on time and expected to be back home around six. Her Dad, who of course understood the importance of the occasion, had offered to swing past the tube station on his way back from the hospital in order to speed things on.

Andrea's bedroom had for years had the aura of forbidden territory to me, a Holy of Holies untainted by testosterone. I didn't even see the upstairs of her house for the first year we were going out and even on that night mounting the stairs was tinged with a sense of danger. Her room had seemed to have been frozen in her teenage years, with pictures of horses on the walls and a dressing table complete with curtains hiding the legs like a Victorian piano. Even the lampshade had an antique feel, with a lace border along the bottom of a pink bell-shaped cover. The floor looked like the local dustbin lorry had decided to tip its load all over it, and it was this, as much as it being her hallowed ground where she could be herself rather than a grown up, which I suspected prevented her from being keen on sharing it with me.

I put the carrier bag I'd brought with a change of clothes on a wicker chair in the corner and looked out of the window. It was practically dark now and it was already possible to make out the dim halo cast on the horizon by the floodlights from the ground. The scene was almost Hollywood-Biblical, as if hundreds of technicians had laboured for hours to create an aura of expectation.

Looking around for somewhere to leave my keys, snot rag and the few coins from the pockets of the more formal trousers I'd worn for my visit to the agency I clocked a photo wallet from Boots on the dressing table. I'd assumed these were from her holiday in Italy and curiosity got the better of me, besides I was sure she wouldn't have minded.

The first few were innocent enough - shots of the Duomo and the banked sides of the Piazza del Campo in Siena and a few around Florence itself and then some taken on a beach. It was towards the back of the deck that things began to change. Totally unexpectedly there was a picture of Andrea and Jacqui topless, sitting on a towel, their knees drawn up, their faces each sporting a wide grin, with Andrea's tell-tale dimples ruling out any chance of a case of mistaken identity. Pulling my eyes to the left of the photos away from Jacqui, who, judging from the evidence before me, was certainly a big girl, I stood and gazed in a state of complete shock.

Two more followed, the next a variation of the first and the last featuring a boy, his arms around both of the girls, his grin, understandably, even bigger than theirs. Long shaggy locks danced around his shoulders like a Rastafarian's dreadlocks and he had both thumbs in the air in a universal gesture of smug triumph. At first I was perplexed more than annoyed. This wasn't the Andrea I knew. I wouldn't have put it past Jacqui, the diminutive but certainly well-endowed slut, but I didn't even know that Andrea owned a bikini. She was always a bit shy of her body in public when I was around and more of a one-piece bathing suit kind of a girl when we went swimming. And anyway, who had taken the photos? There was only one conclusion - there had been two boys, one each in other words. While I'd been lying in hospital she'd been peeling off her top to some bloke she'd just met on holiday. How far had it gone? Surely ...

Just as my imagination began to spiral out of control the unmistakeable sound of the door being opened and voices below had filled the hallway. I hurriedly replaced the photos and went down to meet them.

'Hello Colin, heh heh heh'.

'Frank,' I acknowledged.

'Big one tonight eh?'

'Can't argue with you there, Frank.'

While this exchange was going on I couldn't take my eyes off Andrea. It was the first time I'd seen her dressed up for work and she looked totally different, a complete contrast to the vision I'd just seen of her. Make up had been delicately applied, adding a couple of years to her in a positive way, highlighting a young woman rather than the image of a grown up girl I still associated her with. She was wearing a blue suit, tailored to fit her curves, with what were undeniably shoulder pads in the jacket and a large artificial flower on one of the lapels. The skirt had a pencil cut, leading down to a pair of pointed shoes.

I had read about this look in the Daily Mail at work, they called it power dressing, and on the basis of this first contact with it, it seemed to have the desired effect. This wasn't the Andrea I knew, the happy go lucky, slightly spoilt, demure girl I had spent the last few years hanging around with, this was a confident young woman beginning to make her way in the world. I was torn between being surprised and proud. She seemed to have donned a kind of uniform, complete with American footballer shoulders to allow her to barge her way into the world she'd now entered. Don't get me wrong, it wasn't unattractive; it just wasn't the Andrea I knew.

The need for speed broke the mood and Andrea dashed past me on the way upstairs to lose the outfit I'd just been admiring. It was almost as if I hadn't been meant to see her in it, as if she was the bride in her wedding dress before the ceremony and I was the groom - not that that was ever going to happen. I descended the last few steps, being upstairs while she changed was not a place I could be, and I went into the kitchen with Frank to help prepare the tea. I'd get changed later.

HISTORY

12

SEPTEMBER 28TH 1983 was a day that had the potential to go down in the history of our football club, even if the outward signs didn't look good. The first round, second leg of the UEFA Cup. We were already 3-1 down and needed to score two while stopping them scoring any and so far that season we'd won only two games out of eight. True, the second victory had come the previous Saturday and that had been a 4-0 thrashing of Stoke City away, so we consoled ourselves with the thought that at least the lads had got their scoring boots on.

A deeper look at the statistics told their own story. Goals for: fifteen, goals against: also fifteen. We were still scoring, and so long as we were scoring we were in with a shout. What was more, they were coming in from all over the park. Okay, Barnesy had got five of them but the other ten had come from seven other players. It seemed that in our team anyone could score and that gave us hope.

Any of our first team players perhaps, but seven of them were going to miss the game for one reason or another and we were about to field what amounted to a reserve side, with many of those who did regularly pull on the jersey playing out of position. Gilligan was back in the side, but only the most hard-hearted of managers could have left out our leading, our only, European goal scorer; but Richardson at number eight, tiny half-pint Richardson, we'd never even seen before, and he was pitched against the German international Hans-Pieter Briegel. On paper, at least, it was no contest. The journalists, with their sharp pens, sarcastic prose and lazy thinking were due to turn up in force again, intent, we knew, on finishing the demolition job they'd started two weeks before.

To us it didn't matter who took the field, if they were wearing the shirt then they were our boys, the boys with the chance to show that we were more than just plucky Watford, unfashionable Watford, pump it up the field and hope Watford. We don't want to be plucky, unfashionable or crude, the First Division's equivalent of Scotland, we wanted to win, to show that we were here by right and here to stay. We wanted to progress on merit and, however outrageous it may have seemed, we wanted to win this damned cup - one day anyway.

And there lay the problem. Did we have the self-confidence? The manager kept trying to keep things in perspective, telling us to be patient, that we were building a club and that success couldn't be instant. But he was the one who had taken us through the divisions, to the semi-finals of the Milk Cup, to runners-up spot in the First Division. We'd re-calibrated our expectations, we wanted more than success, we wanted respect, to sit at the top table and for voices to go quiet when we wanted to speak, to hold our heads up high.

September 28th 1983 was our chance to earn that right.

We were all there for the big night. Shifts had been traded, diaries cleared, arrangements made. Groovy, Paully, Trev. Even Freddie was there under Sarah's watchful eye, the next generation coming to the Vic to finish what he'd started in Germany. In an interview in the Watford Observer Taylor promised us one of those special Watford nights. We knew that taste and wanted to sup again from the bowl of greatness.

Glory was so close we could smell it in the air, even if we weren't sure whether the dish was being prepared for us.

At last the referee blew his whistle and we were out of the traps like greyhounds on speed. Out and at them straight away, a typical Watford performance, making up with fury what it lacked in elegance. Terry began the action, the first footballer I ever saw who wore what looked like a sanitary towel across his forehead. He claimed it was to protect scar tissue caused by too much heading of the ball, but we all suspected some kind of weird sexual fetish. Whatever his motivations, he rushed out and passed the ball to our captain Rostron, who collected, looked up briefly and sent Callaghan down the wing, his black shorts and socks standing out in the floodlit glare. Most of the twenty one thousand of us in the stadium started to cheer, to urge the boys forward, to get that early goal we'd all been praying for. To Barnesy, Barnesy, we yelled, bang it over and let him loose at them, one of his magical little wriggles and then whack it into the corner, but the move fizzled out as their goalie collected the ball coolly from a misdirected cross.

It was only the beginning, though, as we pushed and pushed and pushed, all the action in their half, as they defended their two goal advantage with their big German internationals against our inexperienced apprentices and makeweights. But it was someone who could never be called a makeweight who brought the stadium to life. Barnesy, our hero, flicked the ball on to the unknown Richardson who, miraculously, shrugged off his marker and started to make a beeline for their goal. One on one with the goalie, boy against man with a defender homing in, somehow he kept his head and cool as you like slotted the ball home.

The whole place went crazy. Not even ten minutes on the electronic scoreboard and we were ahead on the night. Ahead in a European game, our first ever European game at home. Winning - not by enough it was true, but there were eighty minutes remaining. The Germans still had a cushion and they knew it, but suddenly their guard was down, we'd shown we could breach their Teutonic fortress. We'd barely had a chance to digest Richardson's goal when Palmer, one of our full-backs for God's sake, sent in an angled cross which got deflected by the diving keeper only to bounce into the net off one of their defender's knees. 2-bloody-0! We were now technically ahead, we had the away goal. If it stayed like this, we were through, miracles could and did happen, at least down at Vicarage Road.

There was still a long way to go, but the balance of the game had changed. Suddenly the Germans had to score, and as our national side had learned over the years, there are few things more awesome than a German side that needs to score. But first they had to get the ball out of their half as we kept on going at them, trying desperately to wrap it up. They only needed to score once to deflate our optimism, if that happened we'd have needed to get another ourselves just to make it all square.

Come at us they did. Three times they had realistic chances, but they didn't take them, the most gold-plated of them coming just as the half was drawing to a close, but we survived. The kids were back in the dressing room 2-0 up before we even had time to cheer the whistle. Half time. Orange segments and cups of tea. A chance for the manager to prove what he was made of. Maybe he'd have them running on the spot to keep the momentum going, we wondered? Maybe he'd be telling them to just keep playing like they did in the opening twenty minutes? Maybe he'd got a master plan? The one thing he didn't have was a super-sub to change the mix - every man jack of our fit and able players was out there on the pitch. It was up to them. Only they could make history.

In the second half the tempo definitely changed. The pace was slower, more thoughtful, more like poker than racing patience, with stakes to match. The Germans tried to thread their way through our defence, whilst we tried to hammer them on the break, to break their resistance and book our place in the second round. What would the journalists say then about plucky Watford?

We kept our heads, kept passing the ball, retaining possession, asking them to come and get it if they wanted it, and they did want it; they needed it. They were the ones who had to score. What happened next came unannounced. Richard Jobson punted in a low cross and that man, that titch, that hero in the making Richardson came through again, sliding in with a volley which went up into the air and curved over their keeper's head and into the net. Three, plus the one we got there, which meant we were ahead by rights, not just on the away goals rule.

More chances followed, but little had changed other than we knew this was now ours to lose. If they scored they were right back in it. They'd come with a cushion and had thrown it to the crowd. We didn't even have that luxury. This was Watford, you got used to discomfort. We watched together, on the outside urging the team on but inside lost in our thoughts and what might just be.

Our voices were roused by bouts of action but all we really wanted to hear was the ref's final whistle. We all spent just as much time glancing down at our watches, set on stopwatch mode and faithfully reset when the second half had got under way, or looking behind us at the electronic scoreboard, as we did looking at the action on the pitch.

They had one more chance to snatch our glory away from us. Sherwood, our goalie, failed to gather a ball in the six yard box, but Steve Terry's knee saved us, spinning the ball into safety. This was to be our night after all. Finally, inevitably, the ref raised his whistle to his lips, briefly puffed out his cheeks and blew.

The whole place went ballistic, all our pent up emotion erupted and the players followed suit. The first-formers eleven had beaten the first team. They were heroes and had earned their place in the history of the club. We were their loyal fans, we had been there when it happened. We raised our fists in the air, our scarves tied around them, and almost instinctively it seemed, I turned to Andrea and gave her a glorious long hug.

It was then that I did it. God knows why, blame the emotion, the atmosphere, the sheer light-headedness of it all. It wasn't a real situation, more like a dream. It just seemed the right, the natural thing to do. The ultimate. I pulled her into my arms and, drawing my lips closer to her ear (I think I may have been intending to kiss her) those three little words seemed to slip from my lips like melting ice cream: 'I love you.'

We walked back from that night at the Vic in a kind of delirium. High spirits, but no high jinks, just feeding off the adrenaline transfusion we'd been given. But for Andrea and me there was something else. Incredibly, in nearly five years of seeing each other, including three shared at University, those three words had never been uttered by either of us. The cat was out of its basket. The jack was out of its box. The toothpaste was out of the tube.

We held hands, occasionally applying a little pressure with our thumbs, hanging back from the rest of the gang. As if by some kind of implicit pact they made for the pub and left us to do what ever it was we were going to do. Subconsciously no doubt, the others sensed an atmosphere and kept their distance. I walked Andrea home and we kissed at the gate. She was working the next day and she'd said before we set out that she wanted to get straight home to bed after the match and she was as good as her word.

I wasn't too bothered, going in meant either meeting her mother, which would be unthinkable - my head was already on a full spin-cycle - or creating a situation where there was a chance we'd have to discuss what it was I'd said, or at the very least remind ourselves of it. At that moment it was best left hanging, a reality but one that could be temporarily ignored. I think we both preferred it that way. She smiled as she turned and headed down the path to the front door, turning and giving a final wave before the light inside absorbed her.

I turned and headed back to Groovy's deciding to avoid the pub and be at one with my thoughts. Back at the flat I made myself a coffee and flopped down into the sofa, not bothering to put on the light. Alone, I replayed what it was I'd done and it was only then that I realised that she'd said nothing back, not even given one of her trademark half smiles. Just a hug and a slight tap on the back of my coat, the sort of consolation your auntie might give you if your hamster had just died, and about as comforting.

I sat there for what was probably about half an hour, my coffee only half drunk, with an unfamiliar amber light permeating the bamboo shade from the streetlights outside and casting an appropriately mysterious phosphorescence around the room. Finally gathering up the energy to move I got to my feet just as a rattle of keys outside suggested that Groovy was unlocking the door. He shoulder-charged the door open and flicked on a light.

'Christ! You gave me a fright!' he yelled, literally jumping back a couple of feet as he did so, an exaggerated mime-artist kind of reaction. 'What were you doing in the dark, you daft git?'

'Sorry, sorry,' I replied, 'I was just getting ready to kip down.'

'Yeah, well, fine,' he stuttered back, 'I know there's a worldwide energy crisis and all, but hey, it is okay to use the lights you know.'

I apologised again and turned for the kitchen. Maybe it was something in my body language, maybe he just knew me too well, but somehow I was sending out signals that said that something wasn't right.

'Sit down,' my oldest friend barked at me, turning on the main light as he did so. 'Tell Uncle Groovy all about it.'

'What do you mean?' I asked, unfamiliar with being ordered about by my oldest friend. Sure, we shared most things, but we didn't exactly 'do' open heart analysis.

'Well, call me old fashioned if you like, but there's something up and one thing's as sure as hell, sitting here in a darkened room ain't going to solve it. You're in my flat, taking up my space, eating my food, so you may as well go the whole hog and burden me with your troubles.'

'Hey,' I responded, shrugging my shoulders in a way that managed to combine embarrassment with nonchalance, or so I thought, 'as you say, you're doing enough.'

'Right,' he concluded. 'That means there is something.' He lifted his finger and pointed it at my face, lowering it towards the chair as, in his best Barbara Woodhouse impersonation, he commanded me to 'Sit!', putting extra emphasis on the 'T' and carefully avoiding inserting an 'H' after the opening letter.

I then told him everything that was spinning round my head about Andrea and me, about what we loosely called our relationship, about our love life, about how I saw our future, or indeed if I saw any kind of future at all. What I thought she thought. What I thought she might think I thought and so on. The lot. The whole caboodle. Nothing held back.

I ended it all with what I'd done that night on the final whistle, what I'd gone and said. At a time when almost everyone else in the crowd had been celebrating one of the best nights of their lives I'd gone and crapped all over my own sense of exhilaration. The fact that saying those three words had smothered rather than ignited the end of the evening for both of us spoke volumes.

Groovy was great. He listened. He didn't make any smart arse observations and even pulled back from making the universal wanker sign at me. He sat there in silence, occasionally willing me on with a nod of the head or a raising of the eyebrows, but he listened, taking it all in. It was as if I was a young child back tidying my bedroom at home under orders from Mum, putting things back in place, beginning to see flashes of carpet, restoring order.

Finally, he spoke, this time using his own three little words to address the nub of the problem caused by mine.

'And do you?'

'Love her?' I asked. He nodded.

'Well, there's the thing,' I replied, 'we've been together so long I think we've probably lost sight of what love might feel like. I don't need to be with her all the time. I do think of her, some days when I'm bored I think of her quite a lot, but it's usually around practicalities, when we're going to meet up and where, that sort of thing.'

'Um,' my learned friend contemplated. 'And the sex, or should I say lack of it? What's that all about?'

'Same thing really. Just habit. We agreed not to early on and the pact just seemed to stick. No re-negotiation, nothing serious anyway.'

'Really?' He seemed incredulous, but hid it well.

'Well, some. In fact it's come back on the agenda quite recently, but of course it's tricky now - I mean where do we go? It doesn't seem right to bring her here, her parents' place is right out and my Mum never seems to leave our place, besides it would seem odd if I suddenly started turning up there and using it as a love nest.'

'Point taken - well, points taken actually, oh and thanks incidentally for your consideration, it's me who washes the sheets round here as you know and there is a limit.' He paused, thinking, and I gave him the space to do so, all spent after my great unburdening. Outside a police car sped past, its siren cracking the air open like a chainsaw. Something had kicked off. I glanced at my watch. It was half past midnight.

'Well,' he started, 'at the risk of sounding like 'Ask Jackie', it seems to me that the whole sex thing is getting in the way.

You need to get past that and see if it unlocks any other deeper feelings. At the moment it's acting as a dam, holding you both back from moving forward. In short, my friend, having whammed your sledgehammer against the side of the dam you need to follow through and get into her pants.'

'Concise. To the point. An interesting analogy and remarkable for resisting the temptation to avoid making a joke about little boys sticking their fingers into holes, for which I thank you.'

'It was tempting, I agree, but we're both mature adults now and I didn't think it appropriate. Look mate, it's not really any of my business but we can all see that you're not happy at the moment. With the greatest of respect you need to know where you stand, and I mean emotionally, not just sexually. If Andrea's the girl for you then great. If she isn't, well, there's plenty of other fish in the sea.'

I paused to consider what he'd just said, as it had come as something of a surprise. 'Thanks.' I said, before adding 'I needed that.' It was certainly food for thought.

'All part of the service. Now sod off to bed, some of us have got to go to work in the morning.'

HOPE

13

THE EUROPEAN WIN had a galvanising effect on me. Between jobs again, I returned home in order to conserve resources, at least temporarily. Although Groovy let me stay with him and didn't demand any rent, I did like to contribute and staying with him I inevitably got dragged down the pub most nights, all of which tended to add up to too many favours.

As well as predictability and a base, home also gave me access to the typewriter and I kicked up a gear on the job applications. I had sent a few off during my short stint at the warehouse but enough had come bouncing back for me to become something of an expert in the language of rejection. Understanding the grammar of successful applications was proving tougher to grasp. The banks were the most prolific in their advertisements and also the quickest to respond. I was beginning to take the hint, maybe my letters oozed untrustworthiness? Had they perhaps got wind of the golf ball scam?

I tried different approaches and even adopted coloured paper for the CVs to make them stand out and toyed with (and quickly rejected, on account of the nose) the idea of including a photo, but none of these ploys seemed to deliver. At the same time I began to lower my sights, applying for more generic graduate jobs that didn't have a direct link to my degree, trainee schemes, even the occasional sales job; but the result was always the same. Using my statistical knowledge I even began to try to track trends and created an ornate filing system logging applications by type, location and salary against the time it took for them to come back and reasons given for not 'progressing my application', although these were rarely offered.

No one could fault me for effort, and I knew that all my tapping away on the typewriter pleased Mum and Dad, although for all they knew I could have had a couple of monkeys in my room trying to write Hamlet. They did see my face when the rejections came through though, usually when we were having breakfast before Dad set off for work, and I could tell that they shared in my disappointment. At the same time, although I didn't realise it at the time, all this rejection was having a sapping effect on my morale. The gap between Andrea and her growing confidence and me, with my increasing despair, had become so wide you could walk down it swinging a cat in each hand.

Groovy in the meantime got a promotion. Whereas before he had worked with people to make sure they applied for all the benefits they were entitled to he was now given a role to make sure that people weren't claiming more than was their due and putting together a prosecution case against them if they were. Thatcher's Britain.

Betta Staff also came through again via their Hemel branch, which meant becoming a commuter and taking a bus to work in the dark every morning and evening. The job was with a large camera and film maker, packing special Christmas promotion kits on a conveyor belt with a couple of other temps both, like me, recent graduates, along with Reg, a thirty-something employee who'd clearly been assigned to keep an eye on us.

Reg was what you'd call comfortable. He'd worked at the

company since he'd left school and it had allowed him to earn enough to enjoy life and run his Ford Escort without stretching himself too much. He knew the ins and outs of the place, and he also knew that the whole idea of a Christmas rush for the firm's products was a myth.

'Get them in the shops and they'll shift,' was the boss's mantra apparently, but it wasn't true. 'Keep January free,' he told us, 'you'll be back unpacking these and ditching it all.' He went on to explain that the Japanese who owned the company regularly paid a visit in January and what usually happened was round about the second week of the New Year the management would hire some skips and simply throw away all the excess stock. None of this seemed to annoy Reg, he just saw it as part of the natural way of things.

Radio 1 played constantly in the large industrial unit where we worked, providing a rhythm to the day, the highlight of which was Steve Wright's Love Songs, which often inspired a round of raucous piss-taking which sent echoes bouncing round the hanger-like building where we worked. Before long we built up a pretty good sense of camaraderie, with the regular news breaks in particular provoking lively debates and Reg finding himself having to defend some of his long-established views.

In early October, Neil Kinnock and Roy Hattersley were elected as the new leader and deputy leader of the Labour Party. Reg thought they were the real McCoy, but I for one disagreed, although they represented a move out of Labour's nightmare there was something missing there, and I didn't just mean Kinnock's hair. I saw their election as a bit like moving from the Jurassic to the Cretaceous, the dinosaurs were dead, but the continents as we recognise them now still had to form.

I couldn't yet put my finger on it but the more I got about and experienced different jobs the more I could sense that something pretty fundamental was going on in the country, and it was going to need a massive shift with tradition to counter it. Kinnock and Hattersley weren't in that league, with nuclear disarmament still tearing Labour apart they still had to sort out their own party before they could turn their attention to the rest of us. A nagging portion of me even suspected that some of what Thatcher was doing might be the right medicine, what I disagreed with was her style and all that damned hectoring. Surely there had to be a better way?

In the meantime we cheered ourselves up by making little additions to the gift packs we were making up, adding notes saying 'Happy Christmas from the boys in the factory', and occasionally signing them 'Reg' if he'd been over-playing the whole shop steward angle that day.

As autumn dissolved into winter the journey to and from work became harder and colder, and there wasn't much in the way of light relief from Vicarage Road either, with only one point gained in the whole of October and the same haul in November, including a miserable 2-1 defeat to Luton at home at the end of the month which could only be regarded as a total bloody disaster. At the same time, we got knocked out in the first round of the Milk Cup to knackering Huddersfield of all people and things had begun to look decidedly dodgy. The national journalists, of course, were having a field day and the lads at the factory got a lot of mileage out of reading out their pearls of wisdom to me over lunch breaks.

Against this backdrop it came as a surprise when we managed to follow up the Kaiserslautern result with another win in Europe, this time against Levski Spartak, a win made all the more impressive by the fact that I had at least heard of them before. Despite only drawing one apiece at home we went on to win 3-1 away, which gave us a third round tie against the fancied Sparta Prague. Winning the next one would mean we would still be in the cup over the winter break, which in turn would give us a chance to regroup, and maybe even play Mo Johnson, the new striker we'd just bought from some outfit in Scotland.

A 3-2 loss at home soon put paid to that, and it came as no surprise when the Czechs followed it up by thrashing us 4-0 in the away leg. All of a sudden our first European campaign had fizzled out like a late November firework, a momentarily spectacular flare peppered with a surprise at the beginning, but all too quickly over, a puff of barely visible smoke disappearing into a dark background. It seemed that success in Europe was as difficult as we'd all suspected in our hearts it might be, the early results had simply lulled us into a false sense of security. All the same, it had been fun and at least it had delivered THAT night at home at the end of September.

Around the same time as this happened I left the camera job to take up a job as a Christmas postman, something I'd fixed up for myself beforehand. I wondered about checking my own post at the sorting office, but it was just as well I didn't as - plop, plop, plop - the letters of rejection continued to fall onto the mat by our front door. As fast as they came I replaced them all with fresh applications, my standards falling by the week, although I still held the line against accountancy. My plan was to always have some live applications out there, to improve the odds that any day I might come home to find that I'd been offered an interview. It was like the Premium Bonds, I told myself, and probably with about the same chances of success.

Meanwhile, being a postie suited me down to the ground. Okay, it involved early starts but I was my own boss and could work to my own pace, so long as I didn't get too far behind the regulars. I had my own round, or 'walk' as they called it, and after a while got to know the short cuts, although as I was being paid by the hour I didn't always use them. There was also plenty of overtime in the sorting office if I felt up for it, having re-energised myself from the early start with a subsidised cooked breakfast in the canteen after finishing the walk, and as Christmas got closer there were second posts to contend with too.

I loved the crisp winter mornings the best, when there was a crunch of frost on the grass and my feet left footprints in the virgin whiteness on the ground. Watching people rush to get their working day in gear when you were already half way through yours was also oddly comforting. Most important of all, I was on my own for most of the time, which gave me a chance to get my thoughts together. Generally, my spirits lifted, a process helped by back to back victories from the boys, including a 5-0 thrashing of Wolves at home with the new boy Johnson coming good with a hat trick, which held out some hope that we could extricate ourselves from a dangerous flirtation with the relegation zone.

With the year rapidly drawing to its conclusion I decided to close in on my quest with Andrea. Absolutely nothing had happened during the ten weeks since my heart to heart with Groovy as we'd hardly even seen each other. We'd kept in touch by phone but there always seemed to be a reason why we couldn't get together. Either I was busy or she was, with a lot more of her time apparently taken up at work. This hands-off style of relationship was alien to both of us as we were used to living in each others' pockets, and the phone calls were rarely successful. Plus I had noticed a slight shift in Andrea's tone, she was more self-assured somehow, coming more from a standpoint of what she felt and wanted rather than talking in terms of 'us' and 'we'.

Walking around the residential estates of Watford, however, my brain had convinced me that I needed to use what I'd said after the Kaiserslautern game to open up a wider discussion about where we were headed, before it was too late. There was also the not so small matter of the photos to get to the bottom of, something I'd decided to ignore, convincing myself I was being paranoid.

The night after the 5-0 against Wolves we finally got together and went out to see a film, a comedy, and went on afterwards to have a drink in town. I was feeling really upbeat, like I'd been inflated with air, in a suspended state where my feet only just touched the ground. Despite the job thing, I felt as if life was treating me okay and things would all come out all right in the end. When I was in this kind of mood Andrea and I always got on so much better, conversation seemed to flow more easily, like we were on the same wavelength somehow. I decided to cut the crap and get on with it. As she raised her vodka and orange to her mouth I reminded her of what I'd said that night, being careful not to actually utter the words themselves again.

'And did you mean it?' she asked.

I decided the best tactic was to answer her question with another question and continue with the direct approach. 'Well, I said so didn't I? What about you?'

'Do I love you?' She paused to consider. This wasn't a good sign. Her answer was an almost perfect echo of Prince Charles's response when asked the same question on his engagement to Diana: 'Whatever love means.' I wasn't prepared to let her get away with this and gestured with a swirling wrist that she should elaborate.

'Well, let's be honest, we've known each other for so long now that even if we ever had it we would have grown out of the head over heels stage by now. We've grown up together, know each other - almost too well at times. We're comfortable together, there's a tenderness there, something worth keeping and maybe cultivating.'

'Maybe?'

'Well, there's the rub really, we know what we have, have some idea perhaps of what we could have but don't know what we might have with someone else. Maybe we're cowards, not wanting to jeopardise what we have now, afraid of starting again with someone else?'

Bloody hell, she'd gained in confidence, it was like a totally different woman talking. An image of the topless photos flashed through my mind but I pushed it away immediately, I didn't wanted anything to cloud this conversation but I couldn't help beginning to wonder if she was speaking from a position of knowing what being with 'someone else' felt like.

'Perhaps we owe it to ourselves to have a full relationship, including the physical side, you know, to help us answer that question,' I wondered.

'Yes,' she said, making me almost spit my beer back into my glass, 'I've been thinking that too.'

That was a 'Yes', not a 'Maybe' or a 'Perhaps' or 'Sometime', but a 'Yes'. At the very minimum we were back to where we'd been in the summer, the only issue then being the time and place not the principle, but even then she'd never actually said yes. It was enough for now. I took our conversation as a green light to take the initiative and solve these little inconveniences. If I'd been feeling good before, I was feeling great now.

Having seen Andrea home I popped in at the One Bell for a quick one before heading back to the flat. The place was packed, but one face stood out, sat all on his own in the corner. It was Trev, and he had a face on him like a bulldog with depression.

'Cheer up mate, it may never happen.'

'That's what I thought,' he complained, 'not to me, but it bloody well has.' I got myself a pint and joined him.

'Explain.'

Trev looked around and then into his beer. 'I'm in a mess, Colin, and I don't know what to do.' He took a sip of the comforting brown liquid and plunged on. 'You know that Claire I see?' Trev had so many women in tow it was difficult to know which was which. Sensing my uncertainty he elaborated. 'Long blonde hair, wears a 'Police' T-shirt a lot. Slim. Dancer.'

'Yeah, yeah, got you. What about her?'

'Only up the duff isn't she? Two and a half months.'

143

Every young man's nightmare. It was difficult to imagine, not least the thought of this stick-insect of a girl growing larger by the month. It didn't seem natural somehow.

'And you're ...' I left what in other circumstances might have been described as a pregnant pause.

'Yep,' he confirmed.

'You're absolutely sure?' I asked, 'Don't take this the wrong way or anything but you're certain there's no one else in the frame?'

''Fraid so, we've been seeing quite a lot of each other lately, got quite close, know what I mean?'

'Christ Trev, it's a big one,' I helpfully pointed out, my curiosity driving me to go on to ask 'weren't you using anything?'

'Of course we were, bloody thing must have ripped or something.'

My good mood of an hour before now thoroughly deflated, I tried to keep myself on course to help my friend. All the various options were discussed ranging from getting rid of it through to her having the baby and him supporting it financially, visiting rights and the dreaded 'M' word.

Having gone round the houses, and sinking another couple of pints, Trev came to the conclusion he had probably come into the pub with but hadn't known it. He was going to marry her.

'The bugger is, Colin, I think I love her,' he declared. 'She's special you see and I was beginning to think we may end up together anyway, this has just brought things forward a bit.' More than a bit, I thought, but kept it to myself.

'That's great Trev. I'm pleased for you, really.' And I was. In the light of my conversation earlier that evening I reckoned that if he knew he loved her then that was something to be envious of, sprog or no sprog.

'Cheers Colin, I really appreciate that.' And with that Trev did something I'd never known him do before. He took my hand and shook it. 'Just one more thing,' he asked.

'Um.'

'Would you be my best man?'

You can always rely on your friends to muck your head up again. For the second time in a minute we shook on it, but Trev wasn't done with spoiling my day.

'Oh, and by the way,' he added, changing the subject rapidly as if he had a desperate need to get back onto a subject that was slightly less, well, girly, 'you heard the cup draw?'

In my ebullience I'd let this seminal moment of the season pass me by, the draw for the third round of the FA Cup, the moment when the big boys, and that now included us, joined in the fun and games. It had taken place late that afternoon and had completely passed me by.

'You'll never believe it,' Trev teased, unable to resist sharing his secret any longer. Something in his face revealed the truth to me.

'Not bloody Luton!' I yelled.

'Yep - away an' all.'

Memories of the recent miserable defeat flooded back and together we shared an exasperated chorus of 'Bugger!'

Half Time

It occurs to me, as I sit here remembering all those events of twenty five years ago, how we felt, how we dreamed, how we agonised; not only how long ago it all seems now, but also both how simple everything seemed to be back then and also how trivial. It seems crazy now, but in those days issues such as the score of a football match or whether a favourite band might be about to break up seemed to carry the power to obliterate all rational thought.

At the same time, it was around this time that bigger issues were beginning to demand a fairer share of our consciousness. Earlier I spoke of the significance of births, marriages and deaths and whilst death had yet to rear its menacing black head, that chat with Trev managed to thrust the first two of this trio to the forefront. I guess it was all part of the process of growing up. I'm forty five now and I suppose that, with a bit of luck, I've reached the half way point in my life. Whereas once we used to stand on the terraces at Vicarage Road and, if we were winning, will the minutes to reach that magic number on the electronic scoreboard, I now find myself trying to slow them down.

Back then time didn't matter, now I appreciate just how precious it is. After all, who knows what the next minute, hour, day, month will bring? Although it was absent then, death tends to feature more regularly than births and marriages in my life now, sometimes involving contemporaries, and it's inevitable that as you get older your own mortality seeps into your thoughts with greater regularity.

Reflecting on those golden days before our lives got swept up on a tide of other responsibilities has delivered a fruit and nut of nostalgia and pain. The challenge now, I suppose, is to learn from *these and prepare myself for the next forty five years, plus any other extra time that might be thrown my way. Perhaps everyone should be given the opportunity to stop at some time and take a few minutes out to think about the way their lives are going? Maybe some kind of team talk should be mandatory for us all half way through our lives to urge us on to greater things?*

All this pre-supposes we're in control of our lives though. In my experience fate has a nasty habit of jumping out from behind the bushes and scaring the shit out of me. Which reminds me, it's time we set out on the journey to that second pivotal moment ...

CHRISTMAS. It's like a massive tidal wave heading your way, you know it's coming, you know it isn't going to be good, but part of you looks forward to the experience all the same. Still, for me, that year, Christmas offered the prospect of a good long rest after a spell of working my rocks off, and even though I didn't have anything lined up for the New Year I wasn't too worried as I was beginning to understand that things usually had a habit of turning up. Okay, it wasn't what you'd call a long term strategy, but at that moment all I really wanted to do was stack some Zs and recharge the batteries.

The only slight glitch in this plan was that whichever way I looked at it I was condemned to spend the so-called 'festive season' back at my folks. To borrow a phrase from the Thatch, there was no alternative. Still, I did my best to plan around it and with the final delivery at work taking place Christmas Eve morning and the traditional High Street pub crawl lined up for that evening, I managed to get away with landing at home around one, hanging around a bit and leaving again by six, like a lunar explorer on a reconnaissance. Mum's equally traditional habit of starting the feasting early also meant that I could set out for the night with a well lined stomach, even if it did mean having to share the Nine Lessons and Carols from Kings with Mum on the radio. The fixture list had turned out well too, with a home game on Boxing Day and an away match at Southampton the day after, which Groovy had agreed to drive to, which left just Christmas Day itself to get through.

As they get older most people can at least draw on memories of times when Christmas was fun when they were kids to get them through, but I didn't even have that. For as long as I could remember the season of 'ho ho ho' had been more like one of 'no no no' - no you can't have this, no you can't go there, no we don't do that. When I was growing up it all seemed to be an endless round of church services and visits to elderly relatives whose relationship to me I never could quite work out, and over time it just evolved into a series of metronomic set piece routines slotted into a highly programmed day, done because, well, because they had to be done.

Mum, needless to say, always got up stupidly early to put a ridiculously large turkey in the oven, and if I have one good memory of Christmas it was probably waking up to the smell of roasting meat. She could of course have had at least another hour in bed as the bird was always overcooked and ended up as dry and flaky as peeling sunburnt skin by the time we sat down to eat it.

Breakfast, for some unknown reason, was the wicked extravagance of smoked salmon, either on Ritz crackers or with scrambled egg, during which I was expected to open the stocking my Mum always insisted on getting me, which inevitably included a satsuma and the Watford Yearbook, which had replaced my favourite comic annual half way through senior school.

This particular year the morning was spent peeling sprouts, parsnips, carrots and potatoes to the strains of the Flying bloody Pickets pop-popping their way through 'Only You' on the radio followed by some taped carols. Then there was the ceremony of the opening of the presents. Over the years this routine had got shorter and shorter, which gave Mum an excuse to leap up more often to 'do something in the kitchen' to spin it out, and usually ended with Dad having to run in at some point to open all the windows and possibly the front door too to get rid of the smoke that followed when the skin on the turkey finally caught fire.

This then acted as our cue to sit down and enjoy the lunch itself, 'with all the trimmings' naturally. Seeing as there was only ever three of us by the time we'd finished it was still possible to turn the turkey round and make it look as if we hadn't cut into it at all. This was despite Dad's best efforts with his K-Tel electric carver, an instrument he found so wondrous that it had caused him to abandon his cherished bone-handled carving set the year before and one he had to wield carefully to keep out of the way of his tie, which hung dangerously over the bird. The vegetables were so limp they looked like saturated sponges and the sausages you wouldn't have fed to a dog.

The best bits were always the roasties, which even now Mum seems to have a way with, I think it's something to do with always forgetting to put them in so they only actually end up cooking for a reasonable time. That and the bacon, which was always so crisp and brittle it would explode as soon as you put a knife to it. Naturally, we all sat there like lemons with paper hats on our heads and reading out the jokes from our crackers; it wouldn't have been Christmas otherwise.

Lunch was timed in this way to allow the television to come on for the Queen's Message, after which I helped Mum with the washing up, which always took at least an hour. During this time Dad would slope off and do something in his study. Each year there'd be optimistic talk of going for a walk after lunch, but by the time we'd had our update on events across the Commonwealth and the dishes had been put away the light outside would have turned a gunmetal grey and no one ever seemed to quite feel like it any more.

Then there came 'the silence'. We all knew there were fully four hours to go until the Morecambe and Wise show started. Equally, we all knew, like a child clutching a crayon as their parent comes in and sees drawings all over the wall knows, what was coming next. 'The silence' existed because no one actually wanted to be the one to suggest the inevitable. Once or twice in the past 'the silence' had been stretched long enough for Dad to wander over to the sofa and, suitably anaesthetised by an unaccustomed two and a half glasses of wine, promptly drop off; so I usually played along with it.

Not that year. Despite a half-hearted suggestion during the washing up that I might disappear up to my room and play some music, we were condemned to the annual games marathon consisting of Cluedo, Coppit and, incredibly, Mousey-Mousey; each box needing a year's-worth of dust to be blown off it before being opened. The long hours stretched ahead like a life sentence, alleviated only by the satisfaction of winning each of the board games through a combination of good tactics and shrewd dice-play. Cards followed, in which I was less successful, my parents' generation having seemingly been schooled at their mothers' breasts in the art of card warfare. Around six, Mum could hold herself in no longer and suggested mince pies all round.

Each stage of the journey through the day offered the comfort of familiarity coupled with an unspoken feeling of emptiness that only I seemed to feel. The whole charade (and thankfully that was one game not on the agenda, I don't think I could have stood it) felt dated somehow, as if it was rooted in the soil of a past that had gone stale, unable to nourish the seeds of hope we placed in it.

The weather that year matched the nondescript mood: dark with a steady drizzle throughout, the sort of day that said 'stay indoors and keep dry', not 'play snowballs and make merry with one and all'. Even when we reached the supposed highlight of the day, the Morecambe and Wise Christmas

Show, it was as if the two Christmas jesters had lost the will to go on, that they too were simply going through the motions. The show itself had never really made the transfer over from the BBC, as if someone had taken a favourite sofa and had it recovered in a garish new print.

After Eric and Ernie, as ITV preferred to call them, Dad did us the favour of finally succumbing into the arms of Morpheus, although it was possible he may have done so half way through the show and no one had noticed. This meant the TV could stay on and Mum's knitting could come out - he hated the sound of clicking needles - and we were able to spend the rest of the evening in companionable silence passing only the occasional comment when a programme ended and presented a choice. Three small piles of presents were distributed around the floor like ancient waymarkers, whilst the rainbow colours of the fairy lights on the tree reflected on the TV tube. Just as I dared to think I'd survived another Christmas Mum put down her knitting and asked if I'd heard from Andrea. The answer of course was no, but then I hadn't been in touch with her either. Why was nothing ever straight-forward?

After the festivities a home win and an away loss just about epitomised our current form. The team had been playing better since the arrival of Johnston who by then was only one goal behind Barnesy in his season's tally, with our black-skinned frizzy-haired hero having gone a bit quiet, becoming more the provider than the finisher, but at least we felt we could look forward to the New Year without looking over our shoulder too hard at the relegation zone.

In contrast to Christmas, the New Year had begun to offer promise on other fronts too. Somehow, at the last minute, Paully had managed to talk his parents into letting him have a party at their house. It had apparently been a good year in the estate agency game and Paully's Mum and Dad were jetting off to the Caribbean on the 30th. I say house, it was more of a mansion really, out on Millionaires Row, and by spinning some entirely believable story about Andrea being funny about her privacy I had managed to get him to reserve one of the many spare bedrooms for our exclusive use. He'd even given me a key! What a mate! The end of the year had been my target for us to finally consummate our relationship and now I had the consent, the room and the opportunity it was beginning to look like nothing could go wrong.

After a couple of days indulging in some serious kip I joined the others as usual at the pub before kick off on the day itself. By some stroke of luck the 31st was a Saturday and we were at home, something which confirmed my belief that fate was working for me. This was only reinforced when we managed to sneak a 1-0 win, making it four out of six for December - not too shabby. With another goal from Johnston it was beginning to look like Taylor had got himself a gem.

Afterwards I went straight back to Paully's to help him set up. He'd really gone to town with decorations, coloured lights and signs and even some kind of canopy outside which he said he'd got his parents to hire as it would give him somewhere to point those who'd had too much to drink and we could always fork any sick into the flowerbeds the next morning - although he didn't tell them that bit of course. Under the canopy he'd laid out a number of garden chairs and created a kind of tropical vibe with coconuts and some inflatable palm trees. Paully was great at getting his hands on stuff like that, God knows how he did it.

Inside, we created a drinks area along the breakfast bar in the middle of the kitchen including a barrel of McMullens real ale which he'd had delivered and left for the last two days to allow it to settle. In the lounge we pushed the furniture back against the walls to create a large open area for dancing. Paully had spent most of his Christmas making up some party tapes and we tested these out while we worked.

Our work done, we settled down to test the barrel and swapped stories. I told him how, when I was a teenager I'd read '1984' and calculated how old I'd be when it came around. It had seemed like a massive age, really grown up, yet here we were on the brink of it and I didn't really feel that much different at all, not inside anyway.

Later, when I went up to get changed in 'my' room I noticed that Paully had put a notice on the door calling it Room 101 and remembered the reference to Orwell's classic and how that room was known as 'where the noises come from'. I hoped to God he was right. Then I remembered why it was called that - it was the place people were taken to face what they feared the most. Bollocks to that. The room had its own sink and mirror and I applied a generous dollop of 'Hide and Heal' to cover up the few remaining spots hiding in the crook of my nose.

People began to arrive around half eight and it didn't take long for the party to hit its stride. Andrea turned up with her friend Jacqui and a couple of others as she'd been instructed to get as many girls together as she could, and I felt a small current pass through me when I saw the pair of them together, rekindling a memory I'd pushed back deep down into my subconscious. As soon as Bowie's 'China Girl' came on, as I knew it would from hearing the tape earlier, I dragged her out onto the dance floor and held her close. The initial signals were encouraging, it was looking like this could be one of our good nights.

Just at that moment Paully started up the dry ice machine he'd managed to get hold of and the haze it created weaved a miasma around us in which we got totally lost - and we hadn't even got started on the booze. Everything seemed perfect and I surreptitiously tapped my back pocket where I'd secreted the RJs for later. This time there'd be no discussion, we'd just get down to it, the most natural thing in the world.

The two of us went round together - a couple - for a while, catching up with people we hadn't seen for a while, dancing

155

some more and drinking a bit, although not too much as I wanted to keep a clear head, and I'd noticed that Andrea seemed to be doing the same thing which seemed to signal that we were operating on the same wavelength. I remember checking my watch to see how long there was to go until midnight and noting that it was just under two hours, but after that things become a little more hazy. I know I went to the kitchen to get some drinks but when I came back into the lounge Andrea seemed to have disappeared. I think I'd assumed she'd gone to the loo and so I didn't go looking for her, I felt secure enough that things were going according to plan and wandered outside to catch a breath of fresh crisp air.

Trev was out there, alone, and needed someone to talk to, so as his putative best man I gave him the loan of my ear while he gave me an update on the discussions that had been flying back and forth between him and Claire's parents and between them and his parents and between him and Claire and how it made him envy the Tommies at the Somme who probably had an easier life than his had been over the past few weeks.

By the time this was over I realised I'd finished my drink and had been neglecting Andrea so I went on the look out for her, stopping off via the kitchen for a top up and carrying around her glass of white wine, which had thankfully kept its chill outside. Andrea hated tepid white wine. Inside the lounge the party was really humming and there were people scattered around the hallway and up the stairs too. I don't know where all the people had come from, but the music blaring into the street was probably a pretty effective magnet for anyone left without a party to go to and the whole thing seemed good natured enough, so Paully had clearly gone with the flow. Occasional cries of 'You 'Orns!' flew across the room, penetrating the thick blanket of noise and smoke, a kind of mating call between members of a shared clan. While some danced others gathered in huddles and had earnest conversations while yet others simply got on with the serious business of the night and got off with each other.

Andrea was nowhere to be found and by that time it was gone eleven, still a fair way from midnight but my thinking was that it would have been good to hook up again and rekindle the good vibe we'd had going before. Having exhausted the downstairs I worked my way past the crowds sitting on the stairs, noticing how the music became noticeably duller as I went past the turn in the middle as I climbed my way up, the bass lines pounding into the wood of the staircase.

A light was on in the nearest bedroom and I wandered in, noticing the mountain of coats left on the large double bed in what was one of the guest rooms. A connecting door between this and the next bedroom was slightly ajar and banging in a draught created by an open window, so without even thinking I went over to shut it when I heard a shushing of voices inside.

I paused, not sure I wanted to go in. It could have been anyone, in fact the odds against it being Andrea were astronomical, but some instinct made me go on. On top of that, the ex-schoolboy in me couldn't resist the temptation and I threw the door open whilst at the same time fumbling for the light switch on the wall. The time this took gave whoever was in there the moments they needed to react and as the light came on a great thump hit the floor - one body or two? - leaving nothing to see except a rumpled counterpane which had been partly pulled to the ground on the far side. The room offered no other clues. The furniture was sparse, the wallpaper bland and there was only one mirror, which revealed only the same view of the bed that I already had, except to one side.

Now slightly ashamed of myself, aware that my practical joke wasn't as funny as I'd hoped it might be, I'd offered my apologies in a drawn out sarcastic 'Sor-ry' and turned to leave, reaching once more for the light switch to leave whoever it was to return to whatever it was they'd been up to.

'Colin.'

I looked back and saw Andrea's face peering over the edge of the bed like a naughty child. Her freshly washed, but somewhat tousled auburn hair looked less like a halo in the harsh artificial light than a neon beacon spelling out the single word 'guilty'.

'Andrea,' I replied, with depressing predictability. 'What are you …'

But I never got the chance to finish my sentence as at that moment another face popped up alongside the familiar features of my girlfriend, a Pinky to her Perky. A male face, one I'd seen before, with long black dreadlocks hanging down the sides. It took a few moments to locate where I recognised it from and then I remembered.

It was the bloke in the topless holiday photos. So, he was a local boy, not some holiday romance Eyetie. His still-tanned face carried a look of benign smugness which seemed to carry on it a sense of victory, a look that said that - pissed off as I might be feeling right then - he was the one with the girl and maybe I should just disappear. Lacking any credible alternative response that's exactly what I did.

NEW YEAR

15

AS THE ROOM SLOWLY SWAM INTO FOCUS I dared myself to wake up and work out where I was. My head felt like someone had been trepanning into my scalp and was still turning the handle. I was also convinced that someone, maybe the same person, had snuck into the room in the middle of the night and lined the inside of my throat with cheap carpet, and although I couldn't see it I knew it was grey, the sort of stuff that Betta Staff used to cover their floors. My stomach meanwhile, like pretty much the rest of my body, felt like it had just gone twelve rounds with Leon Spinks.

In my distant consciousness I could hear a voice coming for me from the end of a very long tunnel. Its words were indistinguishable and were echoing against the insides of my skull, ping-ponging around like a pinball, refusing to settle down. My brain meanwhile was fighting back, telling it to PISS OFF, PISS OFF, **PISS OFF**, but still it came. I closed my eyes again and tried to concentrate. It was a woman's voice. Sarah's.

'Happy New Year,' she whispered; considerately.

I think I grunted something back at her, but immediately regretted it as some bile rose up from my gullet. She was holding something, a tray, with a steaming mug of coffee, a glass of water, some white tablets and a plate with toast. I sat up. I could see that the toast had Marmite on it. A thin scraping of pungent, savoury tar. Sarah knew I loved Marmite, but not today, please no, not today.

I rose out of a floral duvet and noticed that I wasn't wearing anything on top, not that it mattered as the central heating seemed to be operating on overdrive. I felt down inside the bedding and discovered I was only wearing my underpants. Someone had undressed me, not Sarah surely - how strange would that be? The clock radio on the side of the bed was flashing 11:37. I'd lost the last twelve hours. Sarah sat on the side of the bed and arranged the duvet so it would take the tray she'd just brought. She picked up the water and tablets and handed them to me, suggesting in her best nurse's manner that they'd make me feel better. I wasn't in any position or mood to argue. She smiled and left me, and I was grateful for both.

Waiting for the plink-plink-fizz to take effect I struggled to reconstruct the evening before. I remembered finding Andrea and leaving her to her new fella. From there I had a vague recollection of heading straight for the kitchen and quickly downing a couple of shorts. Then something happened.

Instinctively I raised a finger to the side of my head. Yes, that was it, I'd strode out of the kitchen and because of the dry ice, which had created a foot high floating mist all over the lounge floor, I'd tripped over the outstretched legs of a snogging couple on the floor and smacked my head on one of the chairs. It had been a bad year for personal injuries, perhaps it was just as well it had finally come to an end.

I took a sip of the still piping hot coffee and racked my brains some more. The next thing I remembered was sitting outside with a couple of the girls - Sarah, she was one of them, that was right, and that Jacqui, Andrea's friend. Sarah had a tea towel full of ice from the cool box pressed to the side of my head, she seemed to be condemned to be my ministering angel, and I was telling them what had just happened - not the trip, but my discovery of Andrea upstairs with another bloke.

'What did he look like?' Jacqui seemed keen to know. I described him, the slick bastard, and she nodded as if she knew him. 'What a cow,' she remarked and I remembered agreeing with her. Insults had been a trademark of that particular conversation, but the real discussion was going on inside my head, and it was loaded with questions.

Who was this bloke, and what was he doing in Watford? Was he really a local, not someone they'd met out there? Had she been seeing him since she'd got back? They seemed to know each other well enough now. Were Jacqui's parents ever in Italy, or was this some kind of two couple thing I hadn't been invited to? Had I been taken for a mug all this time, being strung along like a dead dog on the end of a lead? It would certainly explain why Andrea had been so hard to get hold of lately. Then of course there was the biggest question of the lot, the sixty four thousand dollar question - had the pair of them been at it together? It would have gone some of the way to explaining why she had been so different lately, more confident, a different person somehow.

Then suddenly Sarah wasn't there, why had that been? Oh yes, she'd gone to find Andrea, playing the UN diplomat and taking on the Perez de Cuellar Secretary General role. She'd been keen for Andrea and me to talk, certainly more keen than I was. So, that left me and Jacqui alone. What happened then? I took another mouthful of coffee, to which Sarah had added a liberal spoonful of sugar, and let all the memories come flooding back.

Jacqui had taken my hand and made me stand up. I thought at first this was just part of the treatment for the knock on the head but no, she'd led me to Paully's parents' summer house half way down the garden where we could barely see what we were doing, the music throbbing in time with my head. Showing a determination which indicated she had some kind of plan I went along as by that stage I was in a state of limbo, not really knowing what it was I thought or wanted any more.

The door was unlocked and Jacqui found a light. Looking round she located a padded sun lounger which she unfolded and tested for comfort before turning the light off again and, taking my hand, to which she gave a sharp yank, we both fell onto the seat. Before I'd even had time to think about what was going on she was all over me, sticking her tongue into places I don't think I'd ever had a tongue stuck before.

Meanwhile her hands were all over my back, grabbing the bottom of my shirt and tugging it out of my trousers. Now, I may not be the quickest when it comes to these sorts of situations, but it's funny how quickly pure animal instinct kicks in. While she was pulling at my shirt I'd started to attack it from the top, undoing the buttons and throwing it onto the floor. The T-shirt I'd been wearing underneath soon went the same way then I concentrated on the front of her blouse.

Enough light still filtered down from the house to cast a dusky glow into the summer house - enough for me to appreciate the dazzling whiteness of her bra, and then, seconds later, the glory that was her breasts. I'd seen them before of course, but only in two dimensions. To see them for real, in the flesh as it were, in all their marvellous magnificence, was something else. They were much bigger than Andrea's of course, but not so big that they drooped. Not what you'd call pert, but they were firm enough to jut proudly from her ribcage like two begging puppies. She knew exactly what she was doing of course, and for that I felt quietly grateful. Once she'd displayed her finest assets everything else that followed was inevitable.

Now, having it away on a sun lounger isn't necessarily something I'd recommend, but get the angles right and it's just about possible if you lay the back flat. I thanked God in heaven that my RJ was easily accessible, but just as I grabbed it Jacqui, sensing my urgency, slowed things down and started to run her tongue around other places I certainly couldn't have reached with my own tongue. I reciprocated in kind and when the moment came to pull the top off the foil rectangle I'd been keeping in my pocket for so, so long we were both ready to enjoy it.

By then we were like a giant baked Alaska, except in reverse. Where our skin touched there was a comforting, tepid hot water bottle kind of warmth; but everywhere else was frozen, making it all the more important to keep our hands and other parts of our bodies moving around with wild urgent energy to keep the blood on the go. All my thoughts were focused into keeping going and making the most of this late Christmas present which had been thrown, quite literally, into my lap. I managed to sense when our time was almost over from the shorter and shorter gasps Jacqui gave out, which I was pretty sure were unconnected with the cold. There was no mistaking the moment she finished, which she announced with the kind of 'Yes' which would use up all the 'e's in the average Scrabble set, the word itself trailing off as she finished it. I felt so unbelievably proud of myself that I hardly noticed that I'd finished too, although the evidence was all too plain.

Afterwards we held each other in our arms for a minute or two but by then even our goosebumps had goosebumps of their own and following an unspoken mutual agreement we began to get dressed, rather coyly this time, turning our backs to each other as we did so. Jacqui suggested she leave first and that I follow on a few minutes after and I realised only then that this was the first time we'd spoken. I felt too happy, and frankly dazed, to question her plan, after all she seemed pretty clued up on the whys and wherefores of the situation, so I silently consented as she opened the door and crept back into the house following the edge of the garden out of the light.

I'd duly followed her after a few minutes and I remember bumping into a pruned rose bush at ankle height before going back into the throng inside. Things after that were less clear in my memory. Both Jacqui, Andrea and indeed Sarah, all seemed to disappear and I hadn't really felt like looking for any of them, I was too confused, so much seemed to have happened so quickly.

Sitting up in bed it suddenly struck me that I'd made the target I'd set for myself, and with a few minutes to spare. It wasn't quite how I'd imagined it, and it wasn't with who I'd imagined it with, but hey, what did that matter? It wasn't really my target of course, it had never been as crude as simply losing my virginity, the real target had been to get to some kind of definitive situation with Andrea, but on reflection I supposed I'd done that too, in a roundabout kind of a way.

After that I must have got absolutely bladdered, judging by the state of me. A celebration? Maybe. Pure relief? Probably. It didn't really matter, no doubt I'd been so light headed by then it probably hadn't taken much and the fact that I was paying a price for it now didn't seem to matter, on balance it had been a price worth paying.

With my memory refreshed, I managed to get dressed, rather gingerly, and find my way downstairs where Paully, Groovy and Sarah seemed to be leading the process of tidying up. Furniture was stacked up and there were half-filled bin liners scattered around the floor. Streamers hung limply from the wall and a few balloons remained pinned to the curtain pelmets, wrinkled like an old person's skin. Someone had brought some Silly String and someone else I didn't recognise, a girl, was working hard to get the stain it had left on one of the walls off before it set.

'Evening,' Paully shouted - unnecessarily loudly I thought - as I entered the front room. He was pushing a Hoover around, sucking up the contents of party poppers and other debris from the floor. This was the final straw, so I ventured into the kitchen to see what I might usefully contribute to the effort. Groovy was there gathering together bottles and putting them into cardboard cases for collection, another unnecessarily noisy activity. Sarah in the meantime was washing glasses, and as the draining board looked close to over-flowing I grabbed a tea towel and started to dry.

'Good night?' quizzed Groovy. I didn't know how much he knew - hey, I'd only just remembered what I knew - so I flashed him one of my enigmatic smiles.

'Leave him alone,' suggested Sarah, directing a welcome beam of sympathy.

'Yeah, leave me alone,' I agreed.

'That's all the thanks I get for whipping your kegs off and tucking you up in bed is it?' So it had been Groovy. Thank God.

A couple of minutes later Paully waltzed into the room clearly unhappy.

'Oi, Westlake, you scumbag,' he shouted - he really had to learn not to shout so much - 'When I said people might throw up in the flowerbeds it wasn't a suggestion you know.' As soon as he said this I had a flashback of the countdown to midnight and me hanging over a retaining wall with my face looking into some soil. Three, two, one - cheers and chunder, right into the damp earth, the acrid stink briefly overcoming the reek of freshly laid manure beneath. An appropriate final memory of the year.

'Christ, I'm sorry, mate,' I apologised, eager to make amends. Putting down a glass I followed him outside as I was clearly meant to do and took the fork he had helpfully left leaning up on a wall by the patio. With the evidence returned to the soil, and buried beneath a pile of manure and half digested straw taken from the rosebed, I took the fork back to the summer house and inspected the scene of the, well it wasn't a crime, let's just say the scene of the action.

The opened RJ packet was the first thing I saw, lying lonely but complacent on the floor. I picked it up and quickly pocketed it. The lounger was still up and after inspecting it for stains I folded it up and hung it on the wall, along with the fork. There was still one thing missing though, the RJ itself. What in heaven's name had I done with that?

As gently as I could I picked up various different items of garden equipment from the floor in an increasingly desperate search for the missing used contraceptive. The metal cans and handforks felt cold, the terracotta flowerpots heavy. As much as anything, I didn't think that Paully would appreciate being quizzed by his Dad come the Spring when the damned thing was most likely to reappear if I didn't find it now.

After ten minutes I was still looking when I was distracted by voices from inside.

'Colin? Where the hell have you disappeared to now Colin?' I emerged from the summer house to find Groovy with his thumb and little finger extended and held to the side of his head, making the universal sign for a telephone. He beckoned me over.

'It's Andrea. Do you want to take it?'

The truth at that moment was, I didn't really know.

ALTHOUGH THE THOUGHT of taking a tube in and out of London wasn't exactly one that filled me with joy, we had tickets for Spurs away on the following day. I therefore agreed to meet Andrea afterwards at half past seven, and given the likely seriousness of the discussion I decided to try to make it a home match and was delighted when she agreed to make the venue Groovy's place.

In the event it was a pleasant surprise to discover how much my constitution could recover in twenty four hours and I managed the trip without too many problems, although I passed up on the drinking session beforehand and opted for a long walk down the Seven Sisters Road instead. Just the thought of the smell of stale beer and the noise inside a pub was enough to provoke revulsion. The fact that we ended up winning 3-2 also helped to revive my spirits, with our new hero Johnston scoring two and Barnesy getting back on the score sheet after a rather barren spell of only one in three months. A result all round, in more senses than one.

Andrea looked nervous when we met her waiting on the doorstep back at base, and Groovy opened the door for us before making a strategic withdrawal down to the pub. I put the lights on and made us cups of tea, there was no reason why this couldn't be civilised.

It didn't take long to get to the matter in hand.

'I know it didn't look good when you found me on New Year's Eve Colin,' she said, it was rare for her to actually use my name and it showed, I thought, how desperate she was to connect with me, 'but it wasn't like it seemed.' It was difficult not to scoff at this line, taken straight out of some 1930s melodrama, but I'd resolved to be mature about this and hear her out.

'Go on,' I urged, enjoying the view from the moral high ground, ignoring everything else that had gone on two nights before, partly because she was the one who'd unilaterally changed the rules but more importantly because her whole manner suggested she didn't have an inkling about what I'd done afterwards.

'He'd thrown himself at me and I was trying to push him away when you came in.' This was weak, even by 1930 melodrama standards. I decided to test her, almost unconsciously adopting a slightly Westlake-of -the-Yard type tone.

'Who was he, had you met before?'

'Yes,' she answered, but offered nothing more at this stage. Wise girl, keeping her powder dry and retaining a basis of truth to her answers. Clever. I decided it was time to call her bluff, only wishing that I had the actual exhibit to hand to produce with a flourish.

'Yes,' I confirmed, 'I saw his ugly mug on one of the pictures of you topless on holiday.'

She looked genuinely shocked and even produced a brief blush which stood out against her china-pale cheeks.

'When did you see those?' she demanded.

'That doesn't matter, the point is I have,' I replied, resisting the temptation to add 'things don't look very good young lady, it could well be curtains for you.'

'Okay, I didn't tell you because I didn't want you to get jealous.'

'Jealous!' I almost shouted. 'Why should I be jealous of my girlfriend going away on holiday and stripping off in front of other blokes?'

'Bloke.'

'Bloke then.' I paused, my flow broken. Bloke, as in the singular? 'What do you mean,' I asked, 'are you saying there was only one of them?' This wasn't in the script.

'Um um,' she confirmed.

'Jacqui brought him along at the last moment. She'd met him at the beginning of the summer and they'd become an item. She insisted he came along, said it wouldn't stop us having a good time, but it made the holiday a right bloody misery I can tell you. They were all over each other all the time. I felt like a right royal gooseberry. Her parents weren't too pleased either. He's a real creep.'

'Are they still together?'

'Yes, of course,' she replied, a small catch in her voice colouring her response. 'I haven't told her that he leapt on me at the party. Not yet anyway, I'm waiting for the right moment.'

'So, what you're saying is Jacqui's boyfriend made a play for you in one of the spare rooms at Paully's ...?' I began to summarise, for my own peace of mind as much as anything.

'Yes, I'd gone upstairs to find my coat to get some fresh lipstick. I wanted to look my best for midnight. For you,' she added.

'Okay, and you were trying to get rid of him when I walked in on you, saw what I saw and stormed out.'

'Exactly,' she confirmed, again.

I wasn't sure, it seemed too convenient. Why hadn't there been more of a struggle, I asked, and why didn't she call for help? It seemed the whole thing had just happened and when the light came on she'd seen it less as an opportunity for rescue and more as a potential for discovery, for people getting the wrong end of the stick, which ironically was exactly what happened anyway.

'As soon as I could shake him off I rushed out to find you and bumped into Sarah coming up the stairs and I ended up blurting everything out to her. By the time I'd stopped crying and came looking for you again you were nowhere to be found and I assumed you'd gone home, so I went home too.'

It was beginning to look like I had been made a fool of, but not in the way I thought.

'What about the photos, what was all that about?'

'I hated all that, but you know what it's like when you're in a crowd.'

'What about the one with all three of you, who took that?'

'It was a waitress from the beach bar, another English girl. It was soooo embarrassing.' Andrea's face creased even as she thought of it, and that was the point when I knew she was telling the truth.

'I'm sorry, Colin,' she sighed, clearly pleased to have got it all off her chest, as it were. 'I've really mucked things up haven't I? It was going to be our special night wasn't it? Do you forgive me?'

At that moment it would have been the easiest thing in the world to have said 'Of course I do', take her in my arms and maybe even seize the moment. Despite Groovy's sensitivities when it came to the sheets I'm sure he wouldn't have minded given the circumstances.

But I didn't. At that point I was still wondering what might happen if she laid into Jacqui. I suspected she'd catch both barrels of her soon to be former friend's pique, and as I now knew, Jacqui had formidable barrels.

'No. Yes. I mean I don't know' was the best I could muster. 'I think I need to get my head together.'

She nodded her understanding. 'Look, I'll go now, maybe give you a call early next week?' she asked.

'Yes, do that,' I agreed, and she picked up her coat and waved a goodbye on her way out of the door. And that was that.

What a mess.

A couple of minutes later the door opened again and Groovy walked in after a discrete knock, even though he must have passed Andrea on the way out. He was on his own, which meant he'd come to check up on me.

'All clear?' he asked, as he entered his own flat.

'All clear,' I confirmed.

'How did it go?'

'How much do you know?'

It turned out he knew a lot more than I thought he did. He knew everything that I'd told Sarah, I'd expected that, but he'd also put two and two together and worked out what happened with Jacqui. He was the one who'd undressed me and put me to bed after all. And he was the one who'd found the used RJ half sticking out of my pants.

This was to be the fifth year in a row that the FA Cup was going to start with the third round for us. Gone were the days of being a 'minnow' and praying for those couple of wins that might be rewarded with a payday with one of the big teams on the first Saturday of the year. We had become one of the big boys ourselves, but instead of handing us a convenient underdog the draw had thrown up a fellow First Division team, and not just any First Division team but bloody Luton - for us 'Orns, it was difficult to say 'Luton' without adding the prefix.

I therefore approached the tie with very mixed feelings. On one level our appetite for cup games had been partly satiated by the European adventure, but on another we had developed something of a reputation for good cup runs since Taylor had taken the reins. In truth, in my mind at least, there was a lot of sense in falling back on the old cliché about concentrating on the league, although things seemed to be picking up with the new striker in the pack; results remained erratic. In the end, though, the cup was the cup. The clincher was the opponents. Bloody Luton. There was never a good time to lose to Luton and that recent defeat in the league was still a very raw memory. Knocking them out of the cup offered the prospect of sweet revenge.

So, from initial nonchalance the tie rapidly adopted the mantle of a 'must-win' game. We arrived at the cow shed our rivals called home in plenty of time to secure a decent view given the low eyeline the ground offered. Three o'clock on third round day is always a special day, a day when the pressures of the league are suspended for ninety minutes and the whiff of potential upsets lingers like bonfire smoke on an Autumn evening. The higher you get up the league the more you wish the fire itself is in someone else's garden, but for those from the lower divisions who'd survived to get this far, a feeling we still hadn't quite shrugged off, there was the prospect of possible glory.

For us, this particular day was something different, more personal. A win either way would not be an upset and would not lead the back pages of the Sunday papers, but it would crowd out thoughts of all the other results for both sets of fans. In the end, after what turned out to be a cracking game, a result was the one thing the match lacked. A draw shouldn't have come as a surprise but somehow it did, a bit of a let down in the end, an anti-climax. What didn't come as a surprise were the scorers, Barnesy with a deflected free kick and a Maurice Johnston penalty. Okay, it was a spot kick, but the man was turning out to be a goal-scoring machine and had rightfully earned the nickname 'Mighty Mo' amongst the travelling support. All back to our place on Tuesday then we agreed, when we'd finish this little spat off once and for all. We drove back to Watford content that we were probably ahead on points, but also with an acute sense of unfinished business.

It was the result I'd been dreading on another level too, as I'd arranged to attend a Graduate Job Fair at Olympia in London on the Tuesday and would have to leave early, missing a seminar on CV writing I'd put my name down for. I'd spotted the advert for the Fair in Dad's Daily Telegraph before Christmas and had realised then that this was the sort of thing I should have been doing twelve months before, although at that stage the world of employment had still seemed like a far away country which I had little interest in visiting.

Attending the fair had all the appearances of being just the shot in the arm my job process needed. I'd tried the old boy network and I'd tried answering adverts, I needed to set off down a third track, one with more prospect of reaching the finishing line. The more I thought about it the more positive I felt. On one level I was certainly a year behind, but on another I did now have the advantage of a bucket-load of work experience - I could now bore for England on the range of jobs I'd had, and a revised CV was on the agenda, seminar or no seminar.

Monday was spent getting everyone tickets for the match - they were expecting a sell out and I'd surmised I might not have time to queue on the night - as well as digging into my meagre funds to buy my first ever suit from Marks and Sparks. There was no point in having all this experience if I didn't use it, and the one thing I had taken from the single interview I'd had so far was that in order to be taken seriously, you needed to take yourself seriously.

It was only as I actually got inside the vast echoing hall at Olympia, after queuing for what seemed like hours, I realised I'd got it wrong again. The students looked like, well, feckless students, and kept coming up to me all day with questions, like I was a steward or something. I affected an air of superiority and got on with looking around. The hall was dominated by representatives from the financial industry - the banks, insurance companies and of course the accountants, but by then I knew, as they seemed to know, that we weren't cut out for each other. They tended to have huge flashy stands, usually on the corners of the different aisles, and dished out tacky giveaways such as key fobs and stress balls.

The armed services seemed pretty high profile also, no doubt keen to cash in on memories of, and the need to replace those lost in, the Falklands conflict. The RAF had a small trainer plane you could climb into (in this suit?), whilst the army had pictures of men in camouflage make up and the sort of boots I was more used to seeing worn by skinheads in some of the London away matches. I didn't call in on the sailor-boys.

The rules of the game seemed to be picking up business cards from any of the stands that looked vaguely promising and then following these through with a letter and a CV later, although some were dishing out applications forms too. I knew what I didn't want but the idea was to get some ideas of what else might be out there and from that point of view things went pretty well. There were a few small publishers, most of whom it turned out used print works in Watford, which helped start some conversations off, and a lot of the shops seemed to be looking for graduate trainees.

One stand with what was probably the largest TV screen I've ever seen offered the opportunity to 'get in on the ground floor of an entertainment revolution', and I was pulled in by a series of images on the screen of what turned out to be out of town cinema complexes. I'd heard of a new place at Milton Keynes with an incredible ten screens and they were peddling a message that the whole world of cinema, or 'the movies' as they preferred to call them, was about to change radically. I didn't get it myself, reasoning that video was surely well on the way to strangling the cinema, but maybe this was what was needed - comfortable seats in purpose-built theatres? They were looking for general management trainees and the idea of being in on something new appealed to me.

I managed to traipse up and down all the aisles and leave in time to get home, change and grab a sandwich before the match. As soon as I walked in through the door I could see Mum was upset by the sight of the suit. My ill fated jacket had been a Christmas present the year before and bought specifically for job interviews, this being the sort of thing my Dad wore to work. She managed to bring herself to say how 'dapper' I looked though, and on reaching my room I felt a twinge of guilt when I noticed the jacket finally back from the dry cleaners in a clear plastic sleeve. For all her hurt expression I learned later on that she'd forgotten she'd left it at the cleaners and had had a phone call reminding her that after six months unclaimed cleaning was sent to the Oxfam shop, so it had hardly been at the top of her mind.

A small plastic bag contained the contents of the pockets, a sort of six month old time capsule, including the NUS card, which I picked up and sniffed. Yep, still the unmistakeable odour of puke. I bundled it up in the plastic from the dry cleaners and put the whole lot in the bin outside.

'I've left your post on the sideboard, dear,' Mum shouted as I began to climb the stairs again.

'Thanks, Mum.' Grabbing the envelopes I sorted them out on the way back to my room, brushing off some flour Mum had left on one of the brown ones on the top as I went. Three were replies from applications and it wasn't long before three rejections had joined all the cards I'd been collecting all day on my desk. I would sort it all out in the morning, time was getting short and I needed to get changed.

Two envelopes remained, both too square to be formal letters, both in white envelopes rather than the brown the rejection letters usually came in, like they were the bad cowboy and the white was good. One was slightly thinner and I opened this first. To my surprise it turned out to be a formal invitation to a dinner to celebrate Andrea's 21st birthday that coming Saturday. I'd known it was coming up of course, but given the state of things between us hadn't done anything about it. At least the invitation answered that question, albeit in a fairly cold, hands-off kind of a way. Why the formality I wondered - was it to be a big 'do'? A shiver of cold trembled through my chest: what if, in her innocence, she'd also invited Jacqui?

175

There was no time to worry about that as I stood in the middle of my room in pants and socks. With some impatience I grabbed the other letter. From inside, a folded printed card announced the pleasure that Mr and Mrs Simon Kelly had, probably through gritted teeth, in inviting me to the marriage of their daughter Claire to Mr. Trevor Downing.

Well, they weren't hanging about, I'd give them that.

I was no expert, but I suspected she'd be four or five months gone by then. With some strategically placed flowers she might still get away with hiding her status in the wedding pictures. Checking the fixture list on my noticeboard I noticed that March 10th was a distant away game.

Good lad Trev.

REPLAY

17

REG HAD BEEN RIGHT. A call from Betta Staff had come through mid-morning on the following Wednesday asking if I could do the next two days back in Hemel at the camera warehouse. I couldn't help a chuckle to myself as I said okay and asked if there was anything in the pipeline for the week after. Karen said she'd see what they could do. She was definitely on my case.

Jobs were clearly the theme of that day. I'd been in the middle of a frenzy of applications when the phone had gone, working my way through the various brochures and business cards I'd brought back from the Job Fair. Fluent now in bullshit, I was using the formula I'd picked up in the one seminar I'd managed to attend on writing application letters: don't tell them what you've done, tell them what you're capable of doing for them; don't just repeat the CV and resist the temptation to grovel.

As a result a number of pithy, focused letters had already flowed from my typewriter ribbon and were sitting in a pile on my desk, a CV stapled to the back of each, from now on accompanied by a stamped addressed envelope. A pile of crap, but then again a pile of well-fashioned crap. A feeling that someone had let me into the secret of how to play the job game infused me. Up until then I'd been thrashing around playing water polo when everyone else had been prancing around on horses.

When I woke up I had to stop and make an actual effort to recall where I was supposed to be going that day, a depressing reminder that I didn't so much have a job as work, and even that was doled out to me in rationed parcels. By the time I made it to the factory it was clear that little had changed. All the old faces were there except for one of the temps whose mate told me he'd got a 'proper' job. Reg was in charge of us all again, something he seemed to take in his usual stoic stride.

We'd been told to get there early to meet with Reg's boss as there were some things he wanted to make absolutely clear to us, but in the end we were left hanging around waiting for him to turn up. When he did eventually give us his pep talk the thing he wanted to stress most was confidentiality. It was made very clear to us that if a word of what we were about to do got out then he'd come down so hard on the agency that they'd have to retreat into an nuclear bunker for safety. He then predicted that, should this happen, they'd make sure that none of us ever worked for them again, a prospect that was supposed to fill us with dread.

He was a short thin man with a particularly bad set of teeth, a feature that made most people avoid standing within five feet of him but also one he seemed gloriously unaware of, taking delight in coming right up to you and barking his thoughts straight into your face. He seemed quite proud of both this strategy and his sergeant-major act in general and for a few minutes I felt I knew what it would have been like to do National Service. None of us took him seriously however, and by then, as we'd had nearly an hour to chat, we all knew why we were there and just wanted to get on with it.

We were, of course, there to do the management's dirty

work, the stretcher bearers clearing away the dead after a lost battle. It was great fun though. As Reg had predicted the company had had three whopping great big skips put just inside the shutters at the back of the building and our job was to literally clear shelves' worth of old stock using wheelbarrows hired from a local builders' merchants especially for the purpose. Reg had done this before and we followed his lead when he secured a folded handkerchief over his mouth with rubber bands as the dust rose steadily like a mushroom cloud from the floor and over our heads.

Suitably protected we devised games such as how far we could chuck stuff and producing chemical cocktails from the different bottles that sat on the shelves. From time to time the short arse manager would come out to remind us to keep what we were doing under our hats, but he didn't seem to mind how much noise we made and disappeared around lunchtime never to be seen again.

As soon as he left Reg called a halt and I collapsed into a broken plastic chair outside in the fresh air pulled my handkerchief down and let off a jaw-breaking yawn. I was knackered and my muscles were aching. The previous night had been a late one with the replay stretching into extra time despite us going two up within the first half hour, the second coming off our first corner of the game, a deep cross from Callaghan leaving a relatively simple flick in for the giant Reilly. We could have had a third before half time as well, but instead with typical luck the bastards had managed to sneak one back from a confusion in the penalty area just before the ref blew his whistle.

Barnesy made it three with a rocket five minutes into the second half and that seemed to be that and it could have been four if only Bardsley had made the best of a decent chance. Being hardened 'Orns we knew it could never be that easy though, and sure enough when a stupid back pass led to their second it was quickly followed by another. With Barnsey

179

missing a sitter with a minute to go we had to go into extra time and it was that man Mighty Mo again who sealed it for us in the second period after having an earlier effort cleared off the line.

The relief around the ground had been palpable. To have lost at bloody Luton would have been bad enough, but a replay at home had upped the stakes even more, if that had been possible. To have lost at our place would have wrecked the season, but the fates were with us and it was us singing at the tangerine scarves when the final whistle blew. We were through to the next round and already knew our opponents - Charlton, the next division down. This time we'd be the favourites.

I was just getting my breath back when Reg sidled up to me with his sandwiches. I noticed he hadn't washed his hands and there was a patina of grime overlaid with a rainbow of magenta and yellow powders ingrained into his fingers as he took his first bite.

'You're an educated bloke,' he garbled through a combination of cheese, tomato and the kaleidoscope of chemicals standing out against the white of his bread. I think he saw me as some kind of elder statesman amongst the temps, being just that bit older. 'Do you mind if I ask your opinion on something?'

I was sprawled backwards on the broken back of the chair, staring up at the milky winter sunshine above, trying to catch my breath, but I told him to carry on.

'What do you reckon to this British Telecom privatisation that's coming up?' he asked. It wasn't the sort of question I was expecting and wasn't quite sure how to answer.

'What's on your mind, Reg?' I asked, buying time.

'It's just that I was thinking of trading in the Escort, but there's not a lot of point unless I can get something much newer. I've got a few bob put away but not enough. I was thinking, like, if I hung on and got some of these shares with my savings I might be able to jack up my spending money. The papers are saying it might be possible to double yer money overnight. What do you reckon?'

I knew about the intended privatisation of course, and had read some of the speculation around it in the press, but it wasn't something I'd seen as relevant to me - or indeed to people like Reg. My general view was that the whole thing was a Thatcherite trick, making people pay for something they already owned, a bit like their sale of council homes. Personally it wasn't something I wanted anything to do with. Reg however, was clearly in earnest.

'Well,' I started, 'I guess it depends on your point of view. Have you ever owned shares before?'

He nearly spluttered on his sandwich. 'Don't be daft, 'course not.'

'Well, they do carry a risk.'

'Yeah, I know that, but how much of a risk? I don't want to lose out.'

He was almost desperate now for my opinion, although I sensed he simply wanted to be given the green light for a decision he'd already made. 'Well the way I see it,' I began, 'is that the whole stock market thing is like a giant casino. Do you fancy red or black? If black comes up, you're in clover, if it's red you're dead.'

'Yeah,' he nodded, 'but it's better odds than that ain't it?'

'Probably,' I agreed, 'the point is more, are you a casino sort of person?'

He thought about this for a while and brought his forefinger to his mouth rubbing his lips as he did so, which had the advantage of hiding the mastication process which had been going on throughout this conversation but carried the disadvantage of applying a deep brown chemical lipstick. He came to his decision.

'You know, I think I might be up for a little flutter. Why not?' And with that he got out of his chair and crossed the road to the public phone box opposite, presumably to call his broker - that or his girlfriend, who he usually called around that time every day. The next day was a repetition of Thursday, except the manager didn't turn up until around four, just as we were beginning to run out of things to do. The three skips were full to brimming and we were just in the process of stretching tarpaulin sheets over the tops to hide what was inside. The manager called us over and slipped us a tenner each in cash as we were about to leave. Hush money. Having tried the stick, it seemed he was prepared to offer a carrot to keep our gobs shut as well.

The satisfaction of the Cup win was still tingling in our veins as the weekend approached and there was little appetite for a trek to Coventry for that Saturday's league game, with not even the prospect of gaining revenge for the first day of the season enough to rouse us. The effort we'd all been through simply to get to the fourth round, to say nothing of the emotional toll it had exacted, seemed to emphasise to me that simply wanting something like crazy wasn't enough, you had to work hard to get it too.

This startling insight had led me to forego my usual non-matchday Saturday morning lie in and to start banging away at the typewriter again. I worked through lunch with the aim of stopping around three and, with Mum and Dad out shopping in town, followed the boys' progress on Teletext while generally chilling downstairs. A call had come through from Frank the previous day while I'd been on my way back from work that they would pick me up around seven for Andrea's birthday dinner, but to be honest I hadn't really thought about the evening much.

It was only when Mum was unpacking the supermarket shop and asked to see what I'd got Andrea as a present that it occurred to me that I had yet to get her anything. Luckily I'd been too tired to go out Friday and with the tenner from the factory and my wages I had a fairly full wallet. Jumping on my bike I made it to the High Street in time to pick up a decent enough 18 carat gold neck chain from Samuels, which came with a scarlet mock-leather box that made it look much more expensive than it actually was, which was just what I needed. While I was there I also managed to check whether I could return it if necessary and got a receipt.

I also got paper and a card - nothing too soppy - and wrapped the present up at home. My stomach felt like one of Dad's winemaking demijohns, fermenting nerves instead of gas, although there was no certainty that the one wouldn't lead to the other. Nothing could dispel a growing sense that the evening ahead represented uncertain territory, its outcome unpredictable. News of a 2-1 away win failed to settle me, and not even finding out that our goalkeeper had somehow managed to score was able to act as Milk of Magnesia to the now audible gurgling in my stomach.

I made the decision to wear my new suit, reckoning that this was appropriate garb for a condemned man, and thank God I did. Andrea had pulled out all the stops: a green work two-piece with a wide collar on the blouse which overlapped similarly broad jacket lapels which in turn matched the now apparently obligatory jutting out shoulders, tapering down to where a thick belt accentuated her waist before the ensemble flared out again over her hips and ended just above the knees.

A light silk scarf was wrapped around her neck, hiding what I often regarded as her best feature. She had also had her hair permed, enough for me to notice, which wasn't something I was usually good at, and I remarked upon it flatteringly, something else I usually failed to do. It all added to a certain sense of artifice, or forced formality, as if we were being watched; which whilst not unpleasant, wasn't exactly comfortable either.

The restaurant was only five minutes drive away and we covered the ground in silence. My spirits lifted when we arrived and I noticed that it was only going to be the four of us. Other people might have diluted the atmosphere, but on the other hand only four place settings also meant no Jacqui. I was off the hook and I breathed a sigh of relief as I took my seat. Part of me didn't know why I was there. Groovy's advice had been to make a clean breast of things. In his eyes New Year had been a defining moment and it was down to me to make it actually mean something. During another heart to heart the previous week he'd finally come off the fence. My relationship with Andrea was tearing me apart and holding me back, he reckoned, which when all was said and done was a pretty impressive combination. It was his view that I needed to move on and that I never would until I'd ended it with Andrea. 'Didn't New Year's Eve prove it?' he'd demanded, visibly quite angry by that time.

'Prove what?' I'd asked

'That a large part of you wants to break free, to play the field, to check out all the other fish in the sea.' He wriggled his hand as he said this to make sure I knew what he meant by fish. My only response had been to put my own hand up like a lollipop lady to stop him before he ran out of clichés. Besides, I'd reasoned, show me one twenty one year old virgin who wouldn't have passed up sex on a plate on New Year's Eve, it didn't really mean anything in the way he saw it. As always it all seemed to come down to whether the whole sex thing was the key or it just made things even more confusing.

There was a reasonable chance he was right, but he hadn't taken into account the fact that I was a coward and the price I was paying for that was to find myself sitting in a dark restaurant lit only by candles in wall sconces, with a crimson carpet on the floor and heavy wood panelling on the walls. Heavily starched napkins folded into cones marked out each place setting. Frank and I waited for the ladies to sit down and then joined them, Andrea and me sitting opposite each other rather than together.

It struck me that the heating seemed to be stuck on a

'Turkish Bath' setting as I picked up my napkin and shook it out, noticing just too late that the waiter was doing this for everyone else. Frank quickly followed my lead in what I supposed was a bid to make me feel less uncomfortable. As soon as this ritual was over Andrea affirmed my view on the temperature and took off her silk scarf.

As she did so a dazzling gold necklace caught the light and pulled my eyes towards her delicate-looking neck. Just in case I hadn't noticed the necklace Andrea touched it subconsciously, as if checking it was still there, although its weight alone would surely have acted as enough confirmation. The best way of describing the necklace's style was probably as a series of interlocking Celtic knots stacked vertically, the whole thing acting like a choker, with what looked like a series of small diamonds set in a centre section just below the hollow at the base of her neck. It looked ravishing on her and for a brief second I could imagine kissing that neck and moving slowly down towards ...

'Do you like it, Colin?' she asked, clearly pleased that I'd let my eyes linger on it.

'It's beautiful,' I replied, simply but truthfully.

'It's 24 carat, you know,' interjected Mrs Kendall-Jones, spoiling the mood, and I guessed it had been their present to her. Not 18 carat then, I said to myself, and not from Samuels either I'd be bound as I fingered the outside of the package I had yet to pass to Andrea. Somehow that moment didn't seem like the right time. Having made her contribution, Mrs Kendall-Jones had lowered her nose firmly into the crease in the menu, as if it was the next trough she was going to put her head into, rather than merely a list of its possible components. An awkward silence fell over the party, but good old Frank came to the rescue.

'How's the job search going then, Colin?'

That's right, I thought, go straight for the jugular.

'Good actually, Frank,' I bluffed, my words however carrying the conviction of my recent optimism, 'I've got quite a few irons in the fire.'

185

'Good, good, heh, heh,' he replied, his eyes running from side to side of the menu, only half concentrating on what he was looking at. Experience had told me not to underestimate Frank however, and he didn't let me down. 'Weren't you once interested in advertising too?' he asked, remembering, elephant-like, our conversation in his living room from months ago.

'I've gone off it actually, Frank,' Andrea's eyes flicked up from her perusal of the menu.

'Really? Any particular reason?' There were lots actually. The thought of spending every working day with a bunch of airheads in an industry that symbolised everything that was going wrong with our country as it spun towards an orgy of consumerism was one. Making a living by convincing people to buy things they didn't need and probably didn't even want, was another; but I decided to keep these to myself.

'Nope,' I shook my head in a gesture of non-commitment. Andrea returned to the menu and I followed her. At that moment the waiter returned, pad and pen in hand.

'Would anyone like a pre-dinner drink?' he asked. I was gagging for a pint but joined the others in a G&T out of politeness. 'Chef particularly recommends our special tonight, the Surf and Turf, a perfect marriage.'

Andrea pretended to gag the moment he turned his back to get the drinks, making Frank and me laugh and at last breaking the ice a little. 'Sounds like horsemeat!' she giggled, sending ripples of light to bounce off her new necklace. 'Perhaps it's something to do with the Common Market,' added Frank, keeping up the momentum.

'Perfect marriage!' exclaimed Mrs Kendall-Jones. 'Perfect marriage?' She turned to Andrea. 'I'll say to you what my Mam said to me. A perfect marriage is all about the three 'S's - society, security and sex.'

A hush fell over the table at the mention of the third of the three S's. Andrea nearly choked on the piece of roll she'd recently broken off and only just finished buttering.

'Society because it's nice to have someone around, security because you need to know you're provided for, and sex because it's the price ...'

With perfect synchronicity, Frank coughed to break the flow and announced his choice for main course while Andrea recovered enough to shout 'Mummy!' Andrea and I followed Frank's lead and it looked like we'd all got away with it when Mrs Kendall-Jones started up again.

'Marriage ...' but that was as far as she got before Andrea interjected.

'...isn't something I want to talk about right now!'

Both Frank and his wife turned to look at their daughter, but I got the distinct impression that I was the real intended audience for her words.

'It's something for way into the future - if at all,' she went on. 'I want to make something of my life first, there's a whole world out there and I want to sample it before settling down. Things have changed for women since you were growing up Mummy,' she suggested, directing a glance towards her mother and now apparently into some kind of stride, 'there's oodles of opportunities for a girl like me. This is a new age. We have a woman as Prime Minister, who'd have ever thought that would happen? Maybe I can get to the top of my profession - what's to stop me?'

I'd never heard her this passionate about anything before, certainly not marriage (which was hardly surprising as it was something we'd never discussed at all). She was positively animated, like a new person with her highly polished jewellery, power-dress business suit and generously applied make up. Where had it all come from? There was something about it that was vaguely attractive, but also slightly frightening. She was changing, almost before my eyes, a Pygmalion-like transformation, only without the dodgy accent.

Was it really all directed at me? Was this what she thought

I wanted, or was it what she thought I wanted to hear? Was she showing me the door round the back with the big green sign saying 'Exit' above it, or was she challenging me to respond? The sheer enigma of it all was actually quite exciting. With a snap of the fingers it was over though, as the waiter returned to take our food order. The rest of the meal passed pleasantly enough, with Mrs Kendall-Jones mercifully quiet and Frank his amiable self. It was a while since I'd eaten out like this so I decided just to enjoy it, finishing the whole meal off with a Baileys and a coffee, which left me in a relaxed, mellow state.

I wasn't invited back to their house, I suspected this was something pre-arranged and began to wonder if Andrea's outburst was too. Our house was on the way back to theirs, so they dropped me off at the ridiculously early hour of ten on a Saturday night. Andrea walked me to the door and I finally gave her her present, telling her to open it later. We kissed and gave each other a brother and sister hug.

As I turned to put the key in the door she gently touched my elbow and half-spoke, half whispered the two words: 'Call me.'

THINGS WERE BEGINNING TO LOOK UP - the cinema chain wanted to see me. They didn't call it an interview, they said they wanted to 'see me in order to explore opportunities available within their company', but they weren't fooling anyone: it was an interview. Then, bugger me, if there wasn't another letter the same day from some computer company called Micro or Macro Software or something like that. Maybe all my hard work was beginning to pay off?

I remembered the first of these quite clearly from the Job Fair, they were the ones with the big TV screen, and although they weren't my first choice I remembered that they seemed like nice enough people and had a vague feeling that they could be on to something. The computer company on the other hand had left no impression at all. All I could remember was that they were based in Reading, which had seemed at the time like a backward step. The job was as a software engineer, which sounded suspiciously like it might involve heavy machinery and I wasn't sure if it was my kind of thing. Still, an interview was an interview and I accepted both by return, even honouring them with first class stamps.

In the meantime Betta Staff had come up with a night-shift job at a bank in town, working from ten in the evening to six in the morning, with the potential for overtime. I grabbed it like a starving child, the prospect of getting some financial experience and a bank on my CV being too good an opportunity to pass up. The turn of the year had also made me acutely conscious that the class of 1984 graduates would soon be on my shoulder in the race for gainful employment and my CV was in need of bolstering in any way possible.

The new job was a simple one and had two main components. The first was to man a massive machine the size of a small shed which was based in the back office and created batches of duplicates of microfiche records, which were then sent out to branches across the region each morning. A bunch of bearded weirdos who looked like they never saw the light of day generated the originals from grey box-like computers in a sectioned off part of the basement and it was my job to take these and duplicate or 'dupe' them the required number of times. It was a bit like babysitting, keeping an eye on the machine to make sure it didn't break down, or more accurately waiting for it to break down as it actually had the temperament of a leading ballerina suffering from PMT.

The second part of the job involved working my way through a big box of cheques and picking out from a daily list those that had bounced. The actual cheque itself had to be sent back to whoever had written it so they could physically re-present it. Apparently this had only recently become a separate task in its own right but even in my time at the bank it escalated so that most nights I was trying to pick around a dozen or so cheques out from the haystack. Of course this had to be done at that low point around three or four o'clock in the morning when all your vital signs were slowing down and concentration went out of the window. Never, ever, did I manage to find them all on the first sweep, which meant going through the whole box again, and possibly again after that so that by the end I felt like putting a match to the lot of them.

Once I'd finally found all the cheques I had to put them into separate envelopes and tour the building with them, along with the duped microfiche, pushing an old tea-trolley around the different floors and up the lift and matching the packets to the right desks. After the humming and whirring of the duping machine this was an eerie experience, the offices taking on a cold Marie-Celeste-like quality in the dark, coming only partially alive when I turned on the lights, the room's purpose seemingly unclear unless it was populated by people.

On the surface the whole thing was very simple, but I'd got the job because the manager had been impressed by my degree - degrees being somewhat thin on the ground in the bank apparently. The problems came when things went wrong, and this was where the potential for overtime came in. If everything went well the whole job could be completed in around four hours. If it went badly I could still be there into the morning, fending off desperate cries for microfiche and dud cheques from the faceless voices from 'upstairs' on the phone. The difference between success and failure however was outside my hands, the whole operation dependent on which side of bed the ballerina had decided to get out of that night.

Watching the bearded geeks at work on their computers didn't exactly fill me with enthusiasm for my forthcoming interview with the software people, although I had to admit to myself that what they did was pretty impressive. They seemed to summon up stuff out of thin air, like magicians with doves and top hats, what was more they did it with a general air of nonchalance, as if they were saying 'that was easy, give me another problem'. The lines of green numbers on their blinking screens seemed to move in a form of perpetual motion, scrolling away as if they were alive and, from a distance, looking like a miniature game of Space Invaders. At least my duping machine was mechanical; you could see the moving parts and could diagnose what was wrong with it when it broke down simply by looking at it, or tracing a fault back by the noise it made. I knew which I preferred.

Working at the bank also gave me an insight into, if not exactly the nine to five, certainly the ten to whatever; and also allowed me to gain a deeper appreciation of how other people earned their crust. The night-time atmosphere was a good one, as if we were all survivors cast adrift in the same boat together, and I enjoyed this. There were also clear hierarchies, with temps being once more at the bottom of the pile - second-class citizens, making me yearn all the more to be accepted and 'normal', although if I was being honest with myself I also carried a certain pride in being abnormal, in not being one of the herd. It all reinforced my schizophrenic existence: of the world of work, but not; seriously qualified, but qualified for nothing.

The job made getting to evening games tricky of course. Thankfully only one came up in my time there, a long trek up to Liverpool which we probably wouldn't have bothered with anyway - which was just as well because the team ushered in February with a miserable 3-0 stuffing there, ending our unbeaten run. Bloody Scousers, I hated them almost as much as I hated bloody Luton, they seemed to specialise in spoiling the party.

One of the best things about working at the bank was when we all managed to finish our jobs early when there'd be a whip-round and someone would nip out for a pizza and a few cans - working nights had a way of disrupting the body clock and telling your stomach it needed refilling. The alcohol would then fuel chat, which would then morph into debate.

Sometimes the computer boys, or boffins as they were known, even helped me look for the dud cheques if they'd finished their work early. Unlike practically all of the people I'd worked with on my various temp jobs, the boffins had some brains between them and when time was hanging heavy on their hands they either entertained themselves by loading complicated fantasy games onto their computers or by engaging in a round of goading the temp - me in other words.

They were okay though, the goading was just their way of coping. Topics varied, but often drifted into politics, which they seemed keen to push me onto as I seemed to offer a different perspective to the tabloids most of them still read. Tony Benn was in the news a lot as he struggled to get back into parliament after the humiliation of losing his seat at the previous election. The boffins liked to compare him to the children's cartoon character Mr Benn, who had a habit of assuming a fresh identity after visiting a fancy dress shop in each episode. This was accepted as fitting for someone, we all agreed, who was a left wing nutter with little left to offer anyone.

On the subject of left wing nutters, the scouser Derek Hatton was also a figure of fun, although he seemed to represent a more sinister side of the Labour Party, one of dark corners and secret deals. Taken together, Hatton and Benn seemed to sum up all that was wrong with Her Majesty's Official Opposition, which in truth was hardly an opposition at all. Nominally at its head, Kinnock and Hattersley seemed to have their hearts in the right place, but another vital part of their anatomy was missing - the balls to sort their party out.

We all agreed that Labour was dead in the water, it was just a matter of time before it sank. The boffins were all Maggie's boys of course, being big believers in the free market and making your own way in the world, and it was when I found out that all but one of them (the one without a beard) were temps too that the balance between us seemed to even up a bit. It seemed they could earn more being self-employed rather than on the company payroll and most of them were creaming it with cash.

Another regular topic was the miners, where there was clearly something brewing and the prospect of another national strike. All of us were old enough to remember the power cuts of ten years before. At the time we'd all been quite young and the days of no TV, board games by candlelight and shared baths had all been a bit of an adventure. We remembered how the lucky few got themselves generators to keep their TVs going, the waves of noise from outside their houses distancing them from the Blitz spirit and the need to be British and fight the good fight.

The miners did for Heath of course. He'd called an election on the question of 'Who runs the country?', only to get a resounding raspberry back and the unmistakeable conclusion that it wasn't who he'd thought it was. It had looked like Thatcher was going to take them on herself in the early stages of her premiership, but the ghost of Heath had clearly haunted her and she'd bottled it. We all knew it was a temporary reprieve and it looked like we might be brewing up another stage of the battle, and knowing Maggie this time it might be to the death.

We didn't anticipate a Blitz spirit this time, it was looking more like hand to hand combat with no clear idea who was going to win. The miners had taken on the mantle of representing the unions in general, it felt like something apocalyptic might be approaching, but none of us could quite put our finger on it. All I knew was, I wasn't cheering for either side. No one seemed to share my view of things though, with the boffins, newspapers and TV commentators all coming across like hooligans outside a football ground goading each other to 'fight, fight, fight', as if that was all they'd come for.

It came as something as a shock when Andrea said she'd like to join us in the trip to Charlton for the next round of the Cup, and even more of a shock when she said she'd drive. It seemed the gold necklace had been only part of her present as her parents had also got her a second-hand Mini, a 'runabout' they called it. It was around five years old and its bumpers suggested it had seen a bit of action in that time, although it was in good nick inside, even if the engine was a bit temperamental in the cold. In the weeks we hadn't been seeing each other it seemed she'd been having driving lessons and had passed her test first time - naturally. It came as a bit of a facer to discover how far we'd drifted apart, how whole parts of our lives were going on independently of each other.

In the end we met up and agreed that the train was probably a better option. The car came in useful in other ways though, giving our relationship the transfusion it needed if it was to survive, allowing us to spend more time together and to discover a few pubs out of town, especially along the canal. We used these trips out to make up for lost time, with me listening patiently to everything going on at her work while she listened equally patiently to me re-running some of the arguments that we'd been having at my work. Our differences seemed to have been put on hold, neither of us prepared to face up to our demons.

Sometimes we met up with Groovy and his new girlfriend Kate who he'd hooked up with after the momentous New Year's Eve party, an event which was, by unspoken agreement, never raised in conversation. This radical shift - traditionally Groovy was a love 'em and leave 'em type of guy and never saw anyone for more than two weeks - was something else that had apparently passed me by. Night shifts had a lot to answer for.

Groovy had grown a blanket of face fuzz since I'd last seen him, which allowed him to complete the transition to a fully paid up member of the underbelly of the civil service. It made him look a complete prat of course, like an incomplete door mat clinging to the front of his face, but he thought it made him look older and more serious, although I knew the man underneath it and couldn't see it as anything other than a disguise. He seemed happy enough and Kate was both pretty and companionable, the pair of them fitting together like Barnesy and Johnston, a perfect combination. I found myself having to bat away a slight pang of jealousy at the way she seemed to adopt the position of soul mate I'd so recently occupied.

Despite this warming of the temperature of my relationship with Andrea on the outside, there still seemed to be a frozen core, like an inadequately microwaved pub meal. We were not back to where we had been and the physical side of things remained coy, at best. Still, breaking my duck seemed to have lifted that particular monkey off my back, making it on the one hand less important and on the other giving me an urge to try it again when I wasn't quite so close to being out of my tree.

The trip to South London came as a shock too, with the landscape from the train looking profoundly depressing almost as soon as we pulled out of Charing Cross: mile upon mile of car wrecks, corrugated iron, gangs of kids with nothing to do and bonfires on vacant plots which looked like they were left over from the war. No one looked happy and even the buildings looked suicidal, it resembled something straight out of A Clockwork Orange. Our visit didn't help of course as we thumped the lower league opposition 2-0 and booked our passage into the next round.

Andrea and I had cuddled up on the terraces to fight off the cold, our hands inside each others coats as we watched what seemed like a routine win with Mighty Mo adding to his season's total, aided and abetted by the gap toothed giraffe who went by the name of George Reilly. The best news of all, however, came over the tannoy when we heard that Cup favourites, the seemingly invincible Liverpool, had failed to do what we had done, losing to Second Division Brighton of all people.

We cheered like mad when the result was announced, jumping up and down like we'd won the cup ourselves, although this time I managed to keep my mouth shut as I felt the waves of excitement break over my heart. A little ripple started somewhere in the crowd and grew with each person that passed it on: the field was wide open, it could be anyone's year - why not ours? Eternal optimism sustains every football fan.

The next Monday I stayed up to catch the draw for the next round on the radio. Things were beginning to get serious: the last sixteen. Get the right draw and we could stand by and watch some of the other big hitters knock each other out. In hindsight I suppose what happened next was inevitable as the balls were drawn out of the hat.

Second Division opposition again, great - but did it really have to be the giant killers, Brighton?

FIFTH ROUND

19

ONE TUESDAY NIGHT everything went tits-up at the bank. The duping machine broke down and it had taken three hours to get someone out from the maintenance company; when he'd finally turned up he wasn't the regular guy and he took an age to fix it. This had had an inevitable ripple effect as soon as people started to arrive at their desks upstairs only to find their familiar buff envelope missing. They then started calling down and demanding where their stuff was, which in turn slowed me down even more, creating a vicious spiral. For the first time in my life I could see what people meant when they talked about a bad day at the office.

It was one of those times when being a temp was a bit like being a leper. It wasn't my fault, but I was the social pariah and fair game, the butt of everyone's anger, whether it was justified or not. They could afford to go for me as I didn't matter, whereas I couldn't afford to retaliate because they did. I felt like I needed to rely upon their charity for my continued existence. My only tactic was to make a mental note of who'd been most unreasonable and get back at them during the following nights by re-programming the speed dials on their phones.

What had made matters a whole lot worse was that the

boffins had finished early that night and someone had brought a portable TV in so they had a bit of a party with porno videos. Hardly surprising therefore that no one offered any help with the dud cheques, which I ended up having to go through four times. What made everything totally intolerable was the fact that I had an interview that afternoon in London and really needed some shut-eye first.

So when I finally made it home, I wasn't in the mood to find Mum in one of her occasional silly girl moods. These took place twice a year, as she reverted to childhood to become what Andrea's Mum would have called a 'giddy kipper', almost as if she was high on something - which she was - although it was excitement, rather than anything chemical. She'd taken her pinny off and washed her hands, which either meant she was expecting to handle something important or we were about to have visitors, and the lack of any 'powder', as she called it, on her face led me to expect it was the former.

Fizzing like sherbet on the tongue, she came rushing up to me, her hands full of envelopes of different shapes and sizes. It wasn't her birthday, which meant it was Valentine's Day. Mum always sent me a card on Valentine's Day and loved to watch me open it. Largely out of habit, I'd sent one to Andrea the day before, but otherwise my expectations for the day were so low they'd dug their own hole and gone into hibernation. It came as a bit of a surprise therefore to see Mum holding up a wedge of post, all addressed to me. I picked hers out straight away by its handwriting and opened it with a fingernail. It was the usual cutesy offering, a stylised Hallmark cupid firing an arrow on the front, inscribed with a finger-down-the-throat rhyme inside:

Violets are blue, clovers are green.
You're the cutest Valentine
I've ever seen

I pecked her on the cheek and thanked her.

'You're very popular this year,' she observed as I flicked through the post. I nodded but didn't much care, on first glance it looked like there were three more cards, plus two other business envelopes: one of them white, which augured well, and a brown rejection letter. I opened the white one. It was another interview, although my addled brain had trouble making out what the words were trying to say. It looked like I was being invited to something that was going to take place over a whole day, including a dinner in the evening. The letter was written in a very personal way, as if the sender was an old friend, and signed simply 'Andy' in a flourishing hand and in fountain pen.

Andy? Andy? I couldn't think of any Andys and could only assume this was someone I'd met at the Job Fair, although for the life of me I couldn't place him. On the other hand, most of the people on the stands had had the habit of introducing themselves using their first name and after a while all the names went in one ear and out the other, without pausing to be processed in the middle. I took note of the date and slipped the letter to the bottom of the pile for further scrutiny when my brain cells had decided to start talking to each other again. I looked at the other envelopes and decided they too could wait - I needed to sleep.

There were around sixteen of us in the hired room in an Earls Court hotel, an A4 notice in the lobby having directed us to the Kingfisher Suite with an arrow added in flipchart marker acting as a guide. I'd managed to grab a couple of hours of kip and felt a bit better by the time I'd got there. I guessed most of the others in the room were still at university and few, I noticed, seemed to have made the effort of wearing a suit.

Two I picked out as immediate rivals, one of them a bloke who looked quite old, in his thirties, who was wearing a smart two piece and looked like he'd been round the block a bit, with thin lines around his mouth and eyes simply yelling out 'experience'. He was busy glad-handing everyone in the room and introducing himself, but I knew his game: he was sussing out the opposition. I ear-wigged some of the responses just to see if he was picking anything useful up.

The second was a girl about my age, a bit dumpy with long black hair with a streak of dyed red in the side. The edge of one of her nostrils was slightly inflamed, as if she'd removed a nose ring just before setting out that morning and her skin was beginning to rebel. When I say she was slightly dumpy let me elaborate - she had a roll of fat that was the very definition of a spare tyre around her middle. It looked like the sort of thing that should have been surgically removed, an act that I was sure would have made a difference to her appearance and general attractiveness - so long as at the same time she could have sorted out (and washed) her hair, learnt a little about what, and what not, to wear, desisted from standing with her legs apart like a soldier on parade and got a bra that fitted. She had a look of cold determination, though, which I didn't fancy. She was a rival all right. I could also see why she was attracted to cinema management - all that dark.

We filed into a soulless wood-panelled room like nervous new recruits and listened to a short presentation, complete with overhead slides, from someone high up in Global Multiplex. You could tell he was from Global Multiplex before he even introduced himself because he was wearing a corporate tie with a 'G' and an 'M' interlaced in the pattern. Up until then we'd had to endure over-sincere ministrations from the outsiders they'd hired to run the session, bright over-manicured young things who might on any other day have been seen offering you perfume testers in Boots.

If I'd been a gymnastics judge I'd have held up a 'nine' for his enthusiasm and 'eight' for content, although the presentation itself left a little to be desired - a 'six' at best, which was a bit odd for a company in the film business. He painted an optimistic picture, of cars turning up at their cinemas and disgorging whole families who then inspected what was on offer out of the ten or twelve films being screened and chose which one they all wanted to see. They then were all herded off to the fast food restaurant attached to the complex, bought some popcorn and played a few arcade games before watching their chosen film. On coming out they may then be tempted into a few lanes of bowling and pop into some kind of giant food/clothes/hardware/gardening superstore to spend yet more money before heading home.

It was all a far cry from going to the local fleapit, after picking something out of a choice of three in the paper, turning up twenty minutes before the screening and standing in a queue in the rain. It looked like something out of a science fiction series, or at the least like we'd seen in, well, films; American films that was. Believable certainly, but not what we were used to, very un-British was the best way I could find to describe it, too relaxed and not enough standing in line. A silence had fallen after the presentation and I struggled to come up with an intelligent question, largely because I had yet to form an opinion of whether I liked it or not.

It was at that point that the older guy stepped in - a case study in what to do if you wanted to make a complete maggot of yourself. He'd done some research and wanted to let us know it. What he hadn't taken into account was that the slick bugger up front had almost certainly seen the same research and had an answer to it.

'Latest industry figures suggest that cinema attendance will fall to an all time low this year,' he announced rather smugly, 'and that the total will be half what it was even four years ago'. There wasn't a question there, but the Global Multiplex man stepped in anyway, pointing out that this indicated what an untapped potential there was, how similar trends had been reversed in the States using the approach he was setting out and the profits they were making there already. One down, fifteen to go. Fat girl and me decided to keep our counsel.

After this we were split off into two group sessions of eight each, in which we were given a potential problem and asked to come up with a solution as a team. It was like a Board Meeting, with each of us assigned a different theoretical role and a written brief with issues we wanted to promote and protect. After ten minutes preparation we were told to get on with it while a couple of other Global Multiplex ties sat quietly in the corner and watched us. I'd done similar things at university and settled in quickly, I loved this sort of exercise, just another opportunity for a good old debate.

Next up were some one-to-one interviews, and although these were staggered I was one of the first up. I straightened the back of my jacket, cleared my throat and went in. The suit and tie behind the desk was friendly enough as we went through my CV and had a general chat about what I wanted out of a job and my wider ambitions. It all ended rather abruptly, before we seemed to have got into anything meaty, and I didn't quite know how to take this but decided to go with the flow, collected my travel expenses and caught the tube back to Watford.

When Mum asked me how it had gone I didn't in truth know how to answer her. 'Okay,' I said, 'no, better than okay,' I added after due consideration, 'all right.' She gave me a look that acknowledged that this was as much as she was going to get out of me and changed the subject, her excitement levels clearly beginning to notch up a gear.

'Who were all the Valentines from?'

In truth I'd forgotten all about them and went upstairs to fetch the small bundle. I felt I owed her something, and seeing as Dad was at work, we sat down together to open them. One was clearly from Andrea, we knew this because she'd signed it and had sprayed her favourite perfume all over it, a smell I could detect at twenty yards.

Of the other two one was postcard size and simply carried

an 'X' inside, I had no idea who that was from, unless Andrea had sent me two, as she used to in the old days, whilst the other was a distinctly past the watershed number that my Mum pretended not to understand, although such was her animated state I could see she was trying to repress a giggle. Acknowledging that your parents understand sex jokes, especially oral sex jokes, is a bit like original sin - you can see how it happens, but would rather it didn't. This was only the half of it though, the squiggle under the rhyme looked distinctly like a 'J' - for Jacqui??

Four cards - a record, but by then I was completely saturated with the whole Valentine's thing and wanted to return to the interview letter that had come with them that morning. I still didn't know quite what to make of it, but assumed it was going to be a bit like that afternoon's exercise, just stretched a bit longer. I'd make a call tomorrow and see if I could get any more out of them.

The final brown letter I left to last without much expectation. The slip of paper inside was thinner than usual and closely typed: *'A Valentine's message has been published for you in today's Guardian. All you have to do is buy a copy of today's paper and look down the 'Valentine's Messages' section. Happy hunting!'*

A Mr. Toad-like 'Peep Peep' outside shook me from an unplanned doze on my bed. I recognised it as coming from Andrea's Mini and on going downstairs found her chatting away quite cheerfully with Mum and Dad in the living room in a way they never did with me. She was on her way to picking Frank up from the hospital and had swung by to offer to drop me off at work - she just loved driving around in that Mini.

As soon as we got in the car she leant over and pecked me on the cheek. 'Thanks for the card, it was very sweet.'

'Likewise,' I responded.

'Did you like it?' she wondered, and I had to stop to remember what it looked like. Sodding Valentines Day, I hated it. 'It was lovely,' I replied, conjuring up a generic image of all the non-obscene cards in order to sound at least half-way sincere.

That seemed to be the end of the topic, thank God, although I sensed some unfinished business. Her picking me up meant I wasn't able to pop into the newsagents to pick up a Guardian and I wondered briefly if the message was her handiwork, a way of making up maybe, and that was why she had seemed so dissatisfied by my answer? The whole thing seemed so complicated. I wished I could just make a clean breast of it all, but I was held back by a combination of fear of the consequences and outright flattery. I wanted to see the message first.

Thankfully things had calmed down at the bank. An engineer had come in and done what they called 'Preventative Maintenance' on the dupe machine, which was a bit like closing the stable door after the horse had bolted, run the Grand National and dropped by to take tea with the Queen, but was welcome all the same. I went into the boffins' room and let my eyes adjust to the dark in there before scrabbling around for a Guardian. If there was going to be one anywhere in the building it would be here. I found one in the bin.

The problem with Valentine's messages in the paper is that any number of them could conceivably be for you, what you're really looking for is something that could only be for you, something unique that only the sender and you would recognise. In short, you needed to crack the code. The problem was, I had no idea who the sender might be, every suspect seemed to have been revealed. All in all it was a bit like trying to find the dud cheques. I went through the list time and again, wading through 'Soppy bunnies', 'Coochicoos' and 'Love sausages' but I admit only with half an eye. Absolute concentration was what was needed, and I eventually found the time to apply it before actually getting onto the cheques, just in case I dulled my eye. With a plastic cup of coffee from the machine next to me and a desk lamp illuminating the paper below, I set to work.

Five minutes later I had it:

Do you know how my heart mourns?
Lift me from this dilemma's 'Orns.

It was the apostrophe that did it, that and the capital 'O'. Why else put that in if it wasn't targeted at an 'Orn? It had to be the one - but what did it mean? Could it be Andrea's heart mourning? That seemed the most likely explanation, but if so she hadn't dropped any hints about the message in the car, but that would have been in character. It couldn't have been anyone else though could it? Surely not? Surely it couldn't be Jacqui? Well, there was that other card too.

Jacqui had her virtues of course, quite generous ones as it turned out, but our brief time together had dissolved into history now. Part of me was frankly embarrassed by the whole episode, especially the bit which involved Groovy afterwards, although another part of me of course looked back on it with pleasure. And didn't she have a boyfriend - wasn't that the point? She'd only dragged me into the summer house to get back at him - hadn't she?

I lost myself in the dud cheques, all eighteen of them, another record. Everything was sorted and ready by the time my boss got in at seven. We always had this handover time to talk through the events of the night and for him to pick up on any problems. That day he called me into his office for a little chat. It seemed that the dupe machine had become obsolete. A new system was going to come into effect where the branches phoned into the boffins who would provide the information they previously got from the microfiche direct. This was going to avoid a lot of waste and save on the budget. He seemed pretty excited by the whole thing. The only downside of course was that the change meant they wouldn't be needing me any more. That was another downside of being a temp, they could get away with giving you an ant's blink worth of notice. So, that made the jobless total three million and one then.

It was the first of my jobs where I felt genuinely pissed off at leaving. It had suited me and I felt as if I'd become part of the crowd, but I'd just been reminded of my expendable status, the discarded wrapper on an eaten Big Mac which would soon be forgotten. We shook hands and agreed that there were no hard feelings, although mine were actually pretty solid. My face must have told a story though and he made a throw-away offer to write a reference for me if I ever needed one. 'I'll take you up on that,' I said. I just hoped I'd need to call that particular favour in sooner rather than later.

In the cold light of day things looked more positive. I was getting a flow of interviews, with two still to do and one waiting for a response. The stats on my system were the rosiest they'd ever been, with outstanding letters approaching two dozen and a CV that now positively yelled experience from the nearest cliff top. It was just a matter of time - surely?

Things were feeling rosier around the Golden Boys too. It was February, the half way point in the season had been passed and our perspective became defined more by how many games were left than results so far. It was even warm enough some days to go to the ground without a jacket. After the hiccup with the (bloody) Scousers we had regained winning ways and two more victories had followed, including a classic 5-3 win at Notts County which Groovy had gone to with a few others by car, but I'd dipped out due to lack of funds. Things were well cued up then for the next of our Cup games, a potentially tricky, but home, match against Brighton, the side that had beaten Liverpool, the side we'd most recently lost to. In theory if they'd beaten the side that had just beaten us we were doomed … but sod it, this was the Cup, anything could happen.

But it didn't. 3-1, thank you very much and goodnight. Johnston scored of course, along with the orthodontically-challenged Reilly and the Welshman, Jackett. A sell out crowd and a ticket into the round where we stopped talking numbers and began a countdown to the Final - the Quarters. Eight teams left. Two games from Wembley. In quiet moments we could allow ourselves the luxury of dreaming.

As soon as the final whistle went I glanced down into my programme and checked for our next date with destiny. At that time my diary was pretty much a week to week affair, with the future an uncertain place, as my experience at the bank had shown all too well. March 10th. It rang a bell. In fact it rang wedding bells. I turned to catch Trev up, who by then was half way towards the exit.

'I know, I know, I know,' he pleaded, holding his hands up in supplication. 'Take it from me, it was that or the Semi. There was nothing else I could do.'

'But it's the bloody quarter finals of the Cup, man!' I yelled, making a bid for the 'stating the bleeding obvious' prize.

'I know, I know, but once the women get going there's no stopping them, you know. This whole wedding thing, I just feel like I've been caught up in a whirlwind.' The hands, so recently used to beg forgiveness were now cradling his face. As his best man, I had no option but to retreat. I placed my arm across his shoulder, awkwardly, and consoled him.

'It's fine. We'll go to the semis.'

'Yeah, of course,' he answered, 'If the wife'll let me.' We both laughed and he dropped his hands. I was grateful tears had been averted.

'Look, I'm sorry, mate. I know Watford's your life, but very soon now Claire and the baby will be mine. I'm moving on.' This seemed to be some kind of declaration, but one expressed sincerely, and I'll be honest, it came as something of a slap in the face as it carried such an obvious truth.

But not as much as a slap in the face as what happened next.

Out of nowhere, just as we were passing the Red Lion and the burger stall outside, a Brighton fan came out of their end and lashed out at me, his long black plaited hair billowing out like a curtain caught on a breeze as he swung his body into a punch. Bizarrely, all I registered about the moments before his fist slammed onto my jaw was spotting a couple of skinheads outside the pub who seemed bemused by the whole episode, as if this wasn't part of the natural order of things and a kind of reverse-Sampson rule had came into effect. What I do know is the whole thing happened so quickly I didn't have time to react and within seconds I was experiencing the sensation of hard bone against the side of my jaw and a sudden, throbbing, excruciating pain.

The blow sent me reeling backwards and onto the ground, where the crowds suddenly parted and I could see two coppers already running in from the side of the road. They weren't quite quick enough though as Trev quickly grabbed the bloke who'd hit me and twisted him round into an efficient arm lock, taking the opportunity to land a short sharp blow to the kidneys with his knee as he did so to knock any residual fight out of him, before pinning him to a lamp post. Definitely a Man of the Match performance.

The other two coppers joined him in a blur of blue and nodded awkward police-type greetings at Trev, who they clearly recognised.

'Know him?' they asked, as I staggered back to an upright position.

'Never seen him before in my life,' I replied.

But I had. I'd have recognised those dreadlocks anywhere, although the last time I'd seen them they'd been peeking over the top of a bed with my girlfriend on her knees next to them.

I'VE SPENT TWENTY FIVE YEARS trying to work out exactly what happened when I went to see the software people in Reading. There was a crowd of us, a fairly disparate, or that could have been desperate, bunch; and we were broken up to play what I can only describe as a series of games together, and although these were fun they hardly seemed to constitute a thorough and exacting examination of our credentials as potential software engineers. Unlike the cinema exercise there didn't seem to be anyone observing us, although later on, when I described what had happened to Paully, he told me I was a complete whazzock and that they were probably watching behind one way mirrors. I hadn't thought of that.

The games ranged from the pointless to the bizarre, from erecting matchbox towers to giant logic puzzles to buzz wires like you might get at a village fete. At no point was there a conventional one-to-one interview, human beings actually talking to each other. I was also the only one there in a suit. I had begun to wish that they'd put a recommended dress code on these invitations.

To top it all I was sporting a large purple bruise on the side of my face that they couldn't have missed seeing through their mirrors - so perhaps it was just as well there was so little talking, as talking still hurt. Perhaps they called me 'bruise boy' to themselves all day, although my brief experience of computer people made me think they weren't really the nickname sort. Anyway, the whole thing was bizarre and when they told us they'd be in touch I neither cared when or how, or indeed, if they ever did.

The subject of the whack I'd got after the Brighton game was of course a hot topic amongst my friends, and no matter how much I tried to keep a low profile in the hope that not too many awkward questions were asked in certain quarters, there was simply no getting away from it. Trev had been a hero, not only on the day itself but afterwards, making sure, on my insistence that my assailant got away with a stern talking to and nothing more. I wanted the whole thing dusted and put away like an unwanted present. Groovy had come in on the end of the incident and thought he recognised him from somewhere but I managed to keep him off the trail until one day, when I was sitting in the pub with him and Kate, it came to him.

'Got it! He was at the New Year party wasn't he? That's where I've seen him before.' I heard his words and knew that it was inevitable that the rest of the story would tumble out. Groovy was like a terrier once he got something like this between his teeth. I had two options - to let him work it out or put him out of his misery straight away. Out of friendship, I went for the latter.

'He's Jacqui's boyfriend.'

'Jacqui?' Kate asked. Only Groovy and I knew the whole story, and Kate's reaction suggested that, like a true mate, he'd managed to keep it to himself.

'She's a friend of Andrea's' I enlightened her.

'Ooooh!' she added, knowingly, giving the word a certain Les Dawson-like quality. So he hadn't kept it to himself, the bastard.

Andrea had been giving me the cold shoulder ever since the previous Tuesday when she'd come round to fetch me and I'd managed to work out why. She'd seen all the Valentine's cards on the mantelpiece while she was waiting for me to come down and had asked Mum about them. Mum, being Mum, hadn't kept Mum and had allowed her pride at my popularity to spill over, notwithstanding that she was talking to my girlfriend of the last five years. I suspect she'd taken a good look at each and every one of them - she had that kind of easy familiarity - and maybe even seen the one that looked like it was signed with a possible 'J'. Even if she'd had her doubts, my subsequent whacking by Jacqui's hirsute admirer would have quashed them. I was in big trouble. I decided to tackle the problem in parts and explained the card conundrum to Groovy and Kate.

'Look,' I suggested, gazing straight into Groovy's eyes, 'I need some help here. Why can't you say you sent one of them, as a laugh, you know?'

'But I did, mate!' he revealed. He really could be a bastard.

'So did I,' Kate interrupted. We both jerked our heads to look at her. It was clear she hadn't mentioned this to Groovy. 'Like you say,' she went on, 'for a laugh. That's what Valentine's is all about isn't it?' For a number of reasons, laughing was the last thing on my mind.

'There you are then, mate,' concluded Groovy. 'That's all four accounted for - Andrea, your Mum, me and Kate.'

Except there was the fifth one of course. Only the sender, me and the boys at the Guardian knew about that one. I decided to keep it that way, Groovy was proving to be a leaky sieve when it came to secrets.

'Oh, that's it!' I exclaimed throwing down my glass. 'I've had enough.' Groovy and Kate looked at each other, their glasses both pausing on the way to their mouths. 'All these mind games and sulking, good times, bad times, never knowing where we stand. I'm going to end it once and for all. It's time to move on.'

The others' drinks stayed where they were, but their eyes met and they exchanged smiles. Groovy put his pint down.

'Good call,' he announced. No trying to talk me out of it, just a reinforcing tap on the head to make sure the decision was firmly cemented in. 'Why don't you bell her now, seize the moment?'

'What - now?'

'Phone over there, can lend you some ten pences if you're short,' he offered, digging into the tight top pocket of his jeans.

'Yeah, go on. I will. It's a conversation I've rehearsed often enough, I don't have to think what to say.'

'Good on you,' Groovy continued, still fishing in his pocket for change.

'I'm sure you're doing the right thing,' added Kate, touching my hand reassuringly. If I hadn't been so sure myself I might have thought I was on the end of a conspiracy.

The call didn't quite go as I'd expected. Andrea was in and happy to talk, but I never really got out of first gear. She said she was glad I'd called because she'd been doing a lot of thinking lately and she'd come to the conclusion that she was tired of all the mind games between us, that we would probably both benefit from a break from each other, that whilst we'd had some good times the bad times seemed lately to overshadow them - in fact, she seemed to have most of my lines at her fingertips and all I could do was agree with her.

The only bit of the conversation I hadn't already heard in my mind was the bit where she said she'd been asked out by someone at her work and she wanted to go, but that she wanted to have this conversation first. She wasn't the two-timing kind she said, and for a moment I wasn't sure if she was going to add rather haughtily 'unlike certain people'. By the time we'd both put the phone down we had split up, although it was impossible for me to tell if I'd been the dumper or the dumpee.

It didn't really matter, I was free at last. I felt sad for a few seconds but this was soon overtaken by a huge sense of relief, like someone else's soul had been inhabiting my body and had suddenly been called back to base. At that very moment it was lifting out of my skeleton and drifting skywards. I actually felt physically lighter. I was even glad for Andrea that she was going to see someone else. Frankly, you couldn't really call what we'd had a relationship for some months, years even; there wasn't much left for me to grieve over, it had slipped slowly through my fingers like sand and now it was all gone.

I went back to tell Groovy and Kate the news and noticed that they'd got me another drink in even though I was barely half way through the one I'd got, and even though, as it turned out, I had no sorrows to drown. It was a nice thought all the same. Groovy shook my hand, something he never did, and Kate kissed me on the cheek and gave me a lovely hug.

'Welcome to the big wide world,' Groovy declared, and we all gave a toast to that.

After the software interview that wasn't, in fact, an interview, I had no idea what to expect from the day and dinner invitation which didn't even mention the word interview. The big question of course was knowing what to wear and I settled for my suit trousers with a smart shirt and no tie, but for the evening I took a small bag in which I'd put my suit jacket. Cover all bases, I told myself.

The address on the letter was a large square shaped Georgian house down a side street in St. Albans, a long bus ride away, the sort of place that might have once been a rectory or perhaps more recently a doctor's surgery. I rang the door bell, which was actually a handle a bit like an old-fashioned loo chain, and was greeted by a mousey looking woman who was, I guessed, in her mid-forties. Her manner belied her looks as she buzzed around with energy, taking my bag, asking if I needed the toilet and offering me a coffee all in one sentence.

'Colin! Good to see you again.' I recognised the voice, but it had come from behind me so I couldn't put a face to it. 'Given up on jackets all together now, have you?' he asked, with a chuckle in his voice.

'No, I've got one in …'

Then I saw him. It was the man from the toilets at Victoria station, the one who'd helped me get all the puke off my corduroy jacket what seemed like a lifetime ago. His card had called him Andrew Woodford - Andrew. Andy. He was Andy. The putative shirt-lifter. What had I got myself into?

'I'm so glad you got around to writing, I so wanted to make contact again. Ah! I see you've met Kathy, my wife,' he noticed, as we shook hands. Poor woman. Did she know he hung around in public toilets? 'Has she explained the drill yet?'

I wasn't sure I wanted to know what the drill was and cast my eyes around for where my bag had been taken so I could beat a hasty retreat if need be. If it did turn out to be some sort of kinky party, I didn't want to leave with only half a suit. Before I had a chance to say anything 'the drill' was set out to me, and bit by bit, the fog began to clear. I was to meet with a number of different people and the idea was to keep things very informal. We would all get a chance to chat one to one with 'Keith' and as part of a group with 'the Executive', which sounded like some kind of weird sect.

As the last of the fog finally lifted I realised I was at the St. Albans headquarters of the Alliance, the group formed by the Liberals and the Social Democratic Party, the latter having been formed by the Gang of Four senior Labour politicians who'd finally had enough of the influence of the lefties in their party. I didn't know how it had happened or why I was there, but I was glad it had and I was.

The Alliance was, in my view, a modern day success story, still with plenty of mileage on the clock; one of the very few exciting things to have happened in British politics in the previous few years. At the election the previous year, the day in fact when I'd first met Andy, the two parties combined had managed to get within under a million of the total number of votes won by Labour. Despite this however, and winning over a quarter of all votes cast, the two parties only picked up a

215

combined total of 23 seats. Still, it was a reasonable enough start. 'The Executive' was the umbrella under which the two parties operated locally and, as I was to find out, not one of them was disheartened by the outcome of the election. If anything, they were brimming with confidence for the future and their enthusiasm was curiously infectious. They saw this quarter share as a platform from which to build and they also saw places such as St. Albans, with its strong middle class backbone, as ripe for the picking.

With around four years to go until the next election they wanted a paid agent to work the constituency and give their man a realistic shot at winning it next time round. They were professional politicians - a breed I didn't even know existed and almost instantly wanted to join. I had found my nirvana. The seat was held by an up and coming Tory, but last time out it had been the Liberals who'd taken him on and got within eight thousand of winning, squeezing the Labour vote quite severely on the way. Recruiting the agent was what the day was all about.

'Keith', it turned out, stood a good chance of being their man, his candidature just needed to be rubber stamped by the Executive. I was due to meet him later, but in being passed around the room I learned he was an industry specialist and had his own chain of newsagents in and around the town as well as fingers in a few other investments.

The morning whizzed by and was great fun. It was like being back in the bank in the small hours, arguing the toss on the big issues of the day and having your opinion listened to, challenged, revised and then, finally, given another chance to fly. Everyone there seemed to be like me. They actually enjoyed this stuff. I felt like I'd fallen amongst friends. My opposition, and I saw them as opposition, were formidable enough to get me worried, for as the day wore on I got the distinct feeling that I really wanted this job. They were both blokes, one had served an internship in the House of

Commons, which in anyone's book was better experience than a camera factory, whilst the other was a black guy who'd won debating prizes at public school, the git. Only one thing was bugging me - how had I got to be there? The coffee had flowed freely all morning and it was whilst in the loo - on my own - that the possible sequence of events began to unroll in front of me. That conversation we'd had in the Gents at Victoria was reminiscent of the ones we'd been having today. I remembered treating Andy to one of my rants, and I began to realise how a lot of what I'd said at the time would have chimed with the thoughts of him and his colleagues on the Executive - voting reform, Europe, Foot and Thatcher. The whole nine yards - a lot of it could have been lifted straight out of the Alliance manifesto.

Then there was the card he'd handed me when we'd parted. I could only think it had got mixed up with all the other cards I'd brought back from the Job Fair and I'd fired off one of my generic letters. It must have been sitting in the pile of stuff on my desk. After all my hard work trying to create an opportunity for myself, this one had conjured itself up. Crazy.

During the afternoon I got to take a walk around the town with Keith while we chatted. He was interested in what I'd been doing since university and I was able to regale him with some of the fund of stories I'd begun to build up. He seemed to like them and before too long we were sitting together on a park bench swapping tales of incompetence, cock ups and corruption. It was more like being with a mate than a potential employer, but by then I'd given up on ever having a conventional interview. He was a good laugh.

Dinner was harder, with each of us three candidates clearly on show and trying to both impress and outdo the other, without being too overt about it; it was a delicate balancing trick. The subject of the miners came up and the consensus was that if they did go on strike it would be a defining moment for both the Thatcher government and the country. Keith was of

217

the view that the miners couldn't win. The government had been stockpiling coal and anyway, Scargill was tactically naive to embark on a long strike just as winter was drawing to a close. It wouldn't be pretty, he reckoned, but ultimately, in his view, there could be only one winner.

We then moved onto the subject of freedom, one of Thatcher's favourite words. Each of the applicants was invited to hold the floor for a few minutes on the topic. The black guy was great, drawing on the great philosophers and using a number of rhetorical flourishes and tricks he'd no doubt used a hundred times before. The other guy was simply brilliant and had clearly done his homework, which was one advantage of knowing beforehand why you were there I supposed. He held the audience, a dozen of us in all, in the palm of his hand, he was so bloody reasonable he managed to pilot a middle course that was nigh on impossible to argue against. Then it was my turn. I'd had no time to think about it and most of the obvious stuff had been said by then, but I took as my theme the idea that freedom was all about the freedom to choose, but that it was the government's responsibility to provide the conditions to allow people to make an informed choice.

The problem with the way things were going now, I argued, was that the country was being offered a false Jerusalem, with no real substance behind it. It was bread and circuses, I argued, a phrase I was particularly proud to have dredged out from the furthest recesses of my mind. Thatcher was using the oil money to buy people off with stuff they didn't really need when it should be used to rebuild the country. I carried on like this for a few minutes and once my slot was over I noticed a brief but perceptible silence before the usual polite applause. There was a reasonable chance I'd blown it, but Andy was kind enough to give me a broad smile and a discrete thumbs up, so with a bit of luck he was rooting for me. It was impossible to tell though, and I travelled back on the bus coping with a strange combination of being both wired up but also slightly frustrated.

Back at home there was a definite atmosphere, although whether it was benign or malignant it was difficult to tell. The place had the unfamiliar tang of booze again, but this time it wasn't whisky. A fluted champagne cork on the draining board in the kitchen provided a good clue and when I walked into the sitting room Mum and Dad were both holding a cocktail glass of the sparkling stuff, although Mum was holding hers uncertainly, from the base. Dad looked like he'd just won the pools, although Mum's face had a look that suggested whatever lay behind all this was all a hoax and no one had had the heart to tell him yet.

Dad stood up as soon as I walked in and poured me a glass of my own. 'Good news, son,' he announced. Perhaps he had won the pools. I took a sip of my drink and waited. 'I've been made redundant!'

I nearly spat the champagne back into the glass and Mum grimaced, whether at what I'd nearly done, which she would have noticed, or because she still hadn't got used to the idea of having Dad around all the time I didn't know.

'After thirty years,' he added. 'Twenty five great years and five absolutely miserable ones.' I'd had no idea he hated his job. 'They can flipping well strangle themselves to death for all I care now, what with their endless walk outs and wildcat strikes. I've had enough - I'm out, I'm free of the lot of them at last.'

That night as I lay awake trying to get to sleep I couldn't help but wonder whether I might be on the verge of finally getting a job just as my Dad had lost his, as if the damned things were in finite supply? How weird would that be?

QUARTER-FINALS

21

IF DAD WAS GOING TO BE ON THE DOLE, another DHSS statistic, at least I could act as a temporary breadwinner, quite literally as it turned out as Betta Staff's next trick was to get me installed working a conveyor belt at a local bakery owned by one of the big national conglomerates. The factory, and believe me that was the right word, was a huge shed of a place out on the ring road with a high roof where flocks of starlings nested, swooping down periodically through great gouges in the net put there to stop them shitting into the dough. As the shit was roughly the same colour as the dough no one seemed to mind.

Initial impressions suggested this was going to be a very straightforward job, but it didn't take long to suss out that there were layers of unseen stratification amongst the staff, a roughly fifty-fifty split between men and women, with different tasks commanding different pay rates measured in extra pence per hour with the allocation of roles determined not by the management but by the shop stewards. In fact I never saw a manager on the floor, they were hidden behind a huge glass window at one end of the building, looking out benignly on an empire they didn't really control. It didn't take long for me to realise it was just another crap job for crap pay. When was I ever going to break out of the cycle and get a 'proper' job?

The bakery's most pervading legacy was its stink. After only one day there I couldn't stand the smell of white bread in the toaster anymore, and once I knew what those small indentations in the side of a loaf meant just seeing a white sliced was enough to make me heave. The smell got in your clothes, in your hair and in your pores, and seeing as I didn't want to attend to my duties at Trev's wedding smelling like a Pilsbury Dough Boy I showered and showered and smothered myself in whatever I could lay my hands on in the bathroom every day; although I still couldn't face the smell of Old Spice, even if it was only in talcum powder form.

The wedding was on a Saturday of course, and the streets looked empty as I set out. There were rumours that at least ten thousand local citizens were travelling to the match in Birmingham, our quarter final opponents, and that may have accounted for a lot of the empty space. God, I envied them. What made it more interesting was Birmingham had a reputation as bad-arse bruisers and it looked like it could get a bit tasty.

Not where I was going to be, though. Being in Trev's debt after the last round of the Cup, I'd taken my medicine quietly and had worked dutifully on my speech and been very polite to his parents at the rehearsal. I'd even got a book on the Best Man's responsibilities out of the library, but most of these seemed to relate to a type of wedding that bore little resemblance to what was going to happen that day. I was nervous of course, not so much because of the speech and everything else that went with the job, but more because of the game. They say that no one remembers losing semi-finalists, but at least if you make it to the last four you get that day out, that hope. I reckoned that it was worse to lose at this stage, two games short of Wembley, so near yet so, so far.

Birmingham City were many people's tip to lift the trophy that year, even though they were below us in the First Division table. That probably said as much about other people's lack of respect for little old Watford - flash in the pan, here today, gone tomorrow Watford - as it did for reality. Birmingham was a club with tradition, this opinion seemed to say, they had earned their right to glory, unlike Watford who weren't a proper club at all.

Perhaps my nerves were rooted more in the fact that our good form of late had stuttered. There had been plenty of goals it was true, just not always in the right end - nineteen in all in just three games, with the 'against' column just shading it. In cold hard terms, the outcome had been just four points from those games. We weren't worrying about sliding back down the table, if anything a mid-table finish looked more or less certain by then, but this only reinforced the need to keep going in the Cup to keep our season alive.

The team seemed to be stuck in some kind of neutral, and I knew the feeling well. I'd heard nothing back from any of the interviews I'd been to and the new ones had dried up. Working at the bakery was leaving me shattered, they operated a three shift system which changed every week which meant mornings one week, followed by afternoons and then nights. I'd gone through one cycle of this and it had completely screwed up my circadian rhythms and as a result the momentum for new applications had crashed into a mountain of sticky dough.

Meanwhile, there was a wedding to be got through, the venue a small Methodist chapel on a street corner, which I would normally have passed on the way to the ground and actually knew from my parent's church-going days. In many ways it was just as well we hadn't been drawn at home as I don't think I could have stood being so close and not going. There were double yellow lines both sides of all the local roads so most people arrived either by taxi or on foot, having parked in one of the shoppers' car parks.

Not that we were a big crowd, no more than thirty, the only exception to family being me, and that had been a concession apparently. No Groovy or Paully, who were probably grateful given the circumstances, but no Sarah or anyone else from our crowd either. The wedding was scheduled for one and I had met up with Trev around midday so we could be at the church in plenty of time. It was cold inside, the heating having yet to kick in, and the ends of the aisles lacked the flowers I'd been expecting. In fact it seemed a pretty uninspiring place to pledge your troth, or whatever it was you did at a wedding.

We met the minister, who was short and stocky with a closely shaven beard as if he was slightly over-conscious of wearing one. He also seemed rather casually dressed. We ran through a few practicalities and then fell into an awkward silence. Outside a wind was blowing up and I wondered briefly if they were feeling it in the Midlands too. There wasn't an organ but there was a piano and a pianist, and it was part of my role to meet him and pay him off at the end of the ceremony. Luckily he arrived early (I guessed he'd done this before) and started tickling the ivories to get his fingers warmed up. His rendition of the chorus to 'I'm Getting Married in the Morning' lodged itself in my brain and refused to go away all through the service.

Slowly, people started to arrive and in the absence of ushers I directed people to the correct sides of the church whilst all the time keeping an eye on Trev. During lulls in the action I checked that he was okay and he confirmed that he was cool with everything, so I decided against the traditional question making sure he definitely wanted to go through with it. I was too busy to have time to cope with any last minute dithering. We were well past the point of reconsideration anyway though, as the now clearly visible bump protruding from Claire's front amply confirmed when she arrived on time and waltzed down the aisle.

Of the ceremony itself only the weak singing and mumbled responses were in any way memorable and before we knew it I was seeing people out and was running through my checklist of things I had to do at the church before we signed off. Outside the photographer was in full flow and I reckoned I had a couple of minutes to catch my breath, so I wandered round to the back of the dark grey-stoned building to what stood for a garden in order to get away from all the hubbub. A few early daffodils had bullet sized buds ready to bloom in a solitary flowerbed by the back wall, although a lingering chill on the air suggested that Spring was still a couple of weeks away yet.

It didn't take me long to realise that I wasn't alone. A tall bloke with thinning hair and a yellow tie was having a fag and I noticed a thin string of wire linking his ear to the inside pocket of his suit jacket. I checked my watch and found myself humming 'Get me to the church, get me to the church ...' An hour and a half to kick off.

'Any team news?' I asked.

'Exactly the same as the last round,' he replied, 'Sinnott instead of Atkinson as sub.'

I nodded my understanding. No introductions had been necessary.

'What do you reckon?' he asked.

'Johnston hat trick,' I replied and we smiled at each other in the way only die hard fans infused with relentless optimism can. 'Derby in the semis,' I added, for good measure. Derby were from the Second Division.

'Colin?!' A deep male boom from the front of the church meant I was needed, so I spun on my heel to head back.

'Let me know if anything happens,' I asked, and my new friend raised a silent hand in confirmation.

I could have grown a beard to match Groovy's in the time it took the photographer to finish, but eventually we were in the hired cars to whisk us round to the reception, which was to be held in a small family run hotel the other end of town. Tall schooners of golden sherry awaited us, held on trays by black-skirted waitresses with white lace-trimmed pinnies. Sherry had always been a mystery to me. I never had quite worked out how they managed to extract headaches, distil them and create a liquid. I passed, and although I could have murdered a pint by then I was sensitive enough to appreciate that it wouldn't quite be in keeping.

Trev seemed to relax now the deed was done, and I gave the new Mrs Downing standing next to him a kiss on the cheek to congratulate her. She did look good, but somehow, despite the make up that had been applied to make her look older, she simply looked too young to be married, like the whole thing was a game, the clothes taken from a children's dressing up box. They looked happy enough though, although relief may have been an alternative explanation for their expressions.

A Master of Ceremonies, who I later discovered was actually the hotel's owner, ushered us into a small room at the back of the hotel. I was on the top table of course, next to Claire's sister Mary, who was the Chief, well in fact the only, Bridesmaid. When I say top table, I actually mean at the top of a horseshoe, with our table having wings down either side of it to accommodate our small gathering.

Mary was good company and through whispers let me in on some of the background to the day - her parents' reaction when Claire had told them she was pregnant, their insistence on a church wedding, what had become known as the 'search for a church' and the panic that had set in when the baby had begun to show and they weren't sure if the dress was still going to fit. It had seemed a little tight to my untrained eye.

She was Claire's younger sister, but you wouldn't have guessed that there were three years between them. Brunette, with short bobbed hair which framed her face, Mary was confident for her age, and sat most of the time with her fingers intertwined on the top of the table while she talked. She had long sexy fingers, with a pearl varnish on the nails. It felt good to be having this kind of conversation again, the kind between two unattached young people, talking about yourself without inhibition and listening too and yes, flirting a little also. I hadn't done this for ages and I found myself enjoying the sensation, an open book with no hang-ups, pre-set rules or worries. I reflected that I'd managed to get through the split from Andrea without too much trauma, after all, here I was, back on the scene and performing okay. There was of course another bonus from our split: somehow I'd managed to avoid the whole Jacqui thing coming back to haunt me, getting away scot-free from further recrimination, if you were prepared to put aside the violent assault in the street that was.

'When I get married - if I get married,' Mary corrected herself, 'it won't be like this.' I agreed. 'Not some hole in the wall affair designed simply to get it over with. I will want to go out with a bang.'

'No better way,' I concurred. 'If you're going to do it, do it right.'

'Right!' she added, quickly, completing the words to the song and making us both laugh.

The bloke from the garden entered the room and sat down, his earpiece now gone. Prawn cocktails preceded some kind of chicken in a sauce and a fruit salad dessert and then it was time for the speeches. Despite our numbers the service had been slow, but the hotel had had the benefit of being warm and the company had been congenial, so it hadn't been a problem. Trev stood up and planted his feet firmly apart as if he was going to direct traffic before going through his routine litany of thank you's without much adornment and before I knew it, it was my turn.

I stood up and began by thanking Trev on behalf of Mary for the kind words he'd said about her, although whether he had said anything about her I couldn't remember, I just knew it was what I was supposed to say. Just as I started to reminisce about the first time I'd met Trev a cry of 'Yeees!' came from one of the wings and all eyes turned to my friend from the garden, who was now discretely re-attached to his radio. His clenched fists still hung in the air. I took this as a good sign.

'Thank you sir,' I ad-libbed, 'Can I just ask, is that your own mouth or have you rented it from Arthur Scargill for the day?' A ripple of laughter rolled over the room, even though the joke didn't quite work, Scargill would be more likely to say 'No', but it broke the mood and I was able to look back at the target of my humour who had raised a finger on one hand and formed a circle with the other, before giving the thumbs up. 1-0 up, and not yet half time. Encouraging.

All in all the speech went okay, and Claire's Dad, being a teacher, was able to hold the room well, allowing the whole event to pass by without any untoward incident, which has to be one of the best indicators of success for any wedding. Once all the formalities were over, people began to mingle as the cake was cut and duly distributed. There seemed to be no real plan for the rest of the afternoon and I noticed people getting fidgety to go, as if the only reason they'd hung on was for the cake.

Meanwhile, I couldn't help myself from frequently glancing over to my friend with the radio and shortly after four I wished I hadn't as he rested his hands on top of the table and raised the index finger on each. An equaliser, it seemed, 1-1. He caught my eye and mouthed something, but I couldn't make it out. He said it again and I managed to decipher the two words 'Own Goal'. Shit.

Once one couple had gone the rest seemed to follow by instinct, and it had barely turned half past four when I realised that there were only eight of us left: the bride and groom, both sets of parents and me and Mary. Trev and Claire had a room booked in the hotel so they weren't going anywhere and I could see us getting caught up in some kind of impromptu gathering with the parents unless we were careful. I sidled up to Mary.

'Fancy meeting up for a drink?' I whispered.

'I need to get changed first,' she replied, as if she'd been waiting for the offer and had her answer pre-prepared. So it

227

was that we cut the party by a further twenty five per cent, wishing the bride and groom all the best as we left, agreeing to meet up in town at seven.

I couldn't have planned it better. I got back home in time to catch 'Sports Report' and the glorious, magnificent, gut-curdling news that Les Taylor, only recently back from a three month lay-off, had followed up the own goal with an absolute rocket that had left the Birmingham 'keeper shell-shocked, his first of the season and what a time to deliver it; and then good old Barnesy had followed up his first goal with a second, a toe-poke from a headed on corner.

We were in the last four!

I set the VCR for Match of the Day to catch the highlights and put on my best clobber. A little celebration was in order!

UNIONS

22

SUNDAY EVENING, before going to bed, I put the VCR to use again to tape the draw the next morning, but not before watching the goals from Saturday for one last time, freeze-framing the picture for the moment Taylor's shot ballooned the back of the net. Pure bloody magic. The shift cycle had started again at the factory and the coming week I was back on earlies, six in the morning to two in the afternoon. That meant going to bed around nine, which frankly I needed after a terrific night out with Mary, ending up in a club; something I hadn't done in years.

Back at the factory the stench hit me before I got through the door, making me gag, but within a few minutes it was the noise rather than the smell that really worried me. No one wore any kind of formal ear protection and the few that did used plugs of cotton wool, so conversation was carried out mainly by yelling, which meant that very little was carried out at all. Until you got to the break room that was. This was the fiefdom of the union, with one of the shop stewards usually holding court. There was no escape from them as the pattern was to work an hour on and then half an hour off, and there was nowhere else to go, outside was not an option as it meant getting changed out of the apron.

The way these guys ranted on made it impossible to read and the only two things to do were to listen, debate was not encouraged, or to line up for the toast machine; a ready supply of bread not the problem so much as having an appetite for the result. This seemed to be the accepted state of affairs, but it really made the days drag out. It was a case of be part of their club or leave. This was made very clear to me early on when I was joined in the rest room by a double act not unlike Cannon and Ball, except the tall one was fat and the short moustachioed one was thin. They sought me out when I was whiling away a break with more than half an eye on the clock and entered into what I assumed was a well worn routine, talking through me to each other, as if I wasn't there.

'Looks like a new one,' the tall fat one started.

'Not seen him before,' the short thin one agreed.

'Looks sensible.'

'Oh yes, I'm sure he's sensible.'

'Pay his dues?'

'I'll check, but as you say ...'

'... he looks sensible.'

This was the point where a hint of menace seemed to creep in, but I kept my head down.

'After all, what's thirty seven and a half pence a week?' continued the tall fat one.

'Cheap at half the price,' agreed his companion.

'For protection.'

'Protection.'

'From the management.'

'Oh yes,' came the response, 'from the management.'

'And from accidents.' At this point, I looked up.

'Can be nasty, some of the accidents in here.'

'Fingers.'

'Cut off.'

'Nasty.'

'Thirty seven and a half pence a week.'

'A small price to pay.'

And with that, they got up and left, still as if I wasn't there.

Sure enough, I noticed on my first pay slip that thirty seven and a half pence was being deducted for union subs, even though technically I wasn't even employed by the bakery and I'd never signed anything.

Of all the temp jobs I'd had the bakery was probably the most frustrating. At least at the camera company we'd had a laugh, here laughs seemed to be regarded as a bourgeois luxury. Frustrating, also, because there were clearly a lot of good people there who were being kept down. My favourite was a bloke who looked as if he'd stepped out from a Mr Bunn the Baker card in Happy Families. He would take fresh batches of dough and rather than supervise the machine dolloping them into the tins would weave and plait them into fantastic shapes and put them onto baking trays he'd brought with him before they entered the oven.

Everyone knew who these belonged to and would let them wend their way around the conveyor belts until they came back to the rollers near me, where it was my job to pick up loaves knocked out of their tins and stack them on cooling racks. Mr Bunn represented one end of the process and me the other, with all the other activity taking place in between us. I looked towards him and he looked out onto the entire factory. When his confections emerged from the oven he'd take them from me and let them cool by his side, before quite brazenly taking them home.

I could see why my job was taken by a temp. Other than being on the slicer (a job which commanded an extra twenty pence an hour), it was the most miserable place to be in the whole factory. I was forced to wear industrial-strength oven mitts to handle the bread, but many of these had worn right through and if you weren't careful your finger would peep through and sink into one of the furnace-hot new loaves sending a spear of pain through your hand and arm. This was where the holes in the loaves came from. What we all dreaded were the batches of slimmer's bread, aerated cylinders of puff which would scatter and roll onto the floor. Slimming maybe, mouse droppings, almost certainly - note to self, avoid the raisin slimmer's bread.

Cycling home I passed newspaper placards for the Watford Observer announcing 'Cup Draw', but kept my head down, resisting the temptation for a quick fix. I wanted to savour the experience. The machine was still running when I got home so I stopped it and rewound what was pretty much a whole tape. Mum was sitting outside at the picnic table with a cup of tea, chopping some onions on a wooden board, taking advantage of some early Spring sun. Later she would wander down to the bottom of the garden to put the skins on the compost, you could bet your wages on it.

The news was on first and was dominated by the announcement that the miners had finally started their strike. The screen was full of images of thick set men at the pitheads wearing duffle coats and holding placards with slogans such as 'Coal for Britain, Not Dole for Miners', a reference to the plan to close twenty pits, 'Milk Snatcher Thatcher, Now She Wants Our Jobs' and, more succinctly, standard-issue NUM posters demanding that we 'Save Our Pits'.

The men's faces and the blank looks of the cross-armed policemen facing them spoke of determination and incipient confrontation. The whole scene looked light on good humour. As Keith had predicted at the Alliance interview, it wasn't going to be pretty. I was also fairly convinced he was right about the outcome. It was the journey between now and then we had to be worried about. The whole spectacle and what it represented wasn't uplifting, the only hope being that it represented the last battle in the class war.

It was a relief therefore when the picture switched to the easily recognisable scene of the marbled halls of FA headquarters. Like Black Rod demanding access to Parliament, the BBC cameras waited to be invited into the dark oak panelled vault that was the Committee Room. The draw was simply item six on the Cup Committee's agenda, and the cameras were a barely tolerated intrusion into their business. Two men stood up and picked up a small velvet bag containing four small wooden balls.

Like some kind of bizarre black magic ritual, they rattled the bag and a hushed silence descended.

'Gentlemen. We now reach the next item on the agenda, the draw for the semi-finals of the Football Association Challenge Cup.' Speaking in whispered tones for fear of being thrown out, the BBC commentator reminded us which numbered ball related to which team. There were in fact six teams left, with Derby and Plymouth from the Third Division having drawn their quarter final as had high flying Southampton who'd drawn with Sheffield Wednesday, who were locked in a battle with Chelsea to win the Second Division. Derby or Plymouth was definitely the ball we all wanted.

And we got it. Somehow, miraculously, lady luck looked down on us and gave us the Derby or Plymouth ball. It was an open ticket to Wembley - surely? After all we'd achieved that season, over the previous few seasons, it was beginning to feel at last like our name was on the Cup. Sure, we'd revelled in giant-killer status enough times in recent years to know that the impossible sometimes happens, but surely? Surely?

Back at the factory I'd noticed that Mr. Bunn wasn't the only one taking bread home. Everyone seemed to be at it; it seemed to be an accepted perk. No one left work without a carrier bag full of bread, and when at first I opted out of this arrangement I found myself cornered by two shop stewards the following day outside the rest room who demanded to know if I was a scab or a management stooge.

From then on I had no option but to leave with my own supplies, whether I wanted them or not. Before long our freezer and next door's freezer was full of the stuff, and seeing as I was off bread all together we weren't getting through it at anything like the rate we usually did, so I stopped off at Groovy's one day on the way to a night shift to see if I could offload some there.

Sarah answered the door and let me in.

'If that's Mr Kipling shaking his bucket for the miners, tell him to sod off!' came the dulcet tones of Groovy from inside.

'I come bearing gifts actually,' I said, taking off my knapsack and preparing to reveal its contents.

Groovy started to wander around the room, sniffing theatrically.

'Can you smell something?' he asked no one in particular, keeping up the act. 'Something kind of musty and stale. Are you wearing a new aftershave, Kipling?'

I opened the bag. 'Look, do you want this bread or not?' Groovy and Sarah came over and peered into my rucksack and its contents of four loaves of bread.

'I like bread as much as the next man old chum but …'

'Look,' I demanded, 'just take it, will you, eat it, freeze it, feed the ducks with it, start a sandwich business if you like, just take the sodding stuff, there's no way I can take it back with me.'

The bread was received with bad grace and Sarah made the shape of a 'T' with hands. 'Go on then,' I replied, 'a quick one.'

'Toast anyone?' enquired Groovy.

The TV was on and showing scenes of fights outside a colliery, so naturally we got to talking about the strike. Paully was there too and the three of them seemed surprised that I wasn't speaking up for the miners.

'A year ago maybe, but now I'm not so sure,' I told them. 'Why does it always have to be a fight? Why such entrenched positions? In my opinion the sooner they sit down round a table and sort it all out the better.'

'And everything in the garden will be lovely,' added Paully. No cushion being readily to hand I threw him a sneer. Sarah came in with the tea and we started chatting while the others watched footage from scuffles earlier in the day on the TV.

'Been up to much?' she asked. I gave her a run down of my recent movements, plans for the weekend and how I was spending my time generally. I in turn asked her who she was hanging about with but before she got a chance to answer Paully turned his attention away from the TV and pointed a finger at me.

'I know what I was going to tell you,' he announced. 'Did you know that Trev's got rid of his MG?'

'Not enough room for a baby seat, I suppose, daft idiot,' Groovy added. No one had seen Trev since the wedding and I felt a pang of guilt. I had heard that the two sets of parents had got together and put down a deposit on a rented cottage outside of town. It had a small garden apparently, which would be good for the baby when it and summer came, but it was pretty basic. Paully seemed to have read my thoughts.

'Their place has got a real fire apparently, they could be stuffed if there's a coal shortage.'

'It's coming up Spring, they'll be okay.'

'Apparently Trev's been foraging around in the woods picking up fallen timber and chopping it up with an axe. Hermit-man Downing!' added Groovy, and we all laughed.

'I'm a lumberjack and I'm okay,' I threw in and the laughter continued.

'If you want to see him, the best place ...'

'... other than the woods ....'

'... other than the woods, is B&Q apparently,' Paully added. 'He's DIY man as well now.'

'Or Mothercare.'

The chorus of chuckles continued and now in a groove, the conversation kept going in this vein for a minute or two more, each wisecrack notching up the laughter to another level until suddenly Sarah screamed, like someone trying to stop a child running out into a road.

'Stop!'

All heads turned to look at her and she blushed a deep scarlet. Silence fell like a collapsed ceiling, with much the same shocked effect.

'Stop getting at them, just because they're trying to build a life for themselves,' she demanded. 'Don't you dickheads understand? They're married now, a couple, part of a Holy union. They have to work for and look out for each other, to act as a team, make decisions and do things together - even if they'd rather be doing other things.'

We'd never seen Sarah like this, really worked up and using bad language. In doing so, though, she'd certainly earned our respect and we were probably all ready to apologise, I know I was, but the situation she was in was so unfamiliar to her that she didn't know when to stop.

'You guys, you sit on your arses and take the piss out of them but all they want is to sort themselves out.'

It was at that point that she visibly ran out of steam. Tears starting to well up in her eyes and then suddenly the dam walls burst and she started blubbing. It was all so out of character. As soon as the drops started running down her cheeks she turned and ran into Groovy's bedroom. A stunned silence followed.

'Christ,' uttered Paully from the sofa. 'That was weird.'

'Holy union?' I wondered, incredulously.

'Time of the month?' Groovy suggested, as if that answered everything but saying, in his usual blunt way, what we'd all been thinking.

No one was stirring. I jerked my chin up at Groovy.

'Don't you think you'd better …'

He didn't seem keen. 'Why don't you go?' he suggested.

'Me?' I asked. 'She's your sister, mate.'

'Exactly. She won't listen to me.'

'Good shout - you're the one she'll listen to.' Paully added, nodding agreement.

'Me?' I asked again. 'What makes you think that?'

'She listens to you,' they both said together. I shrugged. It was news to me.

And so it was that I crossed the creaking bare floorboards and opened the door to Groovy's room to see if I could do something about the undulating sobs coming from within.

SEMI-FINAL

23

MARY HAD THREE of those qualities a bloke always looks for in a girl: she laughed at all of my jokes, seemed to breeze through her periods and, after a couple of dates, she loved warming her hand on the inside of my thigh. It seemed incredible to think she was only eighteen, was technically in fact still a schoolgirl; she really seemed to have her head screwed on and yet was also great fun to be around, bubbly, vibrant, keen. She even liked the scent of dough I carried around with me, which she described as 'homely'.

I enjoyed her high energy levels and she enjoyed having an older boyfriend, the boys her age seemed to bore her and there was a certain kudos amongst her friends in hanging around with someone who'd passed through the acne stage, as it was beginning to look like I finally had. Things were going well. We were also able to pace our relationship: she had revision and my life was still directed by what shift I was on, but this was no bad thing, it stopped us racing on too far too fast or falling into a predictable routine. Our meetings had to be earned, which made them more precious.

All this variety, coupled with the need to be more organised, had the perverse effect of making my life seem both more intense whilst at the same time making it seem like time was passing more quickly. This was just as well as after the quickfire matches of the previous rounds it made the long gap before the Semi seem less like purgatory and more of a hiatus, a pause to regain our breath.

Although results were patchy, the good ship Watford seemed to have steadied, and a solid mid-table finish now seemed pretty much a certainty. Although still an achievement, it was only our second season in the First Division after all, there was no getting away from the fact that our season was going to be defined by whatever eventually happened in the Cup.

This feeling had been reinforced when, against the odds, Plymouth managed to beat Derby in their replay with a flukey direct goal from a corner, which left us with only a Third Division team to beat to reach the magical Twin Towers, with the venue for the showdown fixed as Aston Villa's ground to the west of Birmingham. My self-denying ordinance barring me from Wembley until the Golden Boys got there would then be vindicated I felt sure. It was so close we could almost smell the freshly cut and manicured grass.

During the wait Mary and I took advantage of the few moments we spent together to really get to know one another. As I've said, we didn't really mingle with her friends, and although I had introduced her to Groovy and Kate, we didn't really hang out together. We actually got into things I'd never really done before like long bike rides to tea shops, walks in the bluebell woods and occasional trips to the Palace Theatre in town to see plays by new writers. English was Mary's favourite subject and what she hoped to go on to study at university, and even though her going away was an obvious potential cloud over our relationship we were too stuck in the present to let it worry us.

All this had a devastating impact upon my alcohol consumption, which fell through the floor, and I even found that I seemed to be losing weight. Mum was the first one to point it out and she put it down to my having cut bread out of my diet, so she swiftly followed my lead, which meant that our own domestic Bread Mountain grew so high that we would have needed Chris Bonnington to get to the top to plant a flag.

Things were happening on the work front too. Although the flurry of interviews in the New Year seemed to have petered out, I received a call from Karen at Betta Staff who wanted to have a chat with me. My first thought was that word had filtered back from the bread factory and that I was in for a roasting of some kind, but she was all smiles when I got there and I was ushered straight through to her office. It seemed she'd had a call from the bank I'd worked at earlier in the year and they were interested in seeing me to talk about a permanent position helping to run their back office. It seemed they'd sacked the man who had been my nominal boss and re-structured the department. It looked like I could wave goodbye to that reference. As a result there was a vacancy for a less senior role called, ironically, a Senior Administrator, and seeing as I seemed to fit in and knew the ropes would I be interested in being interviewed for the post?

My show of enthusiasm was probably a bit like one of those rockets that takes off from Cape Kennedy only to falter and collapse, like one of Fred Dibnah's chimneys. My first thought was 'great', but then I remembered something Andrea's Mum had once said: 'You want to get a job in a bank, that's the only way of getting a mortgage these days.' Is that why people worked in banks - for what it gave rather than for the job itself? Mortgages? Security? Status? Would it be 'just a job' when what I really wanted was a career?

These doubts were followed by the realisation that, looked at from the outside - and I could see it in Karen's face as we were talking - this choice was a real no-brainer, manna from heaven, just what I'd been waiting for. With so much uncertainty around I'd hit the jackpot, what could be better than a job in a large multi-national bank, and they were asking to see me, not the other way around? By then though, I'd had a flavour of what might be better, but seeing as none of the other jobs seemed to be coming through with anything I couldn't afford to look a gift horse in the mouth. I asked Karen to call them there and then and we got a date sorted out.

Completely unexpectedly I now had four irons in the fire, although some seemed to have fallen to the edge and cooled down - it had been nearly two months since the Alliance interview. The meeting with Karen had shown me the virtue of direct action though, so when I got home I picked up the phone and, heart pumping, tried to get hold of someone at each of the three others. No one was available at any of them, but I left messages and was promised by each of them that someone would call back. Secretly I was quite glad, although the uncertainty was frustrating there were often times, usually half way through a shift, when it was somehow reassuring to know that I had all these potential jobs out there just waiting. It was that Premium Bond thing again, the more live applications I had, the more chance I had of winning.

Like an idiot, I stayed in for the rest of the afternoon waiting for the phone to ring, but it remained obstinately silent, no matter how long I stared at it or how often I checked that doors were open so I could hear it if it did ring. Meanwhile, there was always the prospect of Wednesday night and a batch of slimmers' bread to juggle with - literally.

Before too long it seemed appropriate to introduce Mary to the Golden Boys and Liverpool's forthcoming visit to Vicarage Road seemed like a good opportunity - with the prospect of a full house, some class football and some names she'd probably have heard of to see in the flesh. The Scousers looked on course to follow up their title of the previous season, but they'd lost to Brighton and we'd beaten them at our place last year so there was every ground for optimism. The previous three games had produced two wins and a draw, so it looked like we were emerging from our sticky patch just before the quarters and as the pair of us pushed our way through the turnstiles, we did so full of optimism.

The first thing Mary wanted to know as we entered the ground was where she could find the Ladies. We'd been to the pub beforehand and she hadn't fancied going to the loos there, and being a football virgin she hadn't realised that they would seem like an Arab's bathroom complete with gold taps compared to the ones at the ground. I sent the lads on and hung around to wait for her so I could lead her to where we stood, consoling myself with the thought that at least this meant she probably wouldn't want to go at half-time. I didn't know how bad the Ladies got, but there were usually duckboards in the Gents by half time which you needed if you didn't want to get your trainers ruined.

Just as it seemed we were going to miss the kick off she emerged, wiping her hands dry on the back of her jeans, and she seemed surprised to discover that we would be standing. Luckily, she took this in her stride and we shoulder charged our way to the edge of the crowd, the jaws of which opened up and slowly devoured us like a snake's lunch, passing us through its length until we finally reached Groovy and the others, nodding apologies to those around us along the way. I'd bought her a scarf which she was happy to wear, but it looked startlingly new against our grubby, battle-hardened offerings.

She seemed genuinely interested in the whole of the proceedings, both as a sporting spectacle and as an anthropological exercise in human behaviour. It seemed incredible to me that someone could be born and brought up in the town and never have attended a game and I found I had to nurse her through both it, and the rules.

'Why does the flagman keep putting his flag up when the ball hasn't crossed the line?' she asked, but the prospect of explaining the offside rule in the middle of twenty thousand baying fans was one I ducked. Things weren't going our way.

'Why does the referee keep blowing his whistle?'

'It was a blatant foul.'

'Don't they get sent off for a foul?'

We could have done with a couple of their players being sent off, just to even things up a bit. Then the inevitable happened. It had been coming for some time and when it did, it came with a blaster. 1-0 to the bloody Scousers. Mary clapped and people around us turned round and stared at her suspiciously. That new scarf could be a sign that she was there under false pretences.

'What are you clapping for?' I demanded to know, hissing under my breath, beginning to get a bit irritated and finding it difficult to hide the fact now I was in my natural milieu.

'Well, that was rather a good goal wasn't it?'

'That's beside the point, it was for the other side,' I yelled, rolling my eyes heavenwards.

Things got worse, they scored again and there was no way we were going to score two ourselves against this lot, let alone three. The crowd started to get restless. The game seemed to sum up everything following Watford seemed to represent, not least frustration at the sheer unpredictability of it all. We never knew which team was going to turn up, the gallant heroes or the also-rans who didn't seem able to string two passes together and made basic defensive mistakes. Some of the boo-boys began to yell their disaffection at the players and the manager, but they were soon overtaken by another contingent who seemed to want to take it out on the referee, perhaps in some kind of unspoken pact that we didn't dent the boys' confidence before The Big One at Villa Park. Huge sections of the crowd started to form an 'O' with their thumb and forefinger and jerked their hands up and down towards the man in black, booing him every time a decision went against us.

'Why are they all waving at the referee?' Mary asked, even when a chant of 'Who's the wanker in the black?' got up.

At that point I decided it was time to do the one thing I'd never done before at a Watford match. I left early, taking Mary with me and making my excuses to Groovy and the boys. They gave me sympathetic looks back which seemed to say 'Don't even think about bringing her to Villa Park'.

I wasn't.

Early the following week I got a call from Andy Woodford in St. Albans. He was sorry that it was all taking so long (I didn't tell him it seemed to be par for the course) and that he'd been meaning to get back to me as soon as there was something positive to say. He was able to report that one of the other candidates had pulled out, the public schoolboy. I wasn't sorry to see him out of the frame. That just left me and the black guy, Norman his name was. It seemed the Executive was split between our relative merits and it was likely that they'd want to see us both again. In fact, seeing as I was on the phone was I free for their next meeting in a couple of weeks time?

I pretended to pull out a non-existent diary and put the phone closer to the Thompson's Directory, whose tissue-paper thin pages made an unsatisfactory flutter as I flicked through the pages. Miraculously, it seemed I was free and we agreed a time. Meanwhile a letter came through from Global Multiplex saying they were still in the process of interviewing candidates and would get back to me in due course. I wondered if the letter had been prompted by my call and didn't feel encouraged by it.

With things still a long way from being resolved I had to buoy myself up for the interview with the bank, which if anything was beginning to take on the characteristics of a front runner. If things went well there was a danger that they would offer me a job before the others had sorted themselves out. I was beginning to know what it felt like to be a plate spinner, not really knowing which of the four remaining poles I needed to keep my eye on the most.

As it turned out the interview was pretty routine, the first really proper interview I'd had, one to one over a desk, no fun and games or exercises. I hadn't met the suit behind the desk before and it was difficult to guess where he fitted into the hierarchy. Tall, blond haired and in his mid-thirties I guessed, he was pleasant enough, the only thing that counted against him was that he seemed to have traces of a Liverpool accent, although I suspected he'd worked quite hard to iron it out.

Going in ambivalent about the job also seemed to give me an air of calm and that, combined with the confidence I reckoned I'd gained from being Trev's Best Man, with the speech and everything, all added up to me giving what I regarded as a pretty decent performance. I left feeling that there was a real chance I was going to be offered the job, and even slightly surprised, as well as relieved, that they didn't offer it on the spot.

Meanwhile Mary and I came to an agreement that she'd stay away from the football if I stayed away from her friends. I didn't know what this paranoia was about her friends, and seeing as I'd never met any of them so far this seemed like a good deal so we sealed it with a kiss. In fact the kiss was just the start of it and what with her parents being out we also took the opportunity to seal our relationship upstairs in her bedroom.

This came as a welcome surprise, although not as much as the fact that she turned out to be on the pill, especially as my wallet had been short of one vital element (I'd come to suspect that Mum looked through it and didn't carry one around in it any more). It seemed that Mary was determined not to go the way of her sister. Bright girl. With Mary, making love seemed like a natural progression, not the result of a long drawn out battle, and it brought us closer. I used to meet her after school some days and as a sign of our closeness I brought her family into the bread giving circle, which had become much more sophisticated by then, with members taking orders for particular types of bakery products and at times it had even became difficult to keep up with the demand.

It was when I was on my way to pick Mary up from her aerobics class one day that I bumped into Sarah cruising along the High Street, peering into the shop windows.

'Hiya,' I yelled, crossing over the road to meet her. She was looking great and I told her so. She seemed pleased by the compliment. It was the first time I'd seen her since the time she'd gone off on one at Groovy's and I was still feeling a little bit awkward about the whole afternoon. I'd gone into the bedroom as instructed only to find it in semi-darkness and had banged my shin on an old filing cabinet Groovy had picked up from somewhere on the way to the bed where Sarah has been sitting, still crying at that point. I'd sat down and given her a fairly clumsy hug before letting her rest her face on my shoulder, her tears slowly permeating my T-shirt.

After a few minutes she'd calmed down but she hadn't been keen to discuss what had set her off. The best I could get out of her was that she felt we were all being a bit mean, but there was clearly more to it than that. That hadn't been mean, we could do mean and that hadn't been it. It had been as if someone had peeled away the efficient veneer she'd assumed in the last few years and she'd reverted back to a more vulnerable young girl, one from the past. Once she'd had a chance to tidy herself up it seemed all she wanted was for everyone to forget anything had ever happened, starting with me. As soon as we left the bedroom she headed straight for the kitchen and the lads seemed to pick up her cue. Business as usual.

Now she was a different person, clearly on her way to meeting someone as she had obviously taken a lot of care over how she looked. She wasn't wearing her work clothes, but neither was she in jeans either. In fact I was a little worried that she might be feeling a bit cold, as she shivered slightly in a long pink T-shirt which doubled up as a dress with the words

'Choose Life' spelled out in glitter across her chest, pulled together at her waist with a wide leather belt. She was wearing leg warmers though and some dainty looking pumps.

'Nice hair,' I remarked. Even I could see that she'd done something dramatic with her hair, what had been an elegant bob was now an anarchic frizz, with a matching pink flower inserted into it.

'Do you like it?'

Even at twenty two I'd accumulated enough wisdom to know not to comment on a woman's hair cut in anything but positive tones, so I replied 'It really suits you' with enthusiasm, even though I wasn't really sure if it was 'her'.

'I'm just on my way to hook up with Mary. Where are you off to? Some bloke?'

'Um,' she replied, noncommittally.

'Anyone I know?' I teased.

'Yes, I think you might know him,' she replied, thinking as she did so, her eyes looking skywards, 'he comes and goes, is a bit hard to pin down.'

'Intriguing.'

'Yes,' she agreed. 'But I'm not really sure I know where I am with him, whether to keep up the effort. You know what I mean?'

She seemed to be asking my advice. Perhaps I'd started something when I'd comforted her at Groovy's that time. Ask Uncle Colin.

'Well, don't let him mess you around,' I replied, 'you're much too special.'

She seemed pleased with this. 'I'll remember that,' she mused, before waving a goodbye and wandering down the street to her enigmatic rendezvous. I even contemplated following her for a while to see who this mystery bloke was, but that would have made me late for Mary and I liked to get there early so I could watch the end of the show when the sweat tended to accentuate various features under all those leotards. Perhaps Groovy would be able to fill me in later?

247

Mary was hot and sweaty from the aerobics class and all she wanted when I picked her up was to get home and shower, the primary school where the class was run not quite running to showers. She'd looked young amongst the class, a child amongst women, and a little shunned socially; although there was no contest when it came to who had the best figure. I walked her home, a sensation that felt a little like walking your kid sister home, and we said our goodbyes on the doorstep.

I don't think I'd ever been so nervous before a game as I was before the semi-final. All the pressure was on us. Anything other than a win was unthinkable, especially against such supposedly easy opposition. It was a once in a lifetime opportunity, ninety minutes away from the biggest day of our lives.

And yet, and yet. Stranger things had happened. Our form going into the match had gone down the toilet, so perhaps nerves were getting to the players too? We'd followed up the defeat to the Scousers with a 6-1 tanking to Norwich of all people, the only good thing being that at least Johnston had got the one, which suggested he still knew where the net was.

Groovy, Paully and I had driven up together and were now standing with our heads exposed to the wind whipping up off the park outside. We'd tried to get Trev along too, but he hadn't replied to any of the various messages we'd all left. Inside the ground the sun was shining, shaving the worst of the cold off the wind and both sets of fans were in fine voice. We knew how the Plymouth fans felt, not only because they too were so near to the Holy Grail, but because it hadn't been that long ago that we had been like them, lower division underdogs. It was almost as if we were playing ourselves, but not quite, still we were glad we had got them and not Southampton.

We were grateful when an early goal settled our nerves, a text book cross from Barnesy to George Reilly, who slammed it in from near enough the penalty spot. Unmissable. Minutes later Callaghan had a goal disallowed for offside and if we'd have had seats we'd have sat back and waited for the inevitable goal rush to come. Except it didn't quite work out like that.

From then on it was practically all Plymouth, especially in the second half, and we found ourselves clinging on by our fingernails to the slenderest of leads. The last twenty minutes were pure torture and with only seconds to go one of their players broke free and suddenly found himself unmarked and only six yards out. This was it, we all felt, the equaliser. Somehow however the shot twisted a path across the front of the goal and skimmed the outside of the post, going out for a goalkick.

And that was it.

We were in the Final.

CHOICES

24

IT EVENTUALLY TOOK three hours to get out of the car park at Villa Park, but we didn't care. We sang, we cheered, we listened to the match reports, we learned that our opponents would be Everton who'd also won by the lone goal, beating Southampton at Highbury. Everton. The Toffees. We picked our collective brains - we'd lost at their place and had recently shared eight goals at ours.

It looked like being a cracking final.

And then the long wait started all over again. It was as if a jury had been sent out to decide our fate and we had no idea which way they were going to swing. Luckily I had very little time to think about it as all of a sudden everything seemed to happen at once on the job search front. The first bit of news was a letter from the software company in Reading. It was a 'thanks but no thanks', and I can't say I was too bothered, other than it narrowed the field down to three. If I'd had to choose one to lose it would have been that one, the whole place seemed to exist in some kind of parallel universe only they seemed to understand. I couldn't say that I had.

Then I got a call from Karen at Betta Staff. My heart started to thump against my chest as she paused to choose the right words. It seemed the bank didn't want to take things further either. I was surprised, very surprised. When I asked if they'd given any reason she cleared her throat and gave another of her pauses.

'Yes actually. They suggested that you came across as quite arrogant.'

'Arrogant?'

'Well, cocksure was the word they actually used.'

'Cocksure?' I asked, doing my best parrot impersonation.

'As if you thought you had the job in the bag and weren't hungry enough.'

'Wasn't hungry enough?' I had to stop doing that, so I cut the conversation short with thanks for her help before I made even more of an idiot of myself.

Down to two, but the best two. My meeting in St. Albans was already fixed and my focus shifted to making the most of this, taking on board perhaps some of the lessons from the bank exercise. Then a letter came from Global Multiplex. Three days notice - before St. Albans - but they wanted to see me again for a final interview. It would mean missing a shift at the bakery, and probably a long hot shower to get rid of the accumulated dough, but more importantly it meant I was still in with a shout.

The venue was London again, but not a hotel this time. They had a small suite of offices out Soho way which they'd decorated with huge film posters plastered all over the walls. Darth Vader looked out from behind the reception desk, although it was impossible to tell whether he was offering a welcoming smile. There was no one else there, which made me think they were only seeing a few people and slotting them in when they could. I eventually got called into a smallish room with a desk and a coffee table with some unfamiliar American film magazines scattered over its surface. A set of clear plastic chairs was placed neatly around the table and I was motioned over towards one of these by someone who introduced himself simply as Mason, although I didn't know if this was his first or second name.

He was a stubby looking guy with a double breasted suit and a fine moustache, which gave him a vaguely Mafiosi look and I suddenly had an image of him in a Napoli kitchen being served a huge bowl of pasta by his mother. A giant Arnold Schwarzenegger hung over him from the wall advertising the new film 'The Terminator', which I hadn't seen. I hoped it wouldn't count against me, I'd tended towards more highbrow entertainment since I'd started seeing Mary.

I'd taken the feedback from the bank to heart and really concentrated on making a good impression. There was something about this job that attracted me, I think it was the fact that it represented the chance to do something different and be an innovator, a breaker of conventions. I'd had enough of the predictable, the old fashioned industries with the old fashioned way of doing things. There was something fresh and exciting about Global Multiplex, and something more than a little American and sexy.

I made a special effort to listen closely to what was being asked of me, to pause and give considered answers. I'd also done some thinking beforehand and came with some pre-prepared questions of my own. When Mason was speaking I leaned forward a little to make it clear I was concentrating on what was being said and when I was given the opportunity to contribute I did so in a way I thought came across as intelligently. I asked about projected growth rates, geographical reach and benchmarks of success. They asked where I saw myself in three years time.

'Regional Manager,' I replied without hesitation 'With input to the national strategic overview and responsibility for both target setting and realisation.' I used a lot of stuff like this, much of which I'd picked up along the way from listening to the managers in the various jobs I'd had and from reading noticeboards. It was jargon, spiel, bullshit if you like, but it didn't half sound good, even if I didn't know what half of it meant.

We talked for over an hour and by the end I thought it had gone reasonably well - although I couldn't tell for sure, I'd been so absorbed in the process itself. On balance, I felt this ambiguity was probably a good sign. As I got up to shake hands, trying desperately not to tower too much over Mason, I managed to resist putting on my best Arnie voice and saying the catchphrase I'd heard from clips of the film on the radio: 'Ahhll-be-bahhk'.

None of us wanted to make the trek back to Birmingham the following Saturday for the league game with Aston Villa, there was always the danger that we might get there and the whole semi-final would be declared a dream, so it was a case of lingering around town and generally hanging out with Groovy before going back to his place. His Kate was doing something with her Mum and my Mary had her head down in her books, the imminence of her 'A' Levels now beginning to focus her mind.

It was good to fall back into old ways and generally chew the cud with my old mucker. After around half an hour we'd exhausted the topic of football and moved onto women. He was well-pleased with the way things were going with Kate and I teased him that I'd seen them holding hands in town the other day, something I'd never seen him do before, which prompted a magazine to be thrown at my face. Quite naturally he then asked me about me and Mary and I found myself, quite unexpectedly, sharing thoughts with him that I hadn't even previously shared with myself, let alone Mary.

'It's great, Groovy, you know, the whole thing's as fresh as a daisy ...'

'And yet?' he asked.

'Yes, you're right, there is an 'and yet''.

'Tell Groovy,' he demanded, getting up to turn a tape over.

'Well, she's so young. That's a good thing and a bad thing of course.'

'In what way?' he asked.

'Well, what happens next? Hopefully I'll soon have a job and she'll be off to university.'

'Is that a problem?'

'Less for me I think, I just wonder if it would be fair on her.'

'How do you mean?' he asked. I was having trouble trying to articulate this.

'Well, I don't want to hold her back. She should be free to enjoy university, not be tied down.'

'You mean like you and Andrea?'

And there he had it, the old sage. Yes, like me and Andrea had been. It hadn't occurred to me, but I didn't want Mary to live some kind of semi-existence at university, using me as a prop in the way Andrea and I had used each other. I wanted her to throw herself into it, to immerse herself. To be free. With a jolt I knew there was a right thing to do and it was down to me to do it, like Trev with Claire, except his was an easier choice, marrying her was something he wanted to do, I didn't want to let go of Mary. It would be a wrench certainly, I'd really grown quite fond of her, but I saw at that moment that it was my duty to end the relationship before we got in too deep. We were both potentially at a turning point in our lives and needed to make the most of them.

'Christ, Groovy, you really know how to cheer a bloke up. I came in here full of the joys of Spring, sap rising, a jump in my step and within an hour you've got me chucking a girl I'm having a really good time with and acting all mature. What's happened to us?'

'Your decision, mate, not mine.' He was right.

If my heart had been pounding before going into the Global Multiplex interview, it was ramming down the door demanding to be let out by the time I made it to St. Albans. Andy had called again and told me that they couldn't put a cigarette paper between me and the other candidate and that it was all going to come down to how we performed on the day. No pressure then. He was rooting for me he said, but I wasn't to tell anyone he'd said that. I wondered if he said that to all the boys.

Norman was already there when I arrived and he got up to shake my hand while we wished each other the best of luck. I wondered if he wanted the job as desperately as I did. I doubted it, no one could. Sweat was glistening on his forehead despite the fact that the hallway where we were sitting was quite cold, and I dabbed mine with my handkerchief just in case I was doing the same thing.

We were to go before a formal panel this time, and Norman went in first. Rather than simply sit still and become a complete bag of nerves I paced around the hall to burn them off, picking up and flicking through some of the party literature stacked in crumpled brown boxes on the floor by way of last minute cramming. I did some relaxation exercises that I'd read in a book, which were designed to help in situations like these but felt a complete berk doing them, worried someone might come in and see me. Deep muffled voices came from inside the Committee Room, but no indication of how things were going. No satisfying rows or raised voices, but no self-congratulatory laughter either. After almost exactly an hour the door handle rattled and Norman emerged with Andy, the two shaking hands.

'Thanks Norman, we'll be in touch. Don't worry if it takes a couple of weeks, we need to speak with Keith before we make our final, final decision.' Norman nodded his understanding, offered me a final 'Good luck' and left by the front door. 'Give us a couple of minutes will you, Colin, then I'll come and get you.' I waved my acquiescence and he disappeared back into the dark recesses of the room.

It was more like fifteen minutes before I finally got to sit down in front of my three interrogators. There was Andy, Anne Wyatt, the Chairwoman, who I had met last time, and someone I didn't remember seeing before. Anne was a professional-looking woman with large glasses and lipstick that looked much too bright, and I suspected she was against me. The new guy introduced himself as Simon Peachey from National Headquarters. Unlike the other two he had a few grey hairs and exuded the sort of gravitas that suggested he'd been round the block a bit. He also had a voice as smooth as syrup that seemed to ooze its way into the room.

I decided to direct most of my answers to him rather than trying to scan all three of them all the time, something I always felt might come across as looking shifty. I reckoned his might be the casting vote.

The questioning started off gently enough, mostly going over old ground, largely, I suspected, for the benefit of Peachey; although it was good to get the voice working and the heart rate back to something close to normal. We then went on to exploring my CV and general suitability for doing the actual job, although I sensed that this was pretty much taken for granted.

Then it started to get interesting.

Anne Wyatt asked me to sum up where I thought the Alliance was now. This was a big open question and one I'd thought might come up. I started by reminding them that it had only been two years since we (the use of 'we' was deliberate) had had a ten point lead in the polls and how it had only been the Falklands that had won the Tories the last election. This suggested to me, I hypothesised, that there remained a huge pool of potential support which we - that word again - needed to go out and tap. If our aim was to break the mould of British politics we had only cracked it, I suggested we needed to give it a few more sharp blows.

The Peachey bloke then asked me what I thought the priorities were, his question sliding into the flow like a leak appearing under a door.

'Policy wise or locally?' I asked.

'Let's start with policy.'

To answer this I took a metaphorical step back and talked about the need to capture the centre ground, how Labour and the Tories represented two extremes. I expounded my view that so long as we continued like that all we were going to get was the same old ding-dong of knockabout politics, with the country acting as a punchbag for the ideologues. I said that I didn't believe that this was what the British people wanted and that the future lay more in the centre.

Tactically, I suggested, this meant marginalising the Labour party allowing them to continue tearing themselves apart whilst using this unique opportunity to kick them into oblivion. This seemed to go down well, being received with smiles and nods all round. I was speaking with passion now, and I wasn't sure if it was my choice of language or what I was saying that was pleasing them. I carried on regardless, there was no point in not being myself, I reasoned. Proportional representation was a policy priority I suggested and to get it we needed to aim for a hung parliament at the next election.

'Wouldn't PR leave us vulnerable?' Peachey asked. I replied that the world was changing, becoming more diverse, and that we shouldn't fight shy of a little competition. New parties should be seen as a good thing - look at the SDP, I pointed out.

'What was my view of Europe?' I was asked. I was all for it, especially when we looked over the Atlantic and contemplated people like Reagan. We needed real engagement though, not squabbling and putting people's backs up with histrionic demands for refunds. Europe wasn't a branch of Marks and Spencer.

'The environment?' A pressing issue.

'Transport?' I didn't have a car, that was a sign of my commitment to the environment - although I could learn if it was a requirement of the job, I added a little too hastily.

I was asked my view of Neil Kinnock and gave a one word assessment: lightweight.

'What about the miners?' asked Andy, his first question. We'd discussed this in depth when I'd been there before, and it was a simple job to echo back the tenor of his thinking. The whole strike was doomed and there was a danger that the damage it did could be immense. It was a classic example of what was wrong with the country, confrontation politics, I suggested, using a phrase I'd conjured out of the air from somewhere. Coalmining had only a limited long term future, the City was where the country made its money - that was what the boffins had said at the bank anyway. The trick was to manage that decline, not let confrontation tear us all apart.

'What about the economy?' I was asked. This was my strongest suit, an area where I could claim some real expertise. I argued that it was time for the monetarist experiment to stop. I knew, God knows I knew, that there was a lot wrong with many of the businesses that generated wealth for our country, but there had to be another way of dealing with these problems other than closing them down or nationalising them, it was all so black and white.

I sneaked a look at my watch; I'd been in for over an hour. Was that a good or bad thing?

'One last question, Colin,' Andy interjected. 'Last time you were here you suggested that current Government policy was a form of 'bread and circuses'. Would you like to expand on that?'

Christ, did I? I couldn't remember. What had I meant by that? Then it all came back. The use of North Sea Oil money to buy people off with consumerism rather than tackling some of the core issues wrong with the country. Why not use that windfall to revitalise industry, like Norway was doing? As I spoke I could see that Peachey from Head Office was scribbling down some notes and nodding furiously and I made a mental note to thank Andy for what I suspected had been a soft pass.

I left the room exhausted and after the usual goodbyes and

the spiel on what happened next that I'd already heard, I took a walk around the large park and lake below the Cathedral to collect my thoughts. Like the interview with Global Multiplex I wasn't sure just how well it had gone. I hadn't dropped any obvious clangers and felt I'd done myself justice. That was all I could ask. I was in with a shout for both of them, I concluded. What would I do if I had to choose? It was a difficult one. My head said Global Multiplex, it offered prospects, money, a career ladder, all the things I should be chasing; whilst my heart said Alliance, with all its obvious drawbacks of risk, uncertainty and, if I was being honest with myself, possible ultimate failure. It would be fun though.

Things on the pitch meanwhile certainly couldn't be described as fun, and I hoped this wasn't a bad sign. Draws mingled with lost games, including another thumping, this time 5-1 away to Nottingham Forest. There was one victory however, and a significant one, over Luton at their Kennel, which went some way to make up for the games either side of it, but it came at a price. Wilf Rostron, our captain, Player of the Year the previous season and probably this season too, a central part of our side and our most experienced full back, got red-carded. This ruled him out of the Final through suspension, an unbelievable blow. And it had to be against bloody Luton didn't it?

I was oscillating between home and Groovy's at this time. It had taken Mum a while to get over the shock of having Dad around all the time, it upset all her little routines and I sensed that somehow having him observe how she spent her time on a daily basis made her realise quite what a rut she'd got herself into. Suddenly she was the one leaving the house first thing, leaving Dad at home, as she found new things to do - a morning in a charity shop here, a coffee morning there - and this seemed to inject a new lease of life into her: she smiled more, had more to say for herself and found she was active, not simply busy.

The most delicious irony though, and I use the word intentionally, was that Dad learned to cook. For his birthday I bought him his own pinny and he evolved rapidly from a hobby chef to the main cook of the house, something that would have been inconceivable even weeks before. From English roasts we graduated through to Asia and beyond via the Mediterraean, finding a natural home in curries. The smell of Pledge was soon superseded by cumin and turmeric and strange new colours started to stain our chopping boards and crockery. It actually became a pleasure to eat at home.

The night before the tickets for the Final became available I stayed at Groovy's and the pair of us were at the ground a few hours before they became available just in case. I got two because that was the limit and it seemed daft not to after getting up so early and shuffling along in a queue for what seemed like forever. Besides, only getting one would have made me look like Nobby No Mates.

A few days before I'd got round to breaking the bad news to Mary. She had her 'A' Levels coming up and I didn't want to tell her once she'd started, even though I knew instinctively there wasn't ever going to be a good time to do it. It didn't go well. To say she was livid would be an understatement. If weapons had been allowed I think she'd have ended the discussion facing a thirty year sentence. By the time it was all over I felt wretched but also, in a strange kind of way, vindicated. The whole episode and our respective reactions only served to highlight that she was, when all was said and done, still a schoolgirl, whilst I was the sensible, rationale adult. So my head told me, my heart was going to take a little longer to catch up. The top and bottom of it all was my second ticket constituted a spare, and my first thoughts turned to Trev and after a few tries I finally managed to catch him at work.

'It's out of the question, mate. Claire's due to pop any time around then, and the one thing you can guarantee is that if I do go that's when it'll happen,' he pleaded.

I supposed it was true. He'd made his choice and I'd even been instrumental in helping him make it. I said that that was fair enough and we had a quick chat about how things were generally. He didn't like taking personal calls at work though and pretty quickly he cut the conversation short.

'Look mate, I'll be crossing everything for you guys, fingers, arms you name it, even my legs.'

'Just make sure Claire doesn't,' I suggested. 'Good luck mate.'

'Yeah, and to you and the boys too.'

I hoped for Trev's sake that the kid was a boy, I suspected that was the only way we'd ever get to see him at Vicarage Road again.

SO, I WAS LEFT WITH A TICKET for the FA Cup Final on my hands, which was kind of ironic seeing that it had taken us over a hundred years to get there. How precious was that ticket? Fortunately a solution presented itself when I was walking through the shopping centre with Groovy and Kate and bumped into Andrea and her Mum with the dreaded mutt in tow.

I couldn't just ignore her, we'd been through too much for that, so we stopped, although Groovy and Kate pointedly hung back to look in a shop window. What could have been an awkward situation soon relaxed into comfortable familiarity, but after a couple of minutes Mrs Kendall-Jones shattered this when she started to pipe up with her own parallel contribution, instantly injecting a note of surrealism into the proceedings.

It was just as Andrea was volunteering the fact that her relationship hadn't gone anywhere and I was making a joke about being free and single again myself that her Mum announced in a surprisingly vitriolic tone her view that Andrea had been a very naughty girl who should have known better. Even allowing for a mother's protectiveness this seemed a little harsh and in an instant comfort slipped back into awkwardness as neither of us quite knew how to react. Was she referring to me or the new boyfriend? But she wasn't finished - when was she ever?

'You,' she almost growled, 'you stay away from her.' So I was the target of her anger. Her tone went on to escalate into something vaguely threatening. 'Keep your paws off her you dirty dog.' This was a bit hard to take, seeing as technically it was her who'd dumped me in the end, although if I was honest the macho side of me quite liked being called a dirty dog.

'I'm sorry Mrs ...,' but I didn't get a chance to finish.

'Mummy!' Andrea interjected, but she met the same level of success.

'I've told you time and time again,' she resumed, 'beasts like you should be neutered, you're a menace to society.'

I tried to start another apology but got no further than the first time when suddenly she relaxed, all the muscles in her face which until that point had been visibly tense suddenly fell free, showing folds and creases I was more used to seeing on her dog.

Her dog. Of course, it was the bloody dog, which had been attracting the attentions of an admirer behind our backs which, as I turned around, I could just see being pulled away on a lead by its embarrassed owner.

'Well!' announced Mrs Kendall-Jones, filling her lungs before delivering the denouement I thought I'd never hear again, 'What do you think of that then!'

Andrea and I looked at each other and just laughed. After that we didn't linger for much longer although there was just time enough for conversation to get around to the Final when suddenly it hit me. Andrea was the perfect person for the other ticket. She'd shared whole chunks of the journey over the years and had earned her right to be there, to share the view now we'd reached the summit. It would be fitting somehow, both an appropriate sign-off to our relationship and a way of proving that we could be civilised with each other. She also understood the offside rule. She jumped at the idea with her usual enthusiasm and, after I said I'd be in touch with arrangements, we left it there.

'What was all that about?' demanded Groovy as I rejoined him and Kate. He'd clearly been ear-wigging.

'What do you mean?'

'Asking Andrea to the final? I could have got rid of that ticket for you.' He stared me straight in the eye. 'You're not are you? You're not thinking of getting back together again?'

'Naw, naw.' I assured him with a casual brush of the hands. 'Just friends.'

'There's no such thing with an ex,' Groovy asserted. 'You must be mad,' he concluded, before adding, 'there's just no helping some people.'

In the end I took charge of arrangements for the whole day out for everyone. There had been moves afoot to drive rather than take the tube but I suggested instead that we get one of the official coaches so we could get in on the ground floor of the atmosphere on the day. Although ours was one of the nearest football league grounds to Wembley and the journey would only be a short one, I insisted it would be worth it.

So it was that we all gathered together in a car park on the edge of town on the morning of May 19th 1984. Groovy, Kate, Sarah, Freddie, Paully, Andrea and me. The sky was blue, but our hearts were solid gold. It had already been an odd morning. I'd stopped off at Andrea's to pick her up and she'd only come down in a cobalt coloured fluffy jumper she'd bought especially for the occasion as she thought it looked nice.

Blue was for Everton - we were yellow. I sent her back with playful instructions not to come down until she looked like a true hornet, suggesting she buzz off upstairs. Frank followed her and managed to find an old yellow sweater of his, which

I think he may have used for gardening, whilst Andrea put on a black skirt and red blouse, the whole episode being accompanied, somewhat inevitably, by Frank chuckling away to himself.

Mrs Kendall-Jones was about to say something when Andrea finally descended the stairs and I wrapped a scarf round her neck, using it to pull her out of the house and down the road before her Mum managed to release a word - the first and hopefully not last victory of the day.

Before even that the postman had delivered two letters for me that morning, the contents of which would have made my day anyway, despite the fact that I expected it to get so much better yet. Both Global Multiplex and the Social Democratic and Liberal Alliance (St. Albans Branch) were writing to offer me a permanent job.

At last, I'd done it.

I'd only gone and bloody done it.

It still had to sink in though, and there simply wasn't enough room left in my brain to process the decision I was going to have to make. For the moment I simply wallowed in the fact that my search was over, I was about to join the real world. I just didn't know yet in what capacity.

The club had challenged the town to 'go yellow', and the town had responded amply. As our coach pulled out we were immediately immersed in a sea of banana custard, with occasional flecks of cherry and raisin. A lone voice at the back of the coach started on our signature chants and within a second everyone on the coach was yelling out at the tops of their voices a continuous chorus of 'Cooooome on you 'Orns.'

We hit Wembley around midday, but already the crowds were thick with yellow and blue. Back home I'd set the machine on long play to record all the usual pre-match build up on the BBC - the special 'It's a Knock Out' between rival sets of fans, the coverage of the players eating lunch, the V-signs to the camera by fans in the back of the shot. Then there were the endless interviews, some pre-recorded with celebrity fans (although Everton would struggle to top Elton), and others live. Everyone would be nailing their colours to the mast.

'We're on the march with Taylor's Army' came a voice from outside and we picked up the refrain. Once outside we were on equal terms with the Everton fans. No wishes of good luck to plucky Watford, no sneers of derision from the lofty journalists from the national rags, we had earned the right to be there - even if we were still struggling to believe it ourselves. Both sets of fans were shaking hands with each other; we were both just so delighted to be there.

There wasn't the slightest whiff of hooliganism, and even the policemen seemed to be in good spirits as we finally made the journey we'd all be dreaming of, the stroll up Wembley Way, over the bridge and up towards the famous art deco Twin Towers. We couldn't help ourselves and burst into a throaty rendition of 'Wem-ber-ley, Wem-ber-ley, Wem-ber-ley' as we mounted the ramp to the gates.

We were now surrounded by Watford hats, flags and scarves, the latter worn round necks and tied round waists, despite the beautiful, glorious sun overhead. The noise was absolutely ear-splitting, and there was still an hour and a half to kick off.

Andrea unpacked a bag she'd been carrying and handed round some sandwiches as an unseen hand turned down the volume dial for a while. It didn't take long for the singing to start up again though and soon we were yelling (to call it singing would flatter us) through our whole repertoire.

'There's only one 'F' in Watford, one 'F' in Watford.'

To which came the inevitable refrain: 'No 'F' in Luton, there's no 'F' in Luton', which in turn, and just as predictably, led on to a special one for the cameras: 'Are you watching Luton Town?' Pure bloody magic. The teams emerged in their specially bought cup final suits for a walkabout and then there was some kind of car parade which we hoped didn't churn up the grass.

Talking of cameras, the BBC chose that moment to wheel out our hero, the man who should have been on the pitch with Watford, not plying his trade in the backwater that was AC Milan. Our hero, our man, our Luther: the man who personified our rise through the ranks and the spirit that was Watford. The crowd went ballistic. 'Loooooother!' they yelled, spreading the 'o' out as long as was humanly possible as the great man struggled to make himself heard for an interview down the Watford end. Okay, we had Mighty Mo now, but Luther had been our main man for as long as we could remember, he was as much part of Watford as the Watford Observer clock on the Rookery end. What we wouldn't have given to have him back.

Then the crowd hushed and the band struck up for the once-traditional rendition of 'Abide With Me', specially re-introduced to this final, some said at Elton's request. I had to wipe a tear from my eye, and later learned that I wasn't alone, as our blessed Elton, who along with his new wife Renate was sporting a yellow and red spray of flowers in his buttonhole, finally cracked and showed his emotion.

Finally, the teams came out, wearing ridiculously tight shorts. Andrea had brought a pair of opera glasses and made a big deal of how the shorts displayed their wedding tackle to good effect, a phrase I hadn't heard her use before. A flush of blood went through my cheeks and down the sides of my body, fading away as it reached my knees, which then began to tremble uncontrollably, almost as if they were chuckling with delight. I couldn't bring myself to speak, I was too nervous.

After being introduced to the Duke of Kent and various other suits, all of whom seemed to take it all in their stride, the players peeled off their tracksuit tops and jogged on the spot for a bit, working off their impatience to get going. There they were, our representatives, the eleven men in whom we'd

267

trusted our hopes, our ambitions, for some our lives.

According to the names emblazoned across the front of their shirts we were about to witness a gladiatorial contest between Iveco and Hafnia, but we knew them simply as Watford and Everton. Then at last they broke ranks and ran either side of the regimented square block of men marching up and down with brass instruments that was the combined bands of the Guards Division.

I gave Andrea a hug and Groovy gave me a look. What was his problem? Did he think I was going to propose to her this time? He alone knew how I had let the emotion of the moment carry me away that day back in September and I reasoned that he was concerned that I might do something crazy. It was sweet really, crazy but sweet.

The lads had cued themselves up with a 2-1 defeat of Arsenal the week before in the final league game, but none of that counted anymore. Perhaps more significant was the fact that Everton had already played on the hallowed turf that season in the final of the Milk Cup, losing to Liverpool in a Battle of the Scousers. We tried to ignore the fact that the losing finalists in that competition had won this one for the last two years.

Christ, our team looked young, nine of the twelve were my age or younger, which was simply scary, and it had been said that they were possibly the youngest Cup Final team ever. The Grandad of the bunch was our goalie, Steve Sherwood, a lanky moustachioed thirty year old the papers seemed to have it in for, suggesting he was our weak link. We scoffed at this talk - how many other sides had 'keepers who'd actually scored that season?

Graham Taylor had led the team out and was now sitting on the bench looking relaxed in his grey double-breasted suit and tinted shades. A young manager for a young team. Down on the pitch it was odd to see an advertising hoarding for Dad's old company, like that was part of another life now gone and briefly revived.

The sky remained mostly blue as they kicked off, splashes of yellow in the crowd looking like shafts of sunlight illuminating parts of the ground. Immediately we were on the attack, and Barnesy, with his Afro hair and amazing pace, could have put us ahead in the first minute, a rush to the post which their 'keeper just got his hand to. As the minutes unfolded, it developed into a game of 'keepers, as the ball ricocheted from end to end with neither team making the vital breakthrough. The gap-toothed Reilly, our big number nine, was charging about all over the place, trying to feed the ball to Johnston, but to no avail.

It was anyone's game, expansive, fast paced, plenty of action; not at all like most Cup Finals which tended to be cagey affairs with both sides afraid of conceding an early advantage. We had the most chances, but they seemed the more composed. A glance at the watch confirmed that there wasn't that long to go to half time. I had a theory that we usually went on to win games when we went in 0-0 at half time, with Taylor weaving his magic over the orange wedges and cups of tea.

But then, on thirty eight minutes, the worst thing imaginable happened. Graham Sharp of Everton found himself in space, cued up a shot and we could only watch in despair as Sherwood dived and the ball deflected off the inside of the post and into the net. Despair, followed by silence, but not for long. After the restart we created more chances, but the whistle went and we went in one down at half time.

It was only 1-0, we told ourselves, it wasn't over yet, as once again we pored over the programme and searched for omens in the statistics for reassurance. What we needed to do was go at them hammer and tongs in the true Watford style and regain the initiative. We'd picked ourselves up by the time the teams came out again, once more dodging around the Combined Guards, whose bandmaster we noticed was dressed in yellow and red, maybe that was the sign we were looking for?

It started as we imagined, at least for seven minutes, and

then the most blatant piece of goalkeeper obstruction you'll ever see in your life occurred. Everton's Andy Gray - with our man Steve Terry coming down on him like a steam train - headed the ball right out of Sherwood's hands and into the net. He celebrated, we waited for the referee to declare it invalid. He got what he wanted, we didn't. 2-bloody-0.

That effectively killed the game. The stuffing went out of us and we seemed to lose sight of any kind of game plan. We brought on our lone substitute, but it didn't make any difference. With two goals in the bank the greater composure and maturity of the Everton team effectively squeezed us out of the match. The clock counted down, Johnston had a goal disallowed for a clear offside, and the Cup went north to bloody Liverpool.

On a football level we had few complaints. Hampered by injuries, the loss of our captain and a lack of experience, we hadn't deserved to win on the day. It hurt to say it, but there was no point fooling ourselves. Ultimately, I think the Scousers simply wanted it more than us, on the day we'd been happy just to be there, part of the festival, winning it was for another time; this was just a warm up.

Despite the fencing around the pitch some idiot Scousers got onto the pitch and started running around like madmen, but the police didn't even try to stop them. Elton came down out of his seat and wandered around the pitch too, in a more dignified pitch invasion, dressed in his spangled grey suit and cowboy hat, while the teams went up to fetch their medals. We lost them in the crowd at this point, but their bright yellow shirts congregated at the foot of the famous steps and they began to parade around the fencing.

What happened next was extraordinary.

Rather than hang our heads and clap politely before filing back to the coaches, the Watford fans went absolutely bloody mental. A sea of yellow flags and a hurricane of singing filled the stadium and just went on, and on. Honestly, you'd have thought we'd won, and in many ways perhaps we had, simply by getting there and being in a position to enjoy the moment. We didn't know if we'd ever get to this point again, we hoped so, but you never knew, and so we were making the most of it.

I turned round and saw that Andrea had been pushed a few places down the terracing. She was standing next to some bloke and they were shouting into each others' ears. It looked like they knew each other, sharing an easy laughter and delight. Good for them. Groovy was behind me, still in a state of euphoria, and Sarah to my left, joining in with the cheering like the best of them. While I'd been clocking all this my hands had fallen to my side and I'd stopped singing for a bit, lost in my thoughts.

Groovy leant down and shouted something into my ear, his ridiculous putative beard tickling the side of my cheek.

'What?' I yelled.

'You still don't get it do you?'

'Get what?' I asked, straining to catch his words.

'Do you know how my heart mourns?'

I turned round and grabbed his shirt.

'So it was you - you bastard!'

'You really are a complete prannet aren't you?' he asked again, his vocabulary of abuse could be really quite impressive at times. He pointed at Sarah, who was still singing, but had, I knew at that moment, been following our exchange. Suddenly, she threw her arms around my neck, kissed me full on the lips and shouted, as loud as her lungs would allow her 'Lift me from this dilemma's 'Orns.'

More cheering started, but it was directed at us, not the team. Paully, Andrea and Kate were all looking in our direction, whooping us on, while Freddie looked on bemused. Others around us were turning to see what all the fuss was about. At that moment the noise echoing around the ancient arena seemed to take on a different quality, like someone had put a pillow over the 'speakers and I began to feel as if the whole stadium, crowd, TV cameras, floodlights even, even though the sun continued to fill the sky, were all pointing at us as I lifted my arms up and circled them around Sarah's waist before returning the compliment, landing a great big smacker full on her lips. It didn't feel odd, it felt the most natural thing in the world as we stayed locked together for longer than seemed possible without dying of suffocation.

Sarah was standing one tier up from me on the concrete terracing so I had to lift myself onto the balls of my feet to make myself heard in her ear.

'So, it was you!' I yelled.

She smiled, as if she was the holder of a secret, one I guess I'd known all along but hadn't dared to admit to myself.

'No, silly, it's you,' she replied. 'It's always been you.'

And with that she kissed me again and the crowd returned its gaze to the pitch where the golden boys were at last filing back into the changing room. Their season may have been over, but a new one had already begun for me.

Analysis

My second pivotal moment came just moments before Sarah revealed her love for me, that kiss simply sealed it. It happened as the flags filled the air and the noise created a cocoon for thought. It was then that I realised that every football season brings its highs and lows, like every year life delivers its own surprises and disappointments. The trick, it suddenly struck me, was to enjoy the surprises and learn from the disappointments, rising above them rather than being ground down by them. It would be really boring if life was brilliant all the time, like supporting a team that always won.

As a team we'd found our place, if you like, found our level. That's what getting to Wembley had meant for us. It wasn't so much about winning as about getting there, being a contributor, earning respect. It was about enjoying the day, the moment, not just the result; like the difference between living life and reading an obituary.

Some of the post match analysis said we lacked the killer touch, but perhaps we didn't want that. Not winning wasn't a disaster. It's like that moment when you realise that you're never going to win an Olympic Gold Medal or play for England and realise that actually it's okay. Life, like this game, was about succeeding on your own terms - the tricky bit was discovering what those terms might be.

We didn't recognise it at the time, but the Cup Final was the last time our gang all got together at a big occasion like that. Trev represented the vanguard for the way our lives all soon went, not the exception. There were to be no more late night drives all the way up to Grimsby or Stockport just to see a football match.

Once the dust had settled I'd had my own decision to make, whether to go with Global Multiplex or the Alliance in St. Albans. It was a tricky one. Where did the future lie? Where would be the best place to build, to start, a career? Was it in the leisure field, circuses; or was it in politics, the bread and butter of life? Jacket or suit? What would ignite people in the future, what would they be passionate about, where could I make a difference? Would people rally together to make the country a better place, to use this unique opportunity being thrown their way to break the mould of politics, or would they opt for self-gratification and the pleasure dome?

It seemed obvious to me.

I took the Alliance job.

When I look back I can see that once I was freed from the institutions of school and university, of people telling me what to do, I made one bad decision after another, but that was all part of the journey, the learning experience. It was as if I spent that time going round in some kind of daze, oblivious to reality, scared of it almost - a golden daze.

Following Watford had got me used to coming second - after our first promotion we were always the runner-up, we were even runners-up in our first season in the First Division, and of course, runner-up at Wembley. Coming second wasn't so bad, but I drew the line at coming third or even fourth, and after the next general election in 1987 and the Tory landslide I left the Alliance for pastures new.

After Wembley a lot of the commentators said we'd soon be back, but we never did make it. The closest we got was a few months before that election when once again we reached the semis. In what was becoming a trend, we were let down by the goalkeeping position. With all three of our squad goalies out for one reason or another we ended up playing our Chief Executive's son between the posts, a lad who usually played in a Sunday pub league. Needless to say we got slaughtered, by Spurs.

Shortly after the 1984 Cup Final John Barnes scored what was perhaps one of the greatest England goals ever against Brazil in the Estádio do Maracanã in Rio de Janeiro, dribbling through the entire Brazilian defence before letting go a cannonball into the back of the net. We felt proud to think he was one of ours. An established international, Barnes stayed with us until after the 1987 semi defeat, and when he decided to go we couldn't really blame him, he'd been a great player for us, probably our greatest, and after 65 goals in 233 appearances he didn't owe us anything any more.

He went to Liverpool of all places, where he maintained his form and goalscoring rate and five years later finally he got his FA Cup winners medal - beating Everton, of course, 3-2; although he was to appear as a losing finalist three more times in his career. Meanwhile, after what was a comparatively short burst of brilliance, Mighty Mo was soon lured away by Celtic, a club incidentally that Barnsey went on to manage at the end of the 1990s after he'd retired from the pitch.

We failed to sell our allocation of tickets for the semi in 1987, something that seemed to confirm that the golden days were over. Before long Taylor left for greater things and the fizz went out of the club, and we found a new natural level as also-rans in the lower leagues. In this period I did make one excellent decision though - marrying Sarah, the only downside to which was having Groovy as a brother in law, although it did make choosing the Best Man a simple task, although the gig was probably his whoever I'd have ended up marrying. I quickly fell into the camp that followed scorelines rather than watching them happen, but my life had moved on by then. New job, new wife, new life, although I did find time to make the occasional match and fifteen years later I finally saw the boys triumph at Wembley in the 1999 play-offs. Predictably, their time in the new Premiership was short, only a season.

Paully went on to take over his Dad's estate agency, build it up into a small chain and then sell it to one of the big banks, after which he moved to Spain, while Groovy found himself pulled into the world of computers and it didn't take long before I didn't have a clue what it was he did, although he seemed to do all right by it. Kate and he had two daughters both of whom seemed to prefer horses over football and he became very much an armchair supporter. He never did shave off his beard.

Andrea got married, although I didn't know the fellow and wasn't invited to the wedding, which is a shame as it was an event I would have bought tickets for just to see Mrs Kendall-Jones in action once again. Andrea did well out of advertising but was a victim of the downturn in that industry in the 1990s and left with a healthy payout, although it was around the same time that her marriage fell apart. We still swap Christmas cards and the occasional email. She bought a small cottage in the Fens and writes, romantic fiction I think, which seems a little ironic to me given our time together, but there you go. There weren't any children from her marriage and none since, but she seems happy enough.

I occasionally glimpse Jacqui in Waitrose, and although I'm sure she recognises me I'm prepared to admit she might not remember why, after all it was pretty dark in that summer house. I saw her once loading her four by four in the car park, a couple of bratty teenagers in the back giving her grief, and I must admit I was tempted to go up to her and remind her that she was the woman I lost my virginity to just to see what their collective reaction might be, but I bottled it. Maybe I'll pluck up the courage next time I see her, although it's probably best to keep the lid on that particular can of worms?

Trev did have the son I'd wished for him, born the day after the Final as it happened, as did Sarah and I, a couple of years later, and we kept in touch, having the occasional beer. In 2006 I got us all tickets for another play-off final, this time at the Millennium Stadium in Cardiff, and we were finally able to sit and enjoy the sweet taste of success together. It was typical Watford, winning a trophy for being the best of the rest, not even second. Still, at the end of the day it was a win on a major stage and it sent us back for another short-lived spell in the Premiership.

Despite monsoon-like rain, which meant the roof over the stadium was kept closed, it was a fantastic day and it felt good to pass on to the next generation what it meant to follow a club like ours. Grafting for success, enjoying it when you get it, but also just wallowing in the moment for what it was as much as for what it meant.

I don't mind admitting that for a second time at a major final, I cried.

Acknowledgments

Although many of the events described in this book are based in historical fact the characters and the things that happen to them are a work of fiction. Yes, the miners went on strike and Watford reached an FA Cup Final (hard though this might be to credit), but Groovy, Andrea and even Mrs Kendall-Jones are all figments of my imagination. Any resemblance to people either living or dead is entirely coincidental and unintended. In the same vein, I am pleased to say that I am not Colin, although that is not to say that I didn't share some of the same trials and tribulations as he does in this book and may even, in the distant past, have done some of the same jobs as he did, although usually not with the same consequences.

Others have helped get this book into print and particular thanks go to Marion Moffatt, my editor, who as well as providing much useful technical expertise and some helpful suggestions has also given continued support and encouragement. Thanks are also due to Matt Rowson, the leading light behind www.bhappy.wordpress.com, by far and away the best website and forum for Watford fans, and its much missed predecessor 'Blind Stupid and Desperate', which is a neat summary of what it means to be a Watford fan and contributions to which offered useful reminders of those times. A mention is also due to Graham Taylor and his team, without whom those golden days simply wouldn't have happened, and to the club in general for its support with this book.

Thanks also go out to Pete, who introduced me to Watford and was also my best man and vice versa, although neither of us managed to get off with a bridesmaid (not as far as I remember anyway), as well as Ian, the keeper of the flame, and Tim – you know who you are. Finally, the biggest thanks of all go out to Annette for her continued and unquestioning support and indulgence and for being simply the best thing that ever happened to me, and to Peter and Ed, the latter of whom I managed to steer away from being an Arsenal glory chaser towards the joys of being a Watford fan. For some reason, he's never actually thanked me.